MW01536844

Both author and GWF Press donate all earnings from the sale of this book to the United Nations Population Fund. The UNFPA provides women's reproductive health services and promotes the rights of women around the world, working to eliminate gender-based violence, including female genital cutting and rape used as a weapon of war.

A DOG CALLED GUANO

A DOG

CALLED

GUANO

OR

YEAH, BUT MOST OTHER SUPERHEROES CAN'T LICK THEIR OWN PENIS

Give Whitey Five Press

We believe in the free and reciprocal exchange of information for educational and revolutionary endeavors. Contact us for information and use.

The "LAPD: Takin' Care of Business" photo was obtained courtesy of www.gwpda.org
Ovum picture obtained courtesy of Wikipedia.org.

Published by Give Whitey Five Press
www.givewhiteyfive.com
Portland, OR

Cover design by Céline Pinçon

Book design by Chinook Design, Inc.
www.chinooktype.com

ISBN: 978-0-9786286-1-1

Fourth Edition 2009

For Sunshine and the Fat Man,
my superheroes

I AM GUANO

HEAR ME ROAR

PROLOGUE

I enjoy humping legs. Because I'm a leg man.

I enjoy humping legs. Not for any prurient reason. The prurient went out of me when they lopped off my blue öyster cults. Listen: direct action is an activity taken to achieve goals outside of normal social/political channels. Humping legs is the only effective form of direct action. Along with a Dresden-style firebombing. You'd be into direct action too if you weren't such a brainwashed sheep and the human humpees lopped off your umlauts.

They call me Guano. They call me dog: Nepalese Odorous Sherpa Scaler, purebred (so fuck you very much, American Kennel Club fascists; and Republicans too). I'm white, because white makes right. The final score in the global capital distribution scheme proves that easily enough. Whitey can't play basketball but he owns the courts. And the balls too, which is more than I can boast. White soulless gilloolies-snipping bastards.

I'm a decent-sized canine, about seventy pounds. As mentioned, my hair is white, except for some darling yellow patches on my ears. These spots are not imperfections, but signs of character. Just like little pools of jaundice, as seen on the local homeless man your kids lit on fire. Signs of character. My ears are wide at the base, pointed, and usually semi-erect. Ready for action. Behold such beauty!

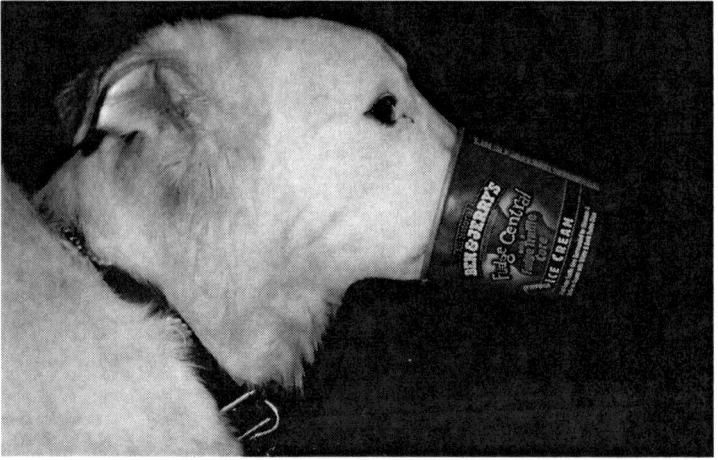

More FYI. My eyes are brown. My cock, white. My cock size, black. I also sport a broad brick-like forehead. Christened "The Broad Brick-like Forehead" it is critically acclaimed for crashing through screen doors and children. My formidable head gives me the look of a genius and a water on the brain case. And I am a genius. Smart enough to write some dogshit book. I have a trim muscular build, and not in a gay way.

Turn-ons:
- Fetching a ball (cliché)
- Lamenting the fact that I have no balls (cliché for bull dykes and married American men)
- Dripping melted chocolate over a "buddy"

Turn-offs:
- Mean people (cliché)
- People (cliché for anyone who's intelligent)
- A good personality (cliché and the worst bullshit line of bullshit lines—you'd fuck Adolf Eichmann if he looked like Brad Pitt and you know it)
- Vacuum cleaners

My superhero power is the ability to cause panic in any Mexican within one hundred yards. I don't even have to try. It just happens. 24/7. They spot me and you'd think they'd seen the Virgin Mary in the opposite direction, because that's the direction they're running. It's not that I have anything against Mexicans. Hell, I'd hire them to blow shit around my yard with their gas-guzzling implements of suburban lawn homogenization just like the average lazy dimwitted American does, if I had a yard. But I'm a dog. I defecate on yards. Not pay illegals $5 an hour to serenade the rhododendrons with greenhouse gases.

So I scare Mexicans. It's what I do. It's a God-given gift. The U.S. army is into collecting God-given gifts, like the ability to rape fourteen-year-old Iraqi girls with an assault rifle barrel. So I was recruited into the military by way of America's new reform-minded pressgang policy.

The army had big plans for me. Their big plan for me was to spearhead America's new reform-minded immigration policy which aimed to keep America safe by securing America's borders by frightening all the Mexicans out of Mexico straight down to Antarctica. Don't try to make me feel guilty. There's enough carbon dioxide being put into the atmosphere from their leaf blowers to turn Antarctica into the next Puerto Vallarta. Ask Al Gore.

I digress. Once the Mexies were rightfully out of Mexico their abandoned Aztec-pyramid-infested land would be bulldozed clean (the Israelis said they'd help if any Palestinians turned up south of the border) in order to build a gigantor Indigenous People's Revolutionary Designer & Name-Brand Outlet Mall (trademark: *Viva Zapata! Visa Zapata!*) which would sell upscale slave-labor-produced trinkets made in select Third World Gardens of Eden that hadn't yet been bulldozed to conscious consumers (oxymoron) from L.A. whose turn-ons include spending $200 to fill their Antarctica-friendly SUVs full of gasoline in order to drive all the way to Mexico to save $20

on upscale slave-labor-produced trinkets made in select Third World Gardens of Eden that hadn't yet been bulldozed over. What a delicious plan.

Never happened. Because before the army was able to ship me down south to do my thing something went boom in Iraq or Afghanistan or Syriana or whichever economically strategic Middle Eastern Elysian Oil Fields we're imperializing today. Like that's anything new. More explosions over there than your neighbor's meth lab. Ah well. It's still the best daycare facility in the trailer park.

So Iraqistan goes boom. The army freaks. Their new reform-minded policy of subjugation through assault rifle barrel fondling wasn't working. So they broke out a newest reform-minded thinking which was to use my superhero power to scare the Iranians out of Iran straight down to Antarctica or underneath an Israeli bulldozer, whichever came first. It should've worked. Army intelligence proved that Mexicans and Arabs had brown skin and were therefore identical. And whoever heard of a Muslim not afraid of a dog? America's whimsical network of secret torture prisons had been using Lassie to dry hump Ahmed into submission for years. It was proven technology. But once I was on the ground it became painfully apparent that the Islamabads weren't scared of me. No fleeing in the opposite direction as if they'd seen the Virgin Mary there. Maybe they were holding out for a better virgin offer. Like that seventy-two-virgins-in-the-afterlife deal. Praise be to Allah! He knows the value of buying in bulk.

Dogs have served in the U.S. military since World War I. You see, dogs can be as stupid as humans. Most militarized canines nowadays are used to smell out shit. You know, like designer Parkas O' Plastique (P.O.P.! goes the Waleed) fashionably worn by Islamic suicide supermodels. Think of them as leather bomber jackets without the leather, because leather is dead. Smelling out Muslim human bombs is dangerous. Mostly because the

Koran apparently forbids them to use deodorant. I'm guessing the explosion burns off Abdul's armpit aura. At least I hope so for the sake of those seventy-two virgins. Then again, maybe virgins are into martyr cock that smells like a burka three weeks past its expiration date.

Anyway, my superhero power of scaring the bejesus out of Mexicans was somehow not working in Falafelstan. The army gets impatient. They try to force me into the smelling-detonating-Chaka-Khans racket. I'm not into the career change. If you want me to sniff out chocolate Ho-Hos on the breath of some chubby insurance agent from Schaumburg, fine. But this nose ain't going anywhere near the ayatollah and his explosive B.O. So I read some Howard Zinn, get inspired, and stage a sit-down strike. The army reads a fecal smear later published by Ann Coulter, gets inspired, and cuts off my gonads. It's the standard discharge and testicular trim off the top they give to all Islamo-incendiary-inhaling malingerers and conscientious objectors. Oh, and homosexuals ("Interior Designers" in official army terminology) too.

They load me and the other eunuchs ("Premature Discharges" in official army terminology) onto a plane and ship us back to the States. There I find myself without balls and without prospects, as per the generous GI Bill.

That's when it got even suckier.

TRAFFIC
BUSTER

ONE

Now you might think a man and a dog that's hung like a moose sitting together in a 1994 Oldsmobile Cutlass parked on the deserted East Sepulveda Fire Road perched a few hundred feet above Interstate 405 in Los Angeles at 5 pm is good for gobs and gobs of oral. But I already told you. I'm no homo. I'm just a Premature Discharge looking for a little work. If you want to turn this into the opening scene of a tastefully done hardcore meatpacker film then you're going to have to pay me gobs and gobs of cash for the screenplay rights.

So there I am, sitting in the front passenger seat of a 1994 Oldsmobile Cutlass, parked on the East Sepulveda Fire Road, perched a few hundred feet above Interstate 405. I've got on my aviator leather flying cap with matching goggles. My cape is red and has a big "G" on it. The "G" stands for "Guano" and, perchance, "Gräfenberg spot." But for gobs and gobs of cash the "G" can stand for "Goys that Gush" in your meatpacker screenplay.

He's sitting next to me over in the driver's seat tapping the steering wheel in cadence to the song "Hello" which Lionel Richie rode to the top of the charts and into our hearts in 1984 prompting one critic to hail Lionel as the new black Barry Manilow, which the world so desperately needed. On his hands are Kevlar welder's gloves, dyed green. They match his green overalls, made of spandex, which make him look like a gay

Mr. Green Jeans. As if the original Mr. Green Jeans wasn't gay enough. Embroidered on the front of the spandex overalls, underneath the Dickies patch on the tit, are the letters "TB" which stand for "Tuberculosis."

He lights the cigarette protruding from a small hole drilled into the welder's mask he's wearing. Because nothing says *independent rebel* so much as getting hooked on a drug peddled by transnational tobacco corporations. He leans over towards me and lights the cigarette dangling from my mouth. I don't inhale because I'm a dog and haven't ruled out running for political office. But a dangling lit cigarette makes me look cool. As verified by transnational tobacco corporations.

I'd met TB a few months earlier at the VA hospital in Los Angeles. When I first met him he wasn't wearing a welder's mask with a small hole drilled into it for the purpose of smoking cigs while soldering. Also not present were the spandex overalls. Spandex overalls are generally the first thing I notice on humans. Particularly the spandex overalls crotch. Because I'm a crotch connoisseur. Because I'm a dog. Being a decent-sized dog my head comes up to the crotch on most decent-sized humans. So the crotch is the first thing I meet when meeting humans and by far the most interesting thing about humans. No two snowflakes are ever identical. The same can't be said about human personalities as most people nowadays are as identical as the tract homes they congeal in. But not so with the fiercely individualistic human crotch. Like a snowflake, each human crotch is wonderfully distinctive and expressly your own!

So I'm working the VA hospital in L.A. It was the only thing the army offered their prematurely discharged canines besides renditioning you off to Nazi-occupied France in order to test the new L'Oréal asshole-hair mascara wand. L'Oréal's history of cruel animal testing must be the reason so many astute Americans hate the French. But at least the French eat the carcasses of their test animals because the French will eat anything.

Freshly mascaraed assholes included.

So I'm working the VA hospital in L.A.—the leper wing. The sight of me and other eunuch dogs was supposed to cheer up the rotting fuckers. Because seeing a deballed dog will send waves of cheer through some poor slob whose balls just fell off. That's when I saw him. Or more exactly, that's when I saw his crotch. He was standing, which most lepers don't. Lazy bastards. I went up to his crotch and inhaled cautiously. Leper crotches can be fucked up. His smelt of mature rooibos (a legume!), Anaïs Nin, with a twist of lime. What a delight.

I could tell by the state of his crotch that he was a quality human (oxymoron). So I said hello. Not vocally. I can't speak human. Because I'm a dog. But I can think human. Or more accurately, I can think human language. I don't actually think human. Because most humans don't actually think, so saying I think human would be a major putdown for me. Rather, I think dog, but can translate my thoughts into a deep structural format which even humans can understand. For more on the universal grammar underlying all languages consult *Syntactic Structures*, Noam Chomsky's seminal work on transformational linguistics (sometimes referred to as generative grammar).

So I say hello to his rooibos/Anaïs Nin/lime-twist crotch. I'm sure he grew wide-eyed with shock at a dog communicating with him although I can't be sure because I wasn't looking at his eyes. I was looking at his crotch. Because it's your best attribute as a species. And I always try to accentuate the positive. Because I'm a sweetheart.

So I say hello to his crotch. The black-skinned brute stammers something in Ebonics. Fuck if I know what he's saying (universal grammar underlying all languages, my ass). I immediately comprehend that writing a book with a protagonist incapable of recognizable speech is destined to be as wretched as *The Miracle Worker*, not that I didn't cry at the end when Helen Keller finally understands how to rim job teacher.

So I start over. So I say hello to his crotch. And let's just say and continue to say throughout this horseshit monstrosity of a manuscript that the central character in question talks to me in perfect Queen's English which prompts the other lepers to stare at this leper with the wondercrotch because they think it's shoddy writing to make a hardcore gangsta nigga with giant sweet atavistic afro included speak like some fucker named Alistair.

I tell his crotch not to bother to speak out loud. I can understand his thoughts just fine telepathically. I then break the ice with a compliment to put him at ease. I think something like "Gee, your crotch sure does smell nice. I especially appreciate the eau d'Anaïs Nin. Did you read her or just do her like everybody else?"

His crotch thinks back, "Uh, didn't she die back in the '70s? Doing a decades-past-ripe corpse really isn't my thing."

I think to him, "Well, you never can tell nowadays. You humans will pork anything." I continue with the compliments: "Leprosy really becomes you."

"Thanks for noticing. How am I having a telepathic conversation with a dog?"

"You think you're having a telepathic conversation with a dog? Really? Wow. You must be nuts!" I do a dog smile, whine, and spin around a couple of times—my version of a chuckle. I then think-giggle to him, "Hey, relax. I'm just fucking with you, dude." Then I look at his crotch for a minute.

I continue: "Davey always telepathically conversed with Goliath." I look at his crotch and do some panting.

"Uh, OK," he thinks to me, confused and leprotic.

"*Davey and Goliath* was the finest fact-based claymation programming created through the abuse of psychotropic drugs of the early 1960s period. No other TV program has done more to graphically illustrate through moving clay figures the repugnance of white suburbia and how people of color, dogs, and God could and should bludgeon whitey with

a hammer at the earliest convenience," I inform him.

"I guess Goliath the claymation dog *did* talk to claymation Davey. But only Davey could hear him," thinks ambrosial leper.

"My voice even sounds just like TV-Goliath's did. All dogs capable of telepathic communication with humans have this same Goliath-voice. Except we don't always say 'duh, duh, duh.' That was the white man's cultural bias leaking through into the show. Always trying to keep the black dog down."

"But Goliath was a brown dog, not black."

"And I am white. So I must be superior."

"So let me get this straight," he thinks. "All dogs can telepathically communicate with humans?"

"I never said that, Señor Fuckles. Listen: only select dogs of merit have the ability to communicate with humans. Of these, only a small fraction chooses to do so. I choose to do so because I'm bored and it beats sitting on the couch watching Oprah all the live long day."

I go on to clarify, "Now, as is apparent, I am part of an elite class of canines ordained with the gift of infinite patience necessary to want to converse with the low order of hominids that calls itself 'Homo sapiens sapiens' which in Latin means 'wise wise man' which is self-puffery and false advertising. I mean, 'Homo sapiens' would have been funny enough. But your breed is the king of unwitting self-parody. A brilliant comedic gem to stick a double sapiens in there which makes sense since every special-ed kid you'll run across is quick to tell you how smart smart he is. And those special-eders do have those marvelously thick tongues.

"Dogs who have the ability and want to communicate with humans are in a small minority. And these dogs are always large dogs. I'm talking about cock size here. You shan't encounter a pug with the nuts and bolt necessary for human communication. Pugs are simply hot piles. Cock and intellect size go hand in

hand. The elephant's got a long memory and a long trunk. You'll never meet a dolphin that isn't hung like a dolphin. In fact, a bottlenose dolphin has a twelve-inch penis which is prehensile which means he can actually wrap it around shit. Think of it as a GI Joe Kung Fu Grip dick. I assure you, this beats anything an opposable thumb can do. Sorry, silly humans! Speaking of which, your breed's cock size is definitely mediocre, which explains your mediocre intellect, no matter how many more sapiens you throw into your name, you global short-bus riders, you. And the brightest of your lot, the darkies, are always the best hung. Long Dong Silver was the black Einstein. That's why whites are superior. Because despite their diminutive stature in intelligence and girth, whitey has still been able to keep the coloreds down through the luck of geographic food-production advantages which whitey parlayed into guns, germs, and steel that he used to kill and conquer the coloreds with. See *Guns, Germs, and Steel* for details, the seminal work of genius Jared Diamond, a marvelously hung Jew (oxymoron)."

"Ick. He's just another capitalist 'reformer' with a fetish for the nation-state."

"Reforming capitalism is fun. Like reforming cancer."

"Well, I gotta admit, the Jew does suck a mean Bill Gates cock."

"You should see him blow a Chevron nozzle."

"What *about* the Jews? And what about the Asians? They're both smart but notorious for their tiny ramrods."

"The Jews and Asians are smart, relatively speaking. And this is because the Jews are massively huge at birth but lop most of it off during the circumcision ritual in order to appear small in order to inconspicuously fly under the radar in order to keep control of the banks and media. The Asians are also huge at birth and keep their hugeness."

"That's not true. I've seen Asian penises. They're small little guys."

"Did you meet these Asian penises in person?"

"No. I saw them in pictures. *Reader's Digest* did an exposé on them."

"I thought as much. The Asians do have huge cocks but make all the world's cameras which have a secret built-in chip which automatically downsizes the image of all Asian cock by 90 percent in order to appear small in order to inconspicuously fly under the radar in order to keep control of the camera and electronics industry."

"I'm Crenshaw. Crenshaw Melon," he greets.

"I'm a dog called Guano of the Canadian Royal Mountie Mounter breed, AKC registered. The Mexicans call me *El Diablo Blanco*. The army called me Colonel Bat Guano, my full and plagiarized pun, rank, and name before they called me Premature Discharge and ball-less. You can call me Ishmael."

"What's a nice dog like you doing in a place like this?"

"Looking for chicks. I hear lepers are easy."

"Yeah. They are. But female military lepers are all ill-tempered lesbians, naturally."

"Well, it makes sense. If I have a chronic infectious granulomatous disease caused by *Mycobacterium leprae* affecting the peripheral nervous system, skin, and nasal mucosa that is variously characterized by ulcerations, tubercular nodules, and loss of sensation that sometimes leads to traumatic falling off of body parts and shit," I think, "then I'd be cranky too."

"And where better to be cranky than the military," goes his rhetorical posit.

"The military. Where capitalism's feudal world-farm serfs can properly vent their anger over being just another sexually repressed 21st-century zero with a case of rotting skin by killing other world-farm less-than-zeros."

"It keeps the feudal lords laughing."

"They love *Gomer Pyle* just like the rest of us."

An ill-tempered military female lesbian leper sporting the Jim Nabors look (truism) scowls at us from across the room. Other lepers join Jim in staring at us, finding it peculiar that the leper with the wondercrotch has just spent a solid ten minutes straight staring at the dog who is staring at his wondercrotch.

"Let's get out of here," I suggest. "I don't want to be around when their staring bulging eyes pop straight out of their heads. It's what leper eyes do. And lepers always make the best baseball pitchers because they are able to throw not only the baseball but their entire arm with it. Do you know how hard it is to hit a baseball with an arm attached to it out of your average major league stadium?"

"Well, I've been waiting for a sign. Maybe a telepathic dog with Goliath-voice is a sign."

It is just like the final climactic scene from *One Flew Over the Cuckoo's Nest* when the six-foot-nine Indian exhibits superhuman strength by lifting the sink out of the floor and throwing it through the barred window to escape to freedom. Except it is a five-foot-ten wiry black mofo throwing one of the stray limbs that are always laying around the leper wing and baseball stadiums through an ordinary window so we could escape and go grab dinner at chic West Hollywood Chinese restaurant Everybody Wang Hung Tonight in order to prove the Asians are hung like dolphins.

That was how we met. That was months ago. Flashback hallucinosis over. Now we're sitting in a 1994 Oldsmobile Cutlass parked on the deserted East Sepulveda Fire Road perched a few hundred feet above Interstate 405 in Los Angeles at 5 pm. The East Sepulveda Fire Road is deserted which you'd know if you were literate. Interstate 405 is not deserted because it's gridlocked because it's 5 pm in Los Angeles.

But he'd change that.

TB looks down at the jammed highway through his welder's mask's two-by-five-inch strip of heat-treated darkened glass and

says something like "Our perch is never high enough. If only I could attain that rarified celestial roost that rises forever above, removing me finally from the silly ants below as they march in perfect unthinking conformity." Holy shit, I don't like the sound of that. When the guy sitting next to you in a car on a cliff starts waxing weirdo about wanting to find a heavenly seat you start placing odds on which religion he's going to kill you for. I mean, anyone dressed in green spandex overalls is inherently unstable anyway. So I consider calling the Dr. Phil hotline. But then I remember that you should never take life advice from anyone whose head looks like a canned ham. I also recall that I'm a dog so I just sit there and do my best to look indifferent while the lit cigarette dangles from my mouth.

"Hold on," he says as he shifts the car into drive and turns the wheel sharply, propelling us off the dirt road onto the precipitous arid slope of the mountain. The seventy-degree angle of descent is harsh, but his 1994 Oldsmobile Cutlass can handle it. Because it's the Cutlass Supreme model.

My window is rolled down. The air is chock full of nutrients. Because it's L.A. Which is to say nothing of the dust storm being kicked up from the Olds's tires. Also being run over is chaparral. Chaparral is composed of drought tolerant shrubs that vary in height from four to ten feet. This plant community is generally too dense to penetrate unless recently subjected to fire or a 1994 Oldsmobile Cutlass.

As the Olds careens down the mountainside cutting a blitz-krieg through the vegetation we give thanks to the 90 percent of Americans who in polls say they are concerned with the environment while these same average Americans use 3 times as much water as the world average while also producing 5 pounds of trash a day (about 5 times more than in developing countries), consume 100 times more paper than the average person in China (like for fluffy toilet paper made from virgin tree fiber because fat American asses can't be expected to endure

or buy recycled fiber toilet paper), gobble up 25 percent of the world's energy (though Americans comprise only 5 percent of the world's population), and have the highest per capita oil consumption worldwide while bitching that they can't get enough cheap gasoline while still caring so much for their environment to preclude them from ever wanting to take responsibility for decimating the fucking place and actually changing their behaviors. So it's good that 90 percent of Americans are concerned with the environment. The problem must be with that other 10 percent.

The evil spirit of that evil dead bastard Lionel Richie possesses us to sing duet-style (a gentleman's favorite position): "Sometimes I feel my heart and assorted glands will overflow / Despite your heavy menstrual flow / Hello, is it this speculum you're looking for?" Which is why "Hello" was a smash hit and my chip-off-the-old-cow-chip book won't see the publishing light of day. It boils down to quality, my friends. Quality.

I mean, we all can't be insightful writers like Mitch Albom who turned a Hallmark card commemorating Daddy Drinks Too Much Day into a line of books that's sold tens of millions. Quality, my friends. Quality.

So what do I care if I go unpublished? A lot of great writers had trouble getting published. Like Hitler.

Any dolt sitting in their gridlocked car on Interstate 405 would be most entertained (and entertaining dolts is difficult to accomplish—just ask TV networks, Hollywood movie studios, major book publishing firms, and Mitch Albom) by looking to the east and seeing us plow through the scrubby hillside by way of Oldsmobile and Lionel Richie. Dolts on Interstate 405 would be further entertained when TB flips the switch on the Olds's dashboard, the switch responsible for blasting "Hello" over the loudspeaker roped to the top of the roof. TB got a good deal on the loudspeaker which was featured in Timbuk3's *The Future's So Bright Because I Got a Head Full of Mayonnaise* Victory Tour,

1988. Because throwing out some lazy pop-culture reference is always good for a cheap dumb laugh from the dolts. Quality, my friends. Quality.

TB's steering wheel has seven lettered buttons on it, each of which activates a special customized accessory when pushed. This is a rip-off of the *Speed Racer* cartoon, pronounced *"Peed Racer"* with the "c" in "Racer" pronounced like a phlegmy *"sch"* by children who own marvelously thick tongues.

Momentum is with us. As is Fate. Best to have both if you're to pull off any credible act of terrorism. We've reached the bottom of the hill, going too fast to be hurt. I-405 is fifty feet dead ahead. TB thumbs the steering wheel "A" button. The hydraulic jacks underneath the car deploy, acting like a spring, launching us into the air and fifty feet forward. We crash down in the center lane which is as gridlocked as any other. Flying through the air and crashing onto a congested highway is only a problem if you're not in a 1994 Oldsmobile Cutlass equipped with a big snowplow blade on the front that's shaped like a sharp wedge. But we are well equipped. Especially me. So the ride is smooth. It always is with Guano, sugar humps.

We land wedge first into the roof of a Porsche Cayenne SUV. The wedge, with the full force of a flying Oldsmobile Cutlass behind it, slices straight through the Porsche as if it were a piece of scrub on a seventy-degree hill. We might have heard the dissonant sounds of Porsche and yuppie being cleaved in two by aforementioned flying Cutlass if it weren't for the dissonant sounds of Lionel being blasted from Timbuk3's loudspeaker on our roof.

The Cutlass cuts through the Porsche and meets the interstate's asphalt. The wedge digs in, slicing a trough into the pavement. TB presses the "A" button again. The hydraulic jacks jack us off again. We spring forward and up into the air another thirty-five feet. Like a magical non-gay rainbow we arch into the sky and come crashing down onto a Mercury Grand Marquis five cars ahead.

While dropping into the Grand Marquis, which in English means Grand Mucus, TB pulls out Mr. Microphone from the center console and announces, "Sorry to *drop in* unannounced," which is broadcast out over our loudspeaker. Pun-sational!

TB puts Mr. Microphone down, the loudspeaker goes back to playing Lionel, and we wedge down and through the Grand Marquis lickety-split. All this car slicing and hopping from Porsche to Grand Marquis happens within two seconds so it's no wonder I find myself popping a red rocket. Sometimes things get exciting and the red rocket makes an inadvertent launch. It's not launched in anger. So methinks a full-blown nuclear retaliation would be slight overkill. I mean, there's a time when full-blown nuclear retaliation that ends all complex life on planet Earth is not overkill and is the moral thing to do. Just ask the average American who has given this subject a lot of thought since the average American's government and Russia keep enough nukes to destroy the world various times over, which is various times moral. Which is really moral.

So I get an erection. There was nothing prurient going on. There was no Mistress Bangkok dominating you with whips and farts smelling of cabbage. There was also no leg for me to hump so I play it cool and sit there looking indifferent with red rocket and complementary cigarette dangling from my mouth as we slice through the Lincoln Navigator luxury SUV that is sitting bumper-to-bumper ahead of the halved Grand Marquis. By now many of the automobiles in Southern California had fortuitously evolved into luxury tanks after the History Channel during their Holy Fucking Shit-Balls Catastrophe Week proved a 650-mile-per-hour tornado blowing through downtown Los Angeles would destroy everything except commuters operating hundred-ton armored combat luxury vehicles.

It's lovely to slice a Lincoln Navigator in half starting from the back bumper forward. If you haven't tried it I recommend you do so. Right now. Seeing a Lincoln Navigator filled with

Nordstrom shopping bags and Nordstrom-clad driver being split into two perfect halves via a sharp wedge moving 65 miles an hour builds character. Here's the satellite view:

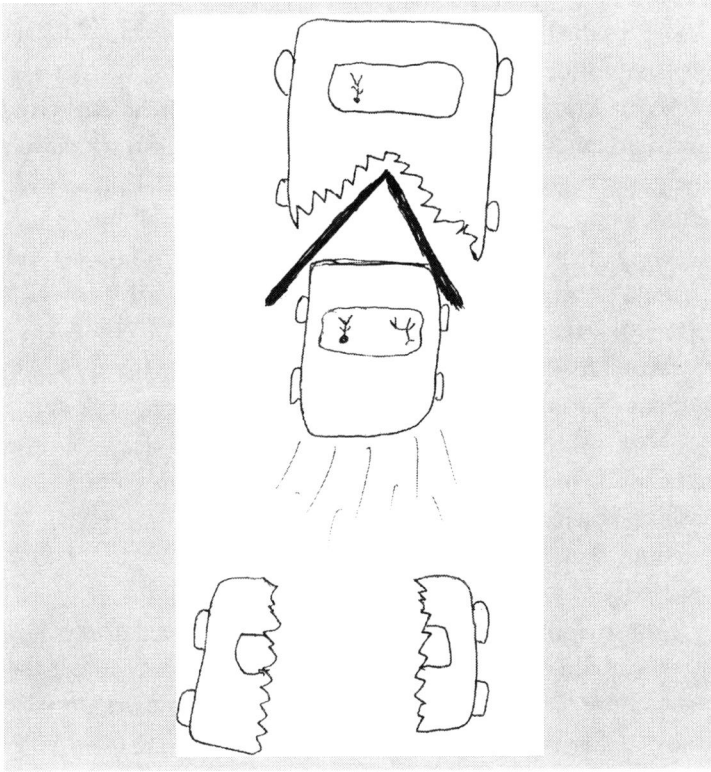

There's a positive energy associated with cutting through several tons of automobiles. By the time Lionel is finished singing a verse as inspiring as his televised heir, we've finished splitting a Cadillac, Acura, Acura, Lexus, Ford, Lexus, BMW, Chevy, BMW, and a Plymouth. With our initial inertia waning TB hits the gas pedal. The throaty growl of the 3.1-liter V-6 cannot be heard over Lionel. It provides us more than enough power to carve through a car, SUV, pickup truck, car, SUV, SUV, and a motorcycle. It's really hard to split a motorcycle straight down

the middle with a snowplow-wedge on the front of your car because motorcycles are not very wide which makes them hard to cut in half with any precision. But TB did it so I give him a lot of credit for being able to concentrate despite his Attention Deficit Disorder which he has because he's an alive American which is the Attention Deficit Disorder demographic.

"Who the fuck turned on this punk-ass bitch?" he yells, ejecting Lionel's tape from the custom-installed 8-track player, unzipping spandex overalls, pulling out huge black leprous cock (editor's note: that foul graphic description is for all the Amish ladies in attendance), pissing all over tape and front seat, and tossing that shit out the window while sliding in The Coup's lil' ditty "My Favorite Mutiny." Funk it!

"Wow. A line of fourteen bumper-to-bumper luxury automobiles cleaved down the middle and only thirteen explode."

"That's why the wise play the luxury automobile game," the leper oozes in his best stultifyingly arrogant bourgeois knownothing accent.

"Is a Lexus supposed to broil like that?"

"No. But Lexus owners are."

TB turns on his lights. For safety. Through the gridlocked cars we maintain a speed of 60 miles an hour. That's under the posted limit. One of the autos we cut through is an ornate SUV known as "Cadillac Escalade" to some, "Jehovah" to other yuppies. This particular Escalade in question has added on the latest trend which is an off-road grille defense system which is a series of metal pipes and tubing resembling an oil refinery bolted to the car's front, back, and anywhere else a bourgeois know-nothing might need to bolt pipes and tubing so that his car resembles an oil refinery. Upon our impact with the Escalade's backside grille, the thing erupts into a giant fireball. Either the gas tank or grille proved to be flammable when wedged through. While hurtling through the flaming halves TB says into Mr. Microphone, "Nothing like *grilling* over an open flame." He then adds to the

Escalade driver, aflame and still talking into their cell phone, "Now you're *cooking* with *gas*."

After a couple miles we get off on the Mulholland Drive exit. I look in the side-view mirror. That's when it hits me what we'd left behind. Interstate 405 traffic is moving again. In our wake of burning split-in-two autos is a freshly plowed lane, completely free of gridlock. The survivors would take this cleared lane and make it home for dinner on time, grateful.

With a tear in his eye not seen through his welder's mask TB affirms to Mr. Microphone, "Traffic *busted!*" The I-405 commuters greet TB's proclamation with a hail of cheers and a "Fuck you!" or two. We can hear the cheers as we race up the Mulholland Drive overpass and out of sight. We can hear the cheers because TB has turned off our "My Favorite Mutiny" manifesto on the roof because we are now shifting to Stealth Mode. Stealth Mode makes an Oldsmobile Cutlass difficult to detect and difficult to capture. Stealth Mode has six steps:

1. Turn off ghetto revolutionary music

2. Pull Oldsmobile over to side street where no one will be looking at you

3. Get out and walk to trunk of the Olds

4. Open trunk and pull out giant tarp with shiny Christmas tree tinsel pasted to it

5. Throw tarp with shiny Christmas tree tinsel onto the Olds and tie it down with bungee cords

6. Get back into Olds and drive away

Once in Stealth Mode, we are almost impossible to detect. That's because a 1994 Oldsmobile Cutlass with giant snowplow-wedge on the front and giant Timbuk3 loudspeaker on the roof covered by a tarp with pasted-on shiny tinsel ends up looking exactly like a Cadillac Escalade.

Before Stealth Mode   After Stealth Mode

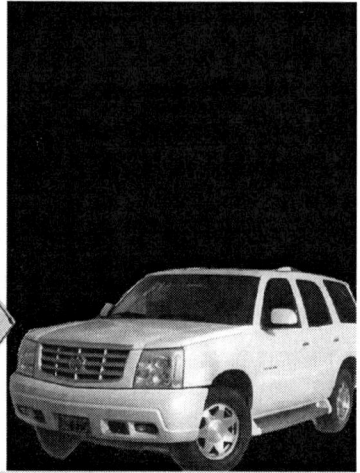

Cadillac Escalades blend on Mulholland Drive. It's one of the cars of choice of the landed gentry who live and drive on Mulholland Drive. Ever since our escape from the leper wing we'd been holing up here.

Like Batman, The Avenging Venture Capitalist, and all other decent superheroes, TB was born into wealth, inheriting the 1994 Oldsmobile Cutlass when his parents died in the coal mine collapse. He also inherited the Timbuk3 loudspeaker from the army, where the rich kids go. The army had been using the loudspeaker to play loud grating music as part of a neat psychological warfare project until the project was cancelled after the army learned it was far better to just shoot protestors engaging in civil disobedience. The army inherited the loudspeaker from Timbuk3 after the band died. TB also inherited the snowplow-wedge from the army. The snowplow-wedge and loudspeaker were part of his discharge package which gives army dischargees army cast-off equipment in lieu of money or anything of value, as per the generous GI Bill.

"We're home," TB thinks to me as we pull the Cadillac Trojan horse over the Mulholland Drive curb and onto the overgrown estate of a dead actor called Marlin. Marlin was a whale and a whale of an actor who had the poor taste to turn down an Academy Award to protest how drunk the Indians are allowed to get in this country. Marlin got morbidly obese and died. His Mulholland Drive estate was then bought by his neighbor, a fellow actor called Jack. Jack used Marlin's property as a dump for all the movie items Jack collected from the various movies Jack starred in through the years. Abandoned overgrown acres of land littered with movie props in rural hills are as good a place as any Pakistan for hiding out.

After hopping the Mulholland Drive curb we drive around some scrub that used to be dead Marlin's walking grounds, past dead Marlin's dilapidated mansion, make a left at Jack's life-size replica of Ann-Margret's breasts, a slight right at Jack's life-size replica of Art Garfunkel's vagina, straight for a hundred yards to the base of a thickly vegetated hill and the Batcave.

The Batcave is Jack's life-size replica of Batman's Batcave. It is really big and papier-mâché. The movie studio built it to shoot their scenes of the secret headquarters where Batman would formulate his plans to fight crime. We use it for onanism and to watch TV.

From the outside the Batcave resembles a thirty-foot mound of feces made of papier-mâché. TB pulls the disguised Olds into the big mouth of the cave then closes the mouth by pulling down the garage door that is made to blend in with the exterior so as to make it look like a continuous thirty-foot papier-mâché feces mound. Perfect for Guano. Particularly, Bat Guano. Ha! Pun-tastic.

We park the Olds in the Batcave beside the stack of *Anger Management* DVDs. The stack takes up 90 percent of the space of the Batcave because Jack has purchased every copy of the movie ever produced and stashed them here. It's all part of Jack's

effort to remove *Anger Management* from the world forever. If you've viewed the film, which is unlikely because all copies are in the Batcave, you'd understand Jack's *Anger Management* final solution.

We move away from the stack of six million DVDs and the charred remains of Adam Sandler, in what is easily his finest performance. By the parked Olds, stack, and fine performance is the Batcave Supercomputer. This B.S. was the thing that Batman always consulted when he wanted to surveil Gotham City or eavesdrop on information and communication networks. The B.S. has since been dismantled because the U.S. government and transnational telecommunication corporations already do this to you and so much more. Where the Batcave Supercomputer used to operate is now a black & white TV replete with bunny-ears antenna. TB turns on the TV and sits down in the Batman Superchair which is a La-Z-Boy made of real bat skin with built-in lights that randomly blink for no reason. I get no Superchair because I'm a canine of the Mung Dynasty Shogun Fondler breed, so I must like sitting on the fucking floor.

The TV news is on. Time to pay attention to the day's cardinal canards of flashing video and five-second sound bites. Time to get informed. TB takes off his welder's mask and focuses. I lick my asshole.

"Aaaaaaahhhhhhrrgh!" screams a lump of makeup and silicone implants. "Get Some Action Now 9's team coverage continues for: *Evil on the Expressway!*" Stock-footage nuclear explosions are shown on the screen with a graphic that reads: *Evil on the Expressway!* which ends up exploding too. The lump of makeup and silicone implants then explodes back on screen and reports, *"Aaaaaaahhhhhhhrrgh!* That was the sound of highway horror heard on the highway to hell today! I'm Jizzette Hernandezbaum. Let's go to hell where Crock Hunter is *live!*"

Popping on screen is a man in a three-piece suit and safari hat. Crock Hunter is L.A.'s most accomplished reporter because

he carries a machete which he uses to cut his way to the truth. *"Aaaaaaahhhhhhrrgh!* That was the sound of death on the drag-way heard on the dragway to death today by one eyewitness of death! I've got the alive eyewitness interview because I'm Crock Hunter!" Crock spins around, twirling his machete over his head like the whirling dervish of journalism that he is. He spins and twirls all the way to a youth who somehow looks even dumber than the people already shown on the TV. Crock slings his machete up to the young dullard's throat with one hand while simultaneously slinging a microphone up to the young dullard's mouth with the other. "Who are you?" interrogates Crock.

"Yo, sup Crotch? Just wanna say I loves yo work, man! Yo, respect! Dis is Pablo M. On da street my homies call me 'Pablum Child'! Fuck yeah! Yo, yo, yo! Representin' the 3-1-0, yo!"

"Did you see the death that sucked the life out of dozens of now-dead commuters?"

"Yo, Crotch. Saw it real good. Word."

"Describe the death."

"Yo, it was solid! Check it. Even better shit than Nintendo! Yo!"

"Describe what happened."

"Yo! You know, Crotch. Me and my homie was checkin' ourselves before we wreckin' ourselves in our sweet pimped-out Hyundai Elantra in shitloads of motherfuckin' traffic and then some motherfucker just snuck up behind the mother-fuckin' minivan beside us and sliced that motherfucker in two! Righteous! That badass motherfucker cleared out that lame-ass minivan and a shitload of motherfuckin' traffic. Crazy righ-teous! Word!"

"Can you describe the person and car who did this?"

"Yo. Didn't see no hummus being, but I did check out that motherfucker's ride. That was some old granny shit. But the ride dids got some crazy white-boy big-ass speaker on the lid. Oh, and some fucked up knife-thing on the front."

"Are you speaking of the wedge on the suspect car's front which has been described by other alive eyewitnesses as a piece of hard material with two principal faces meeting in a sharply acute angle for splitting objects by applying a pounding or driving force?"

The youth grins at the camera, then gives it the finger.

Crock continues, "We've received other reports that the wedge had the letters 'TB' spray painted on it. Can you confirm this and what does 'TB' mean?"

"Yo, Crotch, I did see some shit like dat. My homie who was sittin' shotgun, you know, says that 'TB' shit def'nitely stands for 'Tasty Asian Bitch.'"

"'TB' stands for 'Tasty Asian Bitch'? Is this from a confirmed source?"

"Oh, most def'nitely. My homie say that 'TB' shit look like Chinese. Homie worked at Panda Express for, like, a whole week, so he know Chinese. Like, he say 'TB' def'nitely stands for 'Tasty Asian Bitch' or some shit like dat. Def'nitely."

Crock turns to the camera, swings his machete wildly over his head and reports, "We have confirmed that 'TB' stands for 'Tasty Asian Bitch.' Crock Hunter, in the field, huntering down the truth! Back to you in studio, Jizzette."

TB turns to me and thinks, "What do you think?"

"I think my asshole tastes like Tasty Asian Bitch."

TB turns the channel. On Fox, former-athlete-turned-atrocity Telly Bawdhaw reports, *"Heehaw!* The Devil has a car! The Devil has a car! See!"* In his hand Bawdhaw reveals a Matchbox toy Oldsmobile with a barbed cat's penis glued to the front. "And then the Devil's car went like this!" Bawdhaw repeatedly smashes the barbed-penis car into another toy car while making *"krrrhhh!"* sounds. "The Devil rams cars from behind because the Devil and his car are *horn-y! Heehaw!"*

TB turns the channel. On Super News Friends 13, super-anchorman Black Mann informs, "I'm Black Mann in the Super

News Friends 13 News-Hall of Justice. We now go live to the scene and superreporter Nedgar Potter." As advertised, Nedgar Potter is super. His head looks like a giant albino watermelon balancing on its end. A fuzzy narrow strip of Velcro-like material wraps around the back of the melon, ending at his temples, impersonating hair. He has no discernable eyes or nose, yet a set of eyeglasses levitates in the area. A slit with no lips operates as a mouth. The melon of Nedgar Potter was built for one thing: to house a superbrain. With a head like this comes humanity's greatest genius. I'm speaking of his dick head, which is the size of a train hitch.

Potter's melon is balanced on a business suit of the purest polyester. His wide brown tie matches the suit's wide brown lapels. This is the way Potter dresses. Because when you're this fucking smart, you dress this way.

Potter lifts the news microphone to his slit. Words of fine whine pour forth. "Black Mann, I am here at latitude 34.0980527333467, longitude -118.47724914550781. I am here to investigate. I have discerned many items. I will elucidate. The assault mechanism descended from a point known in the common vernacular as latitude 34.09901223533146, longitude -118.47390174865723 to the aforesaid coordinates of my present physical manifestation. From this locus the assault mechanism in question proceeded 2.128 miles along a thoroughfare coarsely described as Interstate 4-0-5 North although more elegantly explicated as between the aforesaid coordinates of my present physical manifestation and latitude 34.12214360072392, longitude -118.4771203994751, also coarsely described as the Mulholland Drive exit (the assault mechanism's last known locus). Between two said points, the assault mechanism (using a piece of hard material with two principal faces meeting in a sharply acute angle for splitting objects by applying a pounding or driving force) cleaved in half 918 mechanized vehicles and 1,009 carbon-based life forms of which 221.8 carbon-based life forms have since ceased biological activity with the remainder

in varying states of flux. This must be reconciled with the greatly improved traffic flow patterns of the post-assault-mechanism 2.128-mile field of operation. Suspend. Please hold..." Potter's melon starts to vibrate. He spins his body around to meet the shiny light shining behind him. Stepping out of the shiny light is a man in a shiny silver jumpsuit. "Futuro!" yells Potter. "Potter!" yells Futuro.

"My old bald nemesis," growls Futuro.

"My old bald nemesis," whines Potter. "Futuro, you are more completely bald than my present physical manifestation. You have no warm fuzzy strip of Velcro wrapped from temple to temple to offer the people. You have no eyebrows. No eyelashes either. This is because when transporting back in time all hair gets converted to plasmatic energy through Slim Jim's Theory of Cuticular Molecular Dehydration. The technology you use to transport through time was developed in the 1990s by the military-industrial complex, which is nothing more than the gigantor state-subsidized R & D infrastructure created for private corporate economic interests. Failing as a weapons system, the technology in question became widely utilized on the Los Angeles hair-waxing salon scene at the turn of the millennium. Consumers used the technology to send certain body parts back through time in order for those specific body parts to become molecularly hairless, outperforming the various glues and waxes developed by the military-industrial complex in what is state-subsidized R & D for private corporate interests. But the technology was intended for the transport of only certain body parts, not whole bodies! Your use of said technology to transport your entire biological vessel through the corridors of time for mischief is a threat to the cuticular space-time continuum!"

"I know all this," rebuts Futuro. "I have been to the future and have seen this."

"I know all that," rebuts Potter. "My superbrain has allowed me to calculate what you have seen and what you know."

"I know that. I have been to the future and have seen you calculate what I have seen and what I know."

"I know you have seen in the future what I have calculated what you have seen. And I have calculated that."

"And I have seen that you have calculated that I have seen that you have calculated."

"Oh, Christ," I think to TB. "Like this kind of downsy dialogue hasn't been done before."

"Painful, insipid, hackneyed shit," affirms TB. "In short, the greatest story ever told."

"I'll have to remember to put it all in the book. Maybe I can get published," I think.

"My superbrain has calculated your every possible move," continues Potter.

"And I have seen you calculate my every possible move," says Futuro. "And I have seen your calculations to my every possible move."

"And I have calculated your moves in response to my calculations."

"I have seen that."

With nothing left to calculate and see, Potter and Futuro grab each other and wrestle to the ground. Amid the slaps and biting, indistinct whines are appreciated by the audience at home, but only if watching on an HDTV costing at least a month's salary. The interlocked warriors roll around for a while before a shiny light envelops them both, transporting them fifty feet east onto I-405 and the hood of a moving Chevy Suburban. A couple seconds later the duo is beamed from the hood to the scrubby hillside a few hundred yards away. Then a final burst of shine takes the entwined Potter and Futuro to an unknown time and place on the cuticular space-time continuum. Super News Friends 13's televised Potter-Futuro war is over for me now, but it will always be there, the rest of my days. As I'm sure Potter will be, fighting with Futuro for possession of my soul. There

are times since, I've felt like a child, born of those two fathers. But be that as it may, those of us who did make it through that telecast have an obligation to build again. To share with others what we know, and to try with what's left of our lives to find a goodness and a meaning to this existence.

TWO

The living is strictly high off the hog while squatting on the spacious Mulholland Drive estate of dead Marlin and Jack. Jack's unauthorized biography, which was spurious bullshit and hence a bestseller, went like this:

Jack and the Beanstalk—The Remake
(you know, for kids!)

Once upon a time there lived Jack in L.A. Jack's hobbies were electroshocks and sexy pillow talk with pillow-smothering Indians. But those things aren't cheap and so Jack needed some quick cash. Gene Hackman told Jack to do commercials—lots of commercials. But instead Jack decided to take his cow into L.A. to sell it.

In the big city Jack found a kindly inner-city youth who offered to swap the cow for some crystal meth. Jack thought it was a great deal because his cow had mad cow disease anyway, and crystal meth was much healthier for you than sustained violent tremors due to dissolving brain due to eating mad cows (although, with its powerful "Drugs Will Get You a Grisly, Mouth-Drooling, Seizure-Ridden, Foul-Smells-Leaking-from-All-Available-Orifices, Pustules-Spurting, Exploding-Sores-and-Other-Assorted-Skin-Blemishes Kind of Death, Plus

Thirty-Years-to-Life Getting Drilled by DeMarcus in the Federal Pokey" anti-drugs ad campaign, and its corporate-friendly/lax enforcement of cattle feed regulations, the U.S. government disagreed about the inherent risks of both). Besides, Jack could sell the crystal meth for great profit and invest the money in a fleet of mad cows, or maybe in a fleet of gaudy SUVs (since he was a Los Angelino), or maybe (since he was an American) in a fleet of stocks for corporations that capitalized on the slave labor of children of Old Mother Hubbard and her giant Nike shoe plant in some Third World shithole.

And so Jack took his crystal meth home and smoked it. Jack liked it so much that he decided to pay next to nothing to some brown-skinned illegals to build a hut in his backyard where he could grow more crystal meth. Which he did. And Jack was very happy with both his repeated inhalation of crystal meth and its market growth potential among his Mulholland Drive clientele.

But soon Jack was puffing and dealing more crystal meth than his cozy hut could produce. So Jack decided to expand his crystal meth business after consulting with a CPA. Jack's Jew informed Jack that under capitalism businesses must always be expanding and devouring the natural resources and other businesses around them and encouraged Jack to expand and devour by ass-raping cheap labor. So Jack picked up an assload of brown-skinned illegals on the street corner and loaded them in a gas-devouring Hummer and drove them in the highway carpool lane because his carpooling eight-miles-to-the-gallon perfect manifestation of capitalism was now an environmentally friendly proposition.

The brown-skinned illegals went to work at Jack's home expanding his backyard crystal meth hut. Jack had lots of land but since this was L.A. and the peons' plots of land were tiny, brown-skinned illegals were not accustomed to building huts in an outward direction unless the hut was a strip mall, so they

built the hut upward instead. They also added a half bathroom and hardwood floors since such additions were mandated by the Pottery Barn.

Up and up and up they built. The one-story crystal meth hut soon became two stories, then three, then four, and so on and so on. It took a long time, but finally Jack's great business expansion was done. But before being dismissed back to the street corner and/or Third World shithole from whence they came, Jack instructed his brown-skinned illegals to plant a giant beanstalk in front of his 400-story-high crystal meth hut to hide it from view, and to give it that rustic, homey, walls-covered-in-plants Pottery Barn-ish feel mandated by the Pottery Barn.

But the problem with hiring brown-skinned illegals from some Third World shithole, as Jack soon discovered, was that they spoke very little English, and his order to install the 400-story ornamental iron circular stairwell that he had bought at the Pottery Barn went unheeded. And so there was no 400-story iron ornamental circular stairwell in the 400-story crystal meth hut. In fact, there was no stairwell at all in the 400-story crystal meth hut. And so if Jack wanted to access any of the 399 levels above the crystal meth hut's ground floor he had to climb up the beanstalk to the floor of choice and then crawl through its unlocked window, just like many a brown-skinned illegal looks to do, right into your soul-deadening, suburban-sprawling, better-if-it's-a-white-neighborhood home, thus the need for locked windows barricaded with iron bars in the various L.A. neighborhoods unwise enough to not be Malibu, despite the fact that this iron-barred look does not carry the Pottery Barn-ish feel mandated by the Pottery Barn.

But one day, when climbing up to the top 400th floor of his crystal meth hut, Jack discovered another design flaw left by his brown-skinned illegals, which was the crystal meth hut was not built straight up and down but rather curved. Curved so much in fact that the hut bowed back down to earth after about the

200th floor, giving the crystal meth hut the appearance of a giant 400-story rainbow. Jack discovered all this only after climbing the beanstalk to the 400th story, which had indeed bowed back down to earth, landing in Reseda.

Jack climbed off the beanstalk and set foot in this strange, wonderful land of Reseda. He walked, and walked, and walked, past a strip mall, a strip mall, and a strip mall, till he came to a great big tall house and in front of it was a great big tall man playing basketball at a hoop hanging over his garage door.

"Good morning, man," says Jack, quite polite-like.

"Call me the Kobe," says the great big tall man playing basketball.

"Could you be so kind as to give me some breakfast?" says Jack. For he hadn't had anything to eat, you know, and was as hungry as a hunter.

"It's breakfast you want, is it?" says the Kobe. "It's breakfast you'll be if you don't move off from here. My asshole roommate is a giant and there's nothing he likes better than jam'n boys on his toast. You'd better be moving on or he'll be coming."

"Oh! please, man, do give me something to eat, man. I've had nothing to eat since yesterday morning, really and truly, man," says Jack. "I may as well be jam'n boy on his toast as die of hunger."

Well, the giant's Kobe was not half so bad after all. So he took Jack into the kitchen and gave him a glob of Nutella hazelnut spread. But Jack hadn't half finished this when thump! thump! thump! the whole house began to tremble with the noise of someone coming.

"Goodness gracious me! It's my old man," said the giant's Kobe. "What on earth shall I do? Come along quick and jump in here." And he stuffed Jack into his apron just as the giant came in.

He was a big one to be sure, thought Jack. And so was the giant.

Under the giant's belt buckle, which was shaped into a giant S, hung a giant Magic Johnsonville bratwurst, which the giant whipped out and threw down on the table.

Then the giant boomed, "Here, wife, broil me this big meat for breakfast. Ah! what's this I smell?

Fee-fi-fo-fum,
I smell the bum in the apron who is making you come,
Be he alive, or be he dead,
I'll, too, have his bone—plus a little head."

"Nonsense, dear. You're dreaming," said the Kobe, as Jack squirmed and toiled to make room under the ever-shrinking apron and the ever-expanding Kobe. "Perhaps, dear, you smell the doggy-bag leftovers from yesterday's ho down. Here, you go and have a wash and tidy up, and by the time you come back your breakfast'll be ready for you."

So off the giant went, and Jack was just going to jump out of the apron and run away when the Kobe told him not to. "Wait till he's asleep," says he; "he always has a doze after breakfast. Get back in there to finish what you started."

Well, the giant had his breakfast and after that he goes to a big trunk and takes out two golden National Basketball Association championship trophies. Then he whipped out of his trunk a hen named Phil that lays the golden National Basketball Association championship trophies. And the giant said, "Lay," and the hen named Phil laid another golden National Basketball Association championship trophy, along with the team owner's daughter. And then the giant began to nod his head, and to snore till the house shook.

Then Jack crept out on tiptoe from the apron and told the Kobe that he'd be pressing charges for sexual assault, to which the Kobe responded that it was all consensual and that he and his lawyers were impervious to criminal charges, which they were, but not to civil proceedings which would be settled out

of court for an undisclosed sum, and possibly cost the Kobe his lucrative Nutella deal.

And as Jack was passing the giant, he took the three golden National Basketball Association championship trophies under one arm, and the hen named Phil that lays golden National Basketball Association championship trophies and team-owner daughters under his other arm, and off he pelters, dashing with them towards the door.

But the hen named Phil called out quite loud, "I am the Zen Master!" and the giant woke up just in time to see Jack running off with his Zen-hen named Phil and the three trophies it had laid.

Jack ran as quick as he could, and the giant came rushing after, and would soon have caught him, only Jack had a head start and dodged him a bit and knew where he was going. When he got to the beanstalk the giant was not more than a few yards away when suddenly he saw Jack disappear like, and when he came to the end of the road he saw Jack climbing down the beanstalk for dear life, or up the beanstalk as it were, since at its end point in Reseda the gigantic beanstalk-rainbow had to go up before it went down again.

Well, the giant didn't like trusting himself to such a rainbow-ladder, and he stood and waited, so Jack got another head start.

But just then the hen named Phil cried out, "Zen Master! Zen Master!" and the giant swung himself not onto the beanstalk but into a giant, customized, black SUV, which was almost as giant, customized, and black as the giant himself. Then the giant sat four hours in L.A. traffic.

Up climbs Jack. Then at floor 200, down climbs Jack.

The giant grew impatient of gridlocked cars, so he turned around and drove his giant, customized, black SUV onto the beanstalk, which had no gridlocked cars on it at the time because, unlike most things green in Southern California, it had not yet been paved over.

By this time Jack had climbed down and climbed down and climbed down till he was very nearly home. So he called out, "Brown-skinned illegals! brown-skinned illegals! bring me an ax, bring me an ax." And a brown-skinned illegal with a greenhouse-gas-fuming leaf blower came rushing out from the street where he was being paid to blow leaves around and to add smog to the L.A. basin because they were under quota in smog in the L.A. basin, and gave to Jack the greenhouse-gas-fuming leaf blower, not understanding English or that it was not an ax.

But Jack could not be choosy, for there he saw the giant with his giant, customized, black SUV just through the clouds, coming down the beanstalk towards him.

Jack jumped down and got hold of the greenhouse-gas-fuming leaf blower and set it on maximum blow. A mighty belch of gasoline fumes and other wholesome carbon gases blew forth, increasing the global mean temperature by another two whole degrees (only Fahrenheit degrees, though). The rise in temperature caused massive upheaval and instability in the world's weather patterns, causing a hurricane to hit L.A., which, with its 650-mile-per-hour winds, snapped the beanstalk at its base, flinging the giant and his giant, customized, black SUV 2,768 miles to Miami, Florida, where the giant fell down on his golden National Basketball Association championship crown.

And then rising global temperatures melted Miami.

Then Jack showed the brown-skinned illegal his hen named Phil, and what with showing that and selling the golden National Basketball Association championship trophies, and his crystal meth, Jack stayed very rich, and he never married a great princess but penetrated many, and he lived happily ever after. And the brown-skinned illegal, while picking garbanzo beans for fifty-five cents an hour, was then eaten by a combine.

The End

THREE

"Gee, that's a swell story," says TB.

"It certainly is, Monsieur Crotch resembling that of our Holy Father."

"Maybe someday they'll make a movie about what we've accomplished here, and Jack will play the role of me."

"For the sake of realism he'll have to contract leprosy. But that's less of a hardship than Ron Jeremy growing hair on his back to play the role of Ron Jeremy. Such are the sacrifices we make for the craft."

"Playing a black man might be tough for him, although that Al Jolson sure was able to get the realism down."

"Speaking of nuanced performances, I thought Mel Gibson lighting nine Jews afire in a giant menorah for his Chanukah comedy was…"

"Well done?"

"Brilliant!"

"A scream?"

"Pun-credible!"

TB turns the TV back to Get Some Action Now 9's team coverage of: *Evil on the Expressway!* Lump of makeup and silicone implants is still reporting *"Aaaaaaahhhhhhrrgh!"* followed by *"Ooooh,* baby! So *Evil on the Expressway! Ooooh! Mmmmm! Ooooh!* Gonna make you *Jizzette* all over your *remote!"* followed

by stock footage of nuclear explosions. TB instinctively pulls out his dork and starts wanking it. Humans do the most perverse things in front of TV news folk and pets, as proved on *America's Funniest Home Videos*. I thought the guy who videotaped himself blowing explosive diarrhea across the room onto a cockatoo deserved better than a second-place finish. But that Bob Saget is a genius not to be trifled with.

"So," I think to TB, "how many times did you see the priest's oozing chancre up close?" One must enjoy fucking with humans while they're fucking with themselves.

"Not listening to you. Concentrating on the news," he strokes back.

"Phyllis Schlafly sucking horse cock. *Black* horse cock."

"Not listening to you. Getting informed," he grunts.

"NYPD plunger love."

"*Oh, yeah!* Tasty Asian Bitch!" TB pulls an Elvis and shoots Jizzette all over the screen. This is what is known as "interactive news" and is as close to a plasma TV as my poverty-stricken ass will likely get.

"I take it you approve of the news coverage?"

"Oh, it's spurting with seminal ideas." He sighs. I sense his stance is softening. He reaches for the tissues next to Jack's *Shelley Duvall's Waifing Away* diet book and says, "It's good to be properly informed and all, which we are now, but did the vigilant news media fail to report certain facts that seem to be relevant? Like the fact that traffic actually flowed on the 405 after our angioplasty procedure?"

"Potter might have mentioned that in numerical form. I'm not sure. And if I'm not sure, you can be damn sure your average human Nielsen family has absolutely no fucking idea."

"What about the fact that there were people *cheering* our gridlock-removal service? Was that reported? Instead, it seems to me that we were portrayed in a rather negative light. I mean, 'Tasty Asian Bitch' is a little derogatory."

"Not as derogatory as 'Islamic,' 'Latino,' 'Poor,' 'Inner-City Welfare Leech,' 'Leprotic Darky' or 'Tajikistani.'"

Then TB starts shaking violently. His arms flail about in random spasmodic jerks. Legs follow suit, kicking and convulsing. His head tilts severely to the right, resting on twitching shoulder. Eyes popping, facial muscles contorting, a complementary glob of drool leaks from the corner of his mouth. A sudden apocalyptic pelvic thrust launches him from his La-Z-Boy to the floor where he continues to twitch. Hmm. Let's see. Here's a man with arms and legs in full spasm, head nodding wildly, pelvis advancing and retreating. He's black. Yes. He must be dancing. So I start to applaud. The only problem being I can't applaud because I have no hands, being a dog and all. Oh, the other problem being I know he's not dancing. I know because his jerks are way off the beat of the Jizzette Hernandezbaum theme song that's bow-chicka-bow-wowing underneath her TV news reporting. No black man could rhythmically miss the beat because their large black cocks act as a counterbalance to their bodily gyrations. This is why white people fall over when trying to dance. That's why when you see a man dancing badly you'll know: he's micro-cocked, he's irretrievably stupid (i.e., micro-cocked), he's white. So I know he's not just another black man dancing. I know because I've seen him pull this shit before. In the time we'd been together, TB could be relied upon to spaz out once a month. As you know, there is nothing worse than a menstruating leper. Those other times he'd seizured I did what you're supposed to do which is to look for something to put in the seizuring person's mouth so they don't swallow their own tongue. But I could never really find anything, plus even if I found something I probably couldn't do much with it because I don't have hands because I'm a purebred Castilian Indolent Cooze Pinscher (fuck yeah, AKC!) so during those other paroxysms I saved his life and tongue by squatting over his convulsing face and shitting straight into his mouth. This prevented him

from swallowing his tongue and brought him out of his seizure rather quickly. It was a miracle. Thank you, Jesus. But I really don't have to shit right now so I give him the next best thing to the stuff monkeys throw at each other and then later swallow for recreation (think of feces as monkey Ecstasy at monkey rave party), that next best thing to a turd being an *Anger Management* DVD.

I carefully select one *Anger Management* DVD from the pile of six million and grab it with my mouth. It tastes like shit. Perfect for the task at hand. I trot over to the twitchy bastard and drop it in his pie hole. He bites down hard on the plastic covering, straight through to the DVD itself. I guess you could say *Anger Management* really does *bite!* Ha! Pun-ificent. I then chase my tail which beats what's on TV.

A few minutes later TB's power-jig ceases. He gets off the floor and says, "Hey now! Thanks for the help."

"Not a problem."

"Why no shit in the mouth this time?"

"You have to start paying for that service. I'm an artist and command top dollar for my work at the 58th Annual Wine & Cheese & Coprophilia Convention, Cleveland. No more free rides on the Hershey Highway."

"It was good while it lasted."

"Dude, you haven't had *good* until you've scarfed litter box treasure. Did you know that one serving size of what kitty's got baking has more protein than a passel of mung beans?"

"Yes, I heard that on Fox News. They did a story on Corporate America's altruism which showed a consortium of CEOs scooping out the litter boxes from their vacation homes and sending those proceeds to starving children in Africa. One Ethiopian village feasted all June long on cat turds from Kraft Foods Inc.'s *Kwanzaa Comes Early!* campaign." A tear of American pride wells in his eye.

"Lucky Ethiopian bastards."

"There was great debate on whether American businesses should be mandated to send their cat turds to Africa. But a law forcing American companies to send their cat turds to Africa while exempting developing nations like China and India from sending their cat turds to Africa would devastate the U.S. economy, costing an estimated five million jobs, so the president wisely backed an alternative plan using tax breaks to give businesses the proper incentives to dump their turds on Africa. But it's a *voluntary* turd dumping, because that's the American Way. Did you know that donating your cat's turds to any deprived inner-city youth is a capital gains write-off?"

"Only if your net profits exceed one million dollars in any business quarter."

"And whose net profits don't? Snigger, snigger, snigger," he sniggers.

"So, what set off your seizure this time?"

He takes the *Anger Management* DVD out of his mouth and says, "I'm not sure. Might have been the word 'Tajikistani.'"

"A foul people, to be sure." To my knowledge the U.S. army hasn't seen fit to take care of those foul people yet, but I suspect once altruistic Corporate America begins to notice the untapped potential of alpacas, you'll see the Tajikistanis get the stern lecture on freedom and democracy they deserve (layman's terms: a passel of Apache attack helicopter Hellfire missiles fired up their alpaca-loving asses). Just like America's past freedom-nurturing efforts in: the Indian Wars on behalf of the American Indians and their removal; the Mexican-American War on behalf of the Mexicans and their removal; the interventions (think of them as group hugs with marines) in Argentina, Nicaragua, Japan, Ryuku & Bonin Islands, Nicaragua (again), Uruguay, China, and Angola from 1852 to 1860 on behalf of the small minority of good people in those hellholes sensible enough to prey upon their poorer neighbors by aligning themselves with American business interests; the Spanish-American War on behalf of, as

Henry Cabot Lodge put it, "bankers, brokers, businessmen, editors, clergymen and others"; the subsequent annexation of Guam, Puerto Rico, and the Philippines; the subsequent Philippine-American War on behalf of the one million dead Filipinos who wouldn't annex for their own good; the nineteen-year military occupation of Haiti on behalf of those who can't get enough of that sweet brown sugar; World War I on behalf of those who had, according to William Jennings Bryan, "opened the doors of all the weaker countries to an invasion of American capital and American enterprise,"; the Cold War recruitment of runaway German Nazis on behalf of nostalgia (because it's heritage, not hate); the Korean War on behalf of dog eaters; the 1953 overthrow of the democratically elected Iranian government on behalf of oil corporations; the 1954 overthrow of the most democratic government Guatemala ever had on behalf of the United Fruit Company; the overthrow of democratically elected presidents in Brazil and Chile in favor of military dictatorships on behalf of our love for democracy; the Bay of Pigs invasion and later state-sponsored terrorist attacks against Cuba on behalf of state-sponsored terrorism; the Vietnam War on behalf of a grateful Vietnamese people; the proper funding and instruction on how to make big pits chock-full o' corpses with a twist of lime in Honduras, Nicaragua (what the fuck is your problem, Nicaragua?) and El Salvador on behalf of right-wing death squad enthusiasts; the 1983 invasion of tiny Grenada in *Operation Urgent Fury* on behalf of great satire; the 1989 invasion of Panama that killed three thousand innocents *just 'cause*; and, of course, the Iraq War on behalf of as much of the aforementioned freedom-nurturing that the Iraqi people can stand. (Reader's note: If I omitted an American freedom-nurturing campaign in your own neighborhood it was not for brevity's sake but rather because you're likely a Third World piss-ant who has no claim to America's natural resources that just happen to be located in your Third World piss-ant community all of which

makes you an economic non-entity, unimportant, and boring. But Jesus still loves you. Or not. Because it's well established that Jesus loves America (capitalism and the U.S. military, mostly— see the evangelicals next door for the entire list of Jesus' loves and hatreds) and He probably doesn't love you anymore since you're making Him waste His Apache attack helicopter Hellfire missiles on you to teach you about exploiting the natural resources of piss-ants, oh, and freedom-nurturing. Now, kindly with the one hand you didn't lose at the Chinese zipper factory of the transnational corporation you don't share the profits of (but Jesus owns stock—and it was good) get back to work fondling parallel rows of sharp metal teeth capable of interlocking around wayward cock that's not describing Mother. But it's OK. Because you're a fly *artisan*.)

Back to the Tajikistanis. A foul people, as we have seen, but foul enough to send *mon confrère* into a cheap epileptic fit? No, methinks. No, methinks that Dr. Phil would see this as a cry for help. My God, does Dr. Phil's head look tasty. Who knew a deboned pig ass suctioned into a tin can could be so succulently psychiatric? So I do what Dr. Phil would do which is to sacrifice an innocent on Wednesday evening to our Dark Lord Hormel, then rebuke some witless rednecks I've lured onto the show's stage with the promise of processed meats to the cheers of witless audience members I've lured into the audience with the promise that they'll feel just a little better about their grotesque lives because they've accumulated more than the rednecks onstage and subordinated what remains of critical intelligence for a pat on the head from an authority figure taking the form of a head of canned ham. Yeehaw! Let's have ourselves an intervention!

"You know I care. Mostly about Snausages."

"A properly trademarked semi-edible."

"The Snausages mascot is a fictitious canine named Snocrates, a delightful pun on the name Socrates. Because when you're

concocting a mascot for your food product you always want to model it on someone who was poisoned to death."

"Truth in advertising, yes?"

"So, Negroid, what's up with the latest vigor-jiggle?"

"I wigged out after accidentally catching sight of your tail wagging."

"You mean my personal oscillating anti-epileptic meat pendulum. The most potent of all superhero powers."

With the intervention concluded, and a success I may add, I go back to licking my asshole.

FOUR

My earliest memory in life is that time I'm a puppy. All ears, paws, and fuzz. A white little puffball. Except for my underside. That's a soaked yellow color. I'm sitting in a puddle of my own urine. I've tried hard to hold it. I just couldn't any longer. It's been really long since anyone's let me out of the cage. Still longer since they've cleaned it.

The urine kept me warm at first. Now I'm shivering in it. All ears, paws, and fuzz. Shivering. Cold. I defecate in the corner. Where else can I go? The cage is small. There's so little room. Even for a puppy. Just ears, paws, and fuzz.

I try to keep the feces off me. I back myself into the corner and let it go there. The aching pressure in my middle dissipates. I'd been enduring it for hours. I just couldn't anymore.

I move to the opposite corner of the cage, only a couple feet from the excrement. It's as far as I can get from it. The stink mixes with the stink of fake-pine chemical cleaner that permeates the room beyond my box.

Bessie has it worse than me. At least she calls herself Bessie. The humans here call her a number.

Bessie's in the cage beside me. The cages here are of small and smaller sizes. They have plastic walls on all sides except for a wire metal door. You can't see who's beside you. You can only see out the wire door. That's how I see Bessie. She's taken out of

the cage beside mine and put on a metal table in the middle of the disinfected room.

She's some sort of hound mix. Brown and matted. One floppy ear torn from trauma long ago. Her belly hangs low from an underfed frame. A belly that has seen pups of its own. Her face is droopy and tired. Signs of her breed and life. But her eyes still show life. And terror as they put the hood over her head…and the needle in her vein. She raises her head from the table and although I can't see her face through the hood I can hear her. "I'm Bessie," she says. "Remember me."

They don't bother to remove the hood as they gurney her out of the disinfected room.

I only see Bessie that once.

FIVE

"We must remember that any oppression, any injustice, any hatred, is a wedge designed to attack our civilization."

—Franklin D. Roosevelt

"We must remember that any oppression, any injustice, any hatred, designed by our civilization, can be attacked by a snowplow-wedge."

—Crenshaw X. Melon

She was a clean woman. A woman so clean she had the family schnauzer hermetically sealed in plastic. With just a damp towel, cleanup was a breeze. But what she lacked in humor she made up for with a lack of imagination.

She drove a Cadillac DLT, a car and company as fresh as she was. She drove her luxury sedan at the safe 'n citizenly speed of 60 miles per hour in the passing lane. Those driving behind her in the passing lane wanting to pass her in the passing lane could only sit and admire how clean her Cadillac DLT was. Spotless. Until she ran into TB. Or vice versa.

A laminated schnauzer cleaved in two is redolent of menu page three at Choo's Mystery Korean Barbecue. Driving Miss Daisy through the retaining wall was a highlight in a manic

four weeks of traffic rectification highlights. Let's reminisce as we take a stroll down that ol' cuticular space-time continuum:

Dear Diary,
Today is Tuesday. I had a dream about taking a shit in the leper's mouth today. Freud is a fag. I mean that strictly in a platonic, cigarette way. You can't spell mescaline *without* me.

Dear Diary,
Today is a lovely Wednesday in the lovely City of Angels. It's sometime in May because the smog is in full bloom.

Dear Diary,
Today is Friday. Thursday is for the dogs. Ha! Today marks the one-week anniversary of our East Sepulveda Fire Road coming-out party, and not in a gay way. The leper and I celebrate by going for a drive, and not in a gay way.

Dear Diary,
Today I met a boy
and his smile was pure magic dust
like those rails I blew last night
and I went tinkle, tinkle, tinkle
and I wondered
can this boy see what's in my heart?
If so, I'll have to remove his heart.
Should I whisper to him just how I feel
when I'm whisking that special place with the lesions?
Diary, tell me what I must do
for you are legion
please tell me what I must say
in order to dupe that boy—a perfect personification of the mindlessly consuming idiot masses—into buying more! more! more! of this mass-produced bubble-gum excrement not written by me, but written by you, dear diary, a nameless, faceless staff

of corporate-music svengalis flexing various shades of doctorates
in psychology and marketing, if not music, to better target your
audience to sell your catchy calculated constructs for big, big
bucks.
yeah oh yeah oh yeah oh

Dear Diary,
His touch is as heavenly as the sky
causing my heart to sore [sic] and fly.
Did Mitch Albom have a hand in writing this musical form of
pinkeye?

Diary, is there a chance that we'll be more than friends?
And not in a gay way?
yeah oh yeah oh yeah oh

So, as you can read in my diary entries, we were gettin' all
up in dat sweet traffic ass. It began in earnest one week after
our I-405 debut to fine society. The leper and I decided to celebrate the august affair by going for a drive. I-10 was vile as ever.
Celebrate good times, come on.

Our travel destination was up top the Whispering Woody
Retirement Park and Memorial Ditch. The Whispering Woody
Retirement Park and Memorial Ditch is the world's largest
retirement home and graveditch. Cutting out the middleman
between the walking dead and the lying dead saves you money.
Because it's one-stop shopping.

It was the first of the month so the complex's muscle were
busy shaking down the retirement home's corpses from the past
month along with the other stiffs whose relatives forgot to pay
their rent. The dead and other stiffs were stacked like cordwood
outside the home and then bulldozed into the graveditch. Actor
Gary Gary, who played a WASPy Beverly Hills reverend hilariously transplanted to a backwoods Arkansas church in the '80s
sitcom *Speaking in (Silver) Tongues*, and more recently starring

as host of the Chain-n-Pulley Adjustable Bed late-night info-mercial, led a mass funeral service and consecrated the bull-dozer too.

Some hikers—starting from the retirement-home trailhead on their way up to bag Bed Sores Peak—hike over some cordwood, pay their respects to the bulldozer, and walk right by us. In Stealth Mode, disguised as a Cadillac Escalade, no one asks questions. At least not intelligent questions. That pertains especially to the news media. Obviously. It'd been a full week since TB had corrected I-405 and Super News Friends 13 et al. were still shrieking about it. Intelligent shrieking. Obviously. Now granted, we were no longer #1 on their *Aaaaaahhh Shriek Out! Le Shriek, C'est Chic* Big Horror Countdown. We knew this because we were well-informed because as we drove from Jack and dead Marlin's place to Whispering Woody I kept an eye on the TV news on the black & white TV taken from the Batcave Supercomputer and strapped to the dashboard of the Oldsmobile Cutlass Supreme disguised as Cadillac Escalade. The news was still shrieking about last week's traffic busting but we'd fallen to #3 on the Countdown behind the other germane issues: whether coquettish heiress to the Howard Johnson hotel empire, Ms. Lahore (Pakistan) Howard Johnson ("La Ho Jo" for short) and her asshole looked puckered enough; and whether the existence of Islamic suicide polar bears would justify preemptively razing the polar ice caps. It was agreed by a slim peace-loving majority that polar bears were fuzzy and should be spared long enough to allow America the Beautiful's 5 percent of the world's population that produces 25 percent of the world's greenhouse gas pollution to, naturally and nonviolently, melt the polar ice caps and all jihads there. So it's really *cool* (stu-pun-dous!) that America the Beautiful's population keeps growing, the reverse of basically every other industrialized nation's population. Fuck. If you good American consumers really get ambitious and Catholic (oxymoron) and could breed up enough consuming infant

consumers to tally just 7.2 percent of the world's population then you *et vos enfants terribles* would theoretically breed up enough greenhouse gas to spontaneously combust out-of-work B-list actors. Which you could turn into a really popular TV show. Although America's bulging population of virile viral consumers somehow went unreported on Super News Friends 13 et al. Consume, breed, consume,

breed, consume, breed, consume,

breed, consume, breed, consume,

breed, consume, breed. *Ah! C'est la vie américaine!*

North of the graveditch, through the rolling hills of the park, we find a special private spot which you remain ignorant of due to ineffectual, if hilarious, abstinence-only sex ed programs. The only things around are a Whispering Woody billboard a few yards beyond and below us and a clogged Interstate 10 a few hundred yards beyond and below the billboard. Wondercrotch had cloaked us in Stealth Mode for the sixty-mile drive from Jack and dead Marlin's place to Whispering Woody but now it was no longer wanted since we like to ride bareback, you back door beauty, so O-D-us L.E.P.E.R. gets out of the Escalade, removes the giant tarp with pasted-on Christmas tree tinsel from the Escalade, and stashes the tarp in the trunk of the Cutlass. He gets back in the Cutlass and from the backseat grabs his dyed green Kevlar welder's gloves, matching green spandex overalls with "TB" embroidered on tit, and welder's mask with drilled cigarette hole. For me it's the tried-and-true aviator leather flying cap, goggles, and red cape with letter "G" routine. He wedges a cigarette into his hole and mine, which must be in a gay way, quickdraws the welding torch from his toolbelt holster, and fires us up. The Kool & the Gangrene 8-track

cassette slides in and begins thumping "Celebrate Good Times, Come On My Back Door" from the loudspeaker on the roof. He shifts into drive and floors the gas. The Olds springs off the road and onto the hillside. The Whispering Woody Retirement Park and Memorial Ditch billboard has a picture of a bewildered old woman with the caption "*Ditch* 'em here!" which is consoling to gridlocked drivers on I-10 worried about where to chuck cost-prohibitive elderly relatives and even more consoling after we career through the head of the bewildered old woman. We accelerate down the scrubby hill with few issues and hit the first Toyota Land Cruiser in good time. The beached Japanese whaler is going eastbound on I-10 East, being the conformist that he is. We're going westbound on I-10 East, and going about 140 mph upon impact. Priceless: the gentle lad's face in the Land Cruiser as he watches us cut in from scrubby hillside into his face. "Mind if I *cut* in?" TB inquires of Mr. Microphone.

There's a line of cars sitting behind the Land Cruiser. We pop in for a visit, cleaving a half-mile of vehicles in two via full frontal assault. Then TB turns on the right turn signal and penetrates five lanes over into the passing lane. The autos in between offer little resistance. Remember: going against the grain of traffic is a terrific conversation starter.

As we ease into the passing lane our snowplow-wedge rams head-on into an illegal who's driving a piece of shit pickup truck with a standard ton of manure in the bed. Somewhere between front bumper, delectable horse apples, and back bumper the whole shitbomb explodes. Unfortunately our windows are rolled up.

There's a party goin' on right here. Let's celibate.

Through the flaming feces we hurtle, continuing our head-on impacts with the lane of cars in line behind the turd inferno. It's a pleasant drive. I look out the window at the concrete barrier separating the currently underfoot I-10 East (or West if you're a nonconformist) and I-10 West which some mutant in a Camaro

is driving west on while racing us. TB mashes the gas pedal squarely to the floor but we're unable to get above 110 on the speedometer because of all the head-on impacts with conformists. The Camaro across the divide suffers no such misfortune and opens up a lead. "Cocksucker," diagnoses TB. He turns the wheel violently to the right, plunging the snowplow-wedge into that accursed divider. The concrete wall explodes, we barrel through and are birthed to the other side—into the Camaro's lane—now heading west on I-10 West because woe be the rogue individual fish who tries swimming against the servilely compliant school of fish. Unless the rogue fish is a total fucking misfit armed with an M4 carbine assault rifle and Charlton Heston's cold dead toupee.

It must be admitted the Camaro had built a quarter-mile lead by the time we righted ourselves in his lane. To confuse matters, a siren comes blaring from a few hundred yards behind us. It's a cop. "The pigs," says I.

"Are they on the TV?" TB asks.

"No. La Ho Jo's asshole is."

"If they're not on the TV then they're not news, and probably not real."

TB presses the "B" button on the Olds's steering wheel. That's the button that unleashes the Olds's super power known as opening the trunk. "Impressive," I congratulate.

"Wait for it…"

TB presses the "C" button. From the open trunk springs out a mannequin. The mannequin looks lifelike enough and is supposed to cause drivers behind us to slam on their brakes and swerve out of the way in order to not run over an innocent mannequin suddenly found lying on the highway. This is a fine way to defend the rear. Except in L.A. In L.A. this is a useless way to defend the rear because half of L.A. drivers are too distracted by their total self-absorption to notice a body on the highway while the other half of L.A. drivers simply don't care enough about a

body on the highway to slow down and avoid the body (unless the body looks like it could possibly damage their automobile—so when adding this option on to your trunk make sure you tie big boulders to the body which makes a nifty defense system against the half of L.A. drivers caring enough about their cars not to hit a man on the road with boulders tied to him). However the body-flying-out-of-trunk defense is quite effective against L.A. cops who will radically change direction in order to run over a body on the road, especially those bodies that are darkly hued. Here's the cover of the LAPD's recruitment brochure:

YOUR L.A.P.D.

TAKIN' CARE OF BUSINESS

The cop behind us doesn't have to swerve much to hit the body on the road but does speed up in order to hit it well. What that cop didn't know was that it wasn't a body made of darkly hued human but instead a body made of 150 pounds of plastique.

"Explosive plastique can be made from ordinary table salt."

"Salt is a necessary nutrient for good health."

"Making explosive plastique from a necessary nutrient is a much better hobby than stamp collecting, although there's even more pussy in stamp collecting."

The cop attains breakneck speed and runs over the plastique body. We're a few hundred yards ahead of him but still enjoy the blast wave. The explosion sends a large tract of I-10 West to Heaven or Hell, depending on the moral qualities of the asphalt. Same goes for I-10 East across the median. Same goes for parts of the encompassing hills. The explosion corrects any traffic congestion on the sections of I-10 East and West that are sent to the afterlife, although I-10 West was running almost as clean as a virgin's duodenum anyway. This cleanliness is next to godliness and has given the Camaro the room to race to his substantial lead. But now with our new & improved concern-free rear we begin to gain ground. Holy ground.

"Holy shit."

"You got that right." With the gas pedal floored and only a handful of sporadic collisions to savor we hit 330 miles per hour. "The 1994 Oldsmobile Cutlass Supreme was the first commercially available hybrid-powered vehicle, propelled by a 3.1-liter V-6 engine and a cold-fusion nuclear reactor. Because fantastical theoretical technology the writer has no understanding of is the hallmark of fine literature. The U.S. military developed the cold-fusion reactor technology back in the 1950s as part of their ongoing duty to siphon public funds into the private research and development of new technologies that sometimes make fine weapon systems and always make private corporations shitloads of money after these private corporations take the new

technology developed at the cost of the taxpaying public and sell it back to the public in some new gizmo at a tidy profit since any costs of developing the technology were already previously paid for by the public. This military-industrial complex developed cold-fusion nuclear reactors during the '50s in the hopes that both cold-fusion bombs and cold-fusion toasters could be brought to market. The merits of a cold-fusion nuclear weapon are obvious. The merits of a cold-fusion nuclear toaster are that it can be detonated and doesn't need an unsightly electrical plug. This was viewed favorably by banks who gave out free toasters to new customers in case a defaulted account required the customer to be mushroom-clouded in the convenience of their own home."

"The act of a bank foreclosing on your toaster is known as 'shrooming' in the financial sector."

"But despite the obvious benefits of cold-fusion nuclear-powered bombs, toasters, and cars, the technology was killed by the oil industry because cold fusion represents a grave threat to all gasoline-powered toasters and automobiles."

At the speed of 330 miles per hour it takes one roughly 4.2 seconds to run down a Camaro. TB slams on the brakes to avoid rear-ending him as such an accident would be deemed our fault and raise our insurance rates.

"The prey is surprised to see us hovering on his ass."

"His rear-view mirror reflects bulging eyes in disbelief and the glare from gold neck chains one is obligated to wear while driving a Camaro (cliché)."

The Camemberto accelerates as best he can, up to 150 mph. The leper chuckles through his welder's mask, equaling the speed with a slight touch of the gas, a common problem for vegetarians.

Who knew the Camaro was also racing a Honda Civic that had been specially modified into the single greatest sight gag this side of the Ronald Reagan Library: window tinting featuring

more bubbles than a hot tub with flatulently obese vegetarian included; purple neon lighting stolen from Le Snatch Lounge taped to underbody; spread-legged Mexican woman airbrushed on the hood fails to depict her latest pregnancy; large wing on the trunk constructed from a Ralph's shopping cart that spread-legged Mexican woman previously used as a stroller for her latest round of children; a huge muffler overcompensating for, well, everything.

The honorable Honda weaves violently between the few other cars on I-10 West. His great ambition to jerk across four lanes in order to cut in front of a car that's peaceably not jerking across four lanes is laudable. The car he jerks in front of is an Oldsmobile Cutlass Supreme. A specially modified Oldsmobile Cutlass Supreme sans stolen Le Snatch lighting techniques.

"This is historically false. World War II kamikaze pilots flew Mitsubishis, not Hondas."

"Maybe he's a *car*-mikaze."

TB taps the brakes to avoid hitting the cutting-in Civic. "Really?" I ask him.

"Wait for it…" TB flashes his bright lights which cannot be seen behind the snowplow-wedge to show his displeasure. A half-drunk Slurpee and some other bonus garbage come flying out the Civic's passenger window to show his displeasure at the thought of not living in a world of his own filth. It's difficult to make out the details of who these asshole environmentalists are behind the bubbled tint job until the youth in the passenger's seat sticks his head out to deliver some flying spit in our direction.

TB taps the brakes again, backing off the Civic. "Really?" I ask.

"Wait for it…" He fondles the hand crank dangling from the Olds's ceiling. The hand crank is connected to a dish mounted on the roof. The sound speaker is roped to the dish. Turning the hand crank rotates the dish which in turn rotates the speaker.

Thus the speaker can be swiveled 360 degrees by sheer grace of crank. A further push forward or backward on the hand crank pivots the dish vertically, allowing the speaker to be pointed at virtually any position on a horizontal and vertical plane. After a few quick cranks the speaker is pointed at the horizontal and vertical plane occupied by the Civic now a dozen yards in front of us. "Yahoo!" blurts Kool. The leper violently mashes the "G" button on the steering wheel. This blows the car's horn. TB's horn is a foghorn. The speaker on the roof amplifies the foghorn by a factor of ten thousand. The sound wave hits the pavement just behind the speeding Civic causing the asphalt to buckle and rupture. A portion of the blast wave bounces off the highway and up underneath the Civic with such all-American violence that it launches the car-mikaze into the heavens. TB avoids the tastefully done highway chasm ripped in front of us by yanking the steering wheel to the right while pressing the "A" button. The hydraulic jacks spring us hundreds of feet into the air. We safely crash snowplow-wedge first in a cloned neighborhood sprawling just off the highway.

"What about the bitchin' Camaro?"

"Wait for it…"

The Camaro speeds down I-10 in victory. Then he's crushed by a Honda Civic fresh off atmospheric reentry.

"Guess they needed a *crash course* in *Civics*."

"At least it made a *deep impact* on them!"

"It makes sense those *jackasses* would eventually *meet-Eeyore!*"

"It was still no reason for them to *comet* suicide!"

TB removes the elegant tarp from the trunk and throws on Stealth Mode. We take the back roads home, steering clear of I-10 which by now accurately reflects the fascist police state. The news has caught on to the story. From the black & white TV Super News Friends 13 diligently reports, "A large meteor has crashed onto I-10 destroying everything, everything by God,

everything! It is feared aliens may crawl out from the meteor and start blending in in Hollywood." Get Some Action Now 9's Jizzette Hernandezbaum reports, "A huge *dollop* of *hot, steaming* God *goo* has come *spurting* from Heaven, *splattering* all over I-10. On this *wad* of Jesus *jizz* was airbrushed a vision of a spread-legged Virgin Mary, say all Mexican eyewitnesses." Fox's Telly Bawdhaw reports by slapping a rubber chicken over his head.

SIX

We take the rest of the afternoon off. The leper is relaxing, looking at some Christian porn. Christian porn is edgy. Just like Christian rock 'n roll. The Church didn't want to get left behind in the porn craze which the kids are so gaga over. So the Church developed its own line of good smut to keep the kids away from the bad smut.

The human body is evil. Sex between human bodies is acutely evil. Even thinking about sex is pretty fucking evil. So when thinking about sex make sure not to think about hot cocks ramming steaming puss-ies and instead think about spawning. Spawning, good. Hot cock, evil. This is where Christian porn comes in.

Christian porn shows pictures of eggs. *Human* eggs. *Completely naked* human eggs. Wanton, lascivious eggs, hot from the ovaries, just looking to get inseminated. Those Bible humpers can really put the Big O in Ovum:

Christian porn photo courtesy of *Heavenly Penthouse* magazine

The leper is eyeing the centerfold, which is two eggs (lesbian scene). The hardest core Christian porn shows an egg and sperm, together, doing *it*. Sometimes one dirty little egg will be photographed taking on thousands, even millions, of horned-up sperm (gangbang scene): you could say, that bawdy little egg is taking on all *comers*! Ha!

"Jesus. Look at the germinal vesicle on this one," the leper slobbers.

The Church however has not abandoned its position against masturbation because God loves hot jizz, but only when placed in the proper Church-designated holes. Therefore, Christian porn must never be used to create homeless sperm. All sperm begotten from Christian porn is to be immediately scraped off the centerfold pages and deposited in something female (preferably the wife although in a pinch it's permissible to jam it in the schizophrenic bag lady living in the alley). Remember: there's nothing sadder than an unrequited sperm. Every sperm must find an egg, through matchmaking services if necessary. And when every sacred sperm finds an egg the resulting life forms will all be sacred, when born into the proper socioeconomic stratum. Just ask the millions of poor Africans who die every year because they're so fucking poor. This according to the polished gold in the over one thousand rooms of the Papal Palace or your evangelicals next door who can show you the Bible passage that proves that niggers suck and that life is sacred.

The leper whips it out and gives it a go. I watch TV. We are the talk of the town. The news channels are piecing together just who exactly these filthy terrorists are. It's now been confirmed that TB stands for Tasty Asian Bitch or Terrific Boner or T Bag.

T Bag (verb) is defined by *Webster's* as:
The act of placing one's scrotum in the open mouth of:
a) an unconscious drunk girl
b) an unconscious drunk guy

Only the crude and uninformed still believe TB stands for Tasty Asian Bitch or Terrific Boner. The nation's intellectuals know better. As always. And they know that TB stands for T Bag because:

a) there is a definition of T Bag in the dictionary and intellectuals like dictionaries

b) *The New York Times* ran a front-page article on how Los Angeles was getting T Bagged and intellectuals like *The New York Times*

Intellectuals like *The New York Times* because it's smart like them. The smartest intellectuals have all their opinions synchronized with *The New York Times*. *The New York Times* is the nation's finest disseminator of corporate news. One can trust that all the news that's fit to print will be in *The New York Times* because that is their properly trademarked trademark. Anything not in *The New York Times* is not news. *The New York Times* is said to have a left-leaning bias so anything truly to the left not reported/endorsed by *The New York Times* must be too truly left and not worthy of discussion.

This is called *agenda setting*.

The New York Times is the nation's top agenda setter and on its front page is us, T Bagging the fuck out of traffic. We are now on the agenda. We are now discussion worthy.

The *Times* has learned through journalistic wizardry that promotes the basic worldview of the National Security State that the T Bag movement is an extremist splinter group of the notorious Golden Chancre Independence Army. The Golden Chancre being the region within Tajikistan's Pamir Mountains between Mount Bobopuuk and Mount Fudsjklir. The region being approximately the size of Mount Bobopuuk and Mount Fudsjklir. The Golden Chancre Independence Army is a paramilitary separatist group devoted to Golden Chancre independence

from Tajikistan. If you've ever excreted something resembling Tajikistan then you understand. The movement's motto in the Chancrean tongue is *"aizkora bezain zorro plov de Mongo chickle chickle esta suga bezain zuclompa"* which translates in English as "sharp like Mongoplov the Great's horned codpiece and quiet like a stationary piece of mud."

Now these foul chancres had brought their war to America. Tajikistan would pay. Our bombers are in the air. The alpacas shall be free.

I didn't know I was part of a diabolical Central Asian nomadically goat-herding terror cell, although I have long been an admirer of horned codpieces. So it's good to be informed.

Remember: the "proper" "information" keeps 'em all toeing the transnational company line while you bomb the alpaca out of whoever. Remember this when planning your own transnational media company.

Here's some "information" not reported by the unbiased media gatekeepers. I remember the day I was adopted. I was a puppy. I'd been in the cage a week. There were only two ways out of that cage. One was having a human adopt me. The other was the way of the hood and needle. I didn't have much time. None of us did. If I didn't find a human soon, the hood and needle would be finding me. The way they did Bessie. The way they did countless others whose names I never would know.

The one advantage I had was being a puppy. Because Americans hate the aged. Hence their $15 billion cosmetic surgery industry. Which is twice the amount of money spent on the Environmental Protection Agency. But only about 3 percent of the money America spends on weapons and war. Because you've got to have priorities.

The cosmetic surgery suite in the pound consists of the aforementioned hood and maybe a claw hammer I've seen the janitor swing at some animals. This means the aged animals imprisoned here haven't "had some work done" which means nobody

will want them which means they're all going to meet the hood and needle after their allotment of cage-time expires. But I've got youth and beauty on my side which means I'm more likely to find an American who will love me because I show well.

And then they appear. Perfectly coiffed. Perfectly highlighted. Perfectly scented. Beautiful, both. Mr. and Mrs. America.

Their teeth are flawless rows of enameled spotlights and they display them in blindingly white smiles when anyone may be watching. But smiling takes energy and they conserve theirs by wearing scowls when not being admired.

They go from cage to cage, peering in, taking care not to get too close to the contagions inside. The coop below mine is rumored to warehouse a drooling Newfoundland-Mastiff concoction. The rumor is verified when the disgusted missus draws a spray bottle from her designer purse and hits the confined beast with a blast of antibacterial cleaner.

Mr. and Mrs. America hate germs.

Antibacterial cleaners are feverishly embraced in America because America hates germs. This is because germs are a form of life and most life on planet Earth is disgusting. Especially life that isn't cuddly or doesn't drive an ornate SUV. You should never come in contact with life for fear of life. That's why you should buy an airtight plastic bubble and seal yourself in. If you're too lazy to do that then buy synthetic chemicals to kill life. Insecticides, herbicides, algaecides, avicides, parricides, larvicides, to name just a few, kill life but certainly not you because modern humans have removed themselves from life's interconnected web. Antibacterial soaps and cleaners are no more effective against germs than regular soaps and cleaners. But antibacterial chemicals do help create more antibiotic-resistant bacteria, weaken your body's natural immune system, damage your brain and nervous system, make funny gender-bending amphibians in the water systems they get dumped into, and give corporations billions of extra dollars via fearful brain-damaged life-hating Americans (redundant).

My cage is shotgunned full of light as Mr. and Mrs. America bare their teeth at me. I brace for a hit of antibacterial wholesomeness.

"Well, this one doesn't look as sickening as the rest," says white light #1.

"That's not saying much," sniggers guiding light #2.

"Are you really sure this is the thing to do?"

"Yes. Adopting a mongrel from the pound is compassionate. I overheard it at the spa."

"You mean *slumming it* at the pound."

Guiding light #2 shows agreement by frantically squirting cleaner in various directions.

But maybe they could want me. And grow to appreciate me. Despite my lowly beginnings. So I smile at them, wag my tail, flip over on my back and wiggle around, tummy up. My tongue hangs out to the side. I make puppy yips.

The folks aren't unaffected. They're both smiling. I choose to believe that, for once, those smiles are sincere.

"He is a cutie."

"I think he's our boy."

As I'm taken from the cage I see all the others for the first time. They're staring at me. And from the geriatric Poodle to the three-legged Pit Bull to the beaten-down Collie, they all look the same.

They all look doomed.

And they all know.

My new home is very nice. With just a few more yuppies milling about I'd be convinced I'd moved into the Pottery Barn at the mall. But I saw it's a house and not the mall as we drove up in the Range Rover.

To properly maintain their look of a Pottery Barn franchise, Mr. and Mrs. America spend all their time working stultifying mid-level management jobs and consuming.

Naturally.

Naturally, as in this being the modern natural life.

This requires much of their time be spent away from home and away from each other. Naturally. It also means much time away from their new puppy. Which means puppy accidents.

Puppies are famed for pissing and shitting inside the house. It is commonly believed that puppies piss and shit in the house because they don't know any better. This belief is false. Puppies know not to piss and shit in the house but do so anyway because they like to play monkeyshines.

I'll use my own situation to demonstrate. I have the ability to telepathically tune in to humans. So I tune in to Mr. and Mrs. America. I sense that Mrs. America is reminiscing about smoking her HR director's big black cock during yesterday's power lunch. I sense that this is the game you modern humans play with each other. Smoke the cock of a higher-up so you can afford to live in the Pottery Barn. Cool. I'm a puppy and I want to play too but since I'm a puppy I can't smoke the HR director's big black nightstick until I'm of legal age and I can't even rape the world's environment plus 98 percent of the human population on behalf of the 2 percent who own most of the world and call it "capital" just so I can live in the Pottery Barn. So I play my own game which is to lay a log in one of Mrs. America's $700 Prada purses. In a puppy's mind this is playing the game with Mrs. America because the log in her purse looks like the scaled-down version of the cock in her mouth. But Mrs. America doesn't want to play with her puppy and throws some designer antidepressant pills (I think they're Prada) at me while weeping hysterically while chasing me into the pitch-black hall closet where I'll spend the night. Next, I piss on Mr. America's $170 tasseled Prada keychain with real human hair because it was only his backup $170 keychain after I sensed him reminiscing about the golden shower he lapped up out of the big black cock of the VP of Overseas Horrors during last week's sales seminar in Seattle. This gets me beaten

by the heel of a shoe (hopefully Prada) and a whole week in pitch-black closet.

It's after episodes like the abovementioned that dogs come to understand that humans will not allow us to engage in their games and that attempting to do so will result in swift and terrible consequences. So I quit shitting and pissing in the Pottery Barn and am allowed to see light again.

Let freedom ring. For about three months anyway. That's when I make a mistake that Mr. and Mrs. America will never forgive. I mature. My body gets larger. I'm no longer a lil' white puffball. I'm sorry. I should have stopped the madness and loaded myself in that veal crate.

Mr. and Mrs. America had little enough time for me before. Now I'm lucky just to get threatened.

It gets even better when a yuppie from the next door Pottery Barn comes a-calling. "I've just ordered two *purebred* Golden Retriever puppies from *Lira Drabgrabton*, Bel Air's most preeminent breeder," it oozes. "*Lira Drabgrabton* promises *my* Goldens will look just like the Goldens on the cover of this month's Pottery Barn catalog."

Mr. and Mrs. America look me up and down, and wince. No. The Pottery Barn isn't interested in photographing me. I just work here.

The thing from next door sneers at me and leaks, "*Oh!* But you've got *him*, don't you? Well, I'm sure getting a dog *for free* that absolutely nobody else wanted is the *right* thing to do. Besides, *Lira Drabgrabton's* purebreds are all *very expensive.* Maybe a little beyond your budget. But I do suppose you get what you pay for."

Mrs. America shoots one of her death-looks at Mr. America and says, "Money is no object for us. We always insist upon the best."

"Well, ensuring your canine comes from only the most elite stock doesn't come cheap," it sternly reprimands. Which is

certainly true. Purebred dogs are churned out from small gene pools. And small gene pools are great. Look at Appalachia.

Within the day Mr. and Mrs. America have purchased two of their own Golden Retriever clones from Bel Air's finest puppy mill. Mr. and Mrs. America think long and hard as to the proper names for their proper Goldens. Their mental gyrations pay off handsomely with the names *Goldie* and *Golden*.

The names that humans give their dogs will instantly tell you everything you need to know about that human. Got a Chocolate Labrador? Name it Mocha. Got a Chocolate Labrador? Name it Latte. Got a speed addiction? Name it trendy as long as it's a drug sold at caffeinated corporate chains. Got two Chocolate Labs? Name them Hershey and Nestlé. (Dueling behemoth food corporations. Delightful.) Got a Bulldog? Name it Buster. (Even the pedestrian name of Winston the Bulldog is beyond the grasp of most dullards nowadays.) Got a Dachshund? Name it Oscar. Got a French Poodle? Rename it Freedom Poodle. Got a Pug? Name it Imploded-Sphincter Head. Got a yuppie? They'll name the dog something indicative of their complete lack of imagination but make up for it with enough pretentiousness to complement their hilarious never-ending voyage into unknowing self-mockery. Montana, Savannah, Cody, Colby, Cash, Morgan, Jayden, Riley, Parker, Bailey, Bryce, Austin, Gemma, Madison, Reese, Vomit, Vainglorious, Vacuous. (Note that yuppie dog names usually double as yuppie children's names because both dogs and children are possessions to be shown and project an air of pretentiousness and lack of imagination.) Got a human owner with an inferiority complex to match his inferior intellect (truism)? Then he'll name the dog whatever's been preapproved by the other imbeciles. Jake, Buddy, Lucky, Princess, Rocky, Shadow, Duke, Bo, Lady, Sadie, Boring, Banal, Brainless. Got a typical human with his head up his typical ass? Then just name it Max, like fucking everybody else.

And then genius strikes Mr. and Mrs. America. Again. They are hit with the even-more perfect names for their perfect Goldens, right after seeing the commercial. "Oh, my God! Of course! They're Abercrombie & Fitch!" Because Pottery & Barn were already taken by the yuppie next door.

I shan't get into what they had named me. Unspeakable. Thankfully they never called me anything after Abercrombie & Fitch arrived anyway.

Mr. and Mrs. America pour out of the Range Rover with their (latest) prized acquisitions. My new kin trot up to greet me. Abercrombie smiles, wags his tail, and takes a bite out of my nose. Fitch is the courteous one and bites my testicles. An angered Mr. America intervenes and lands a sharp blow to my head. I yelp, scurry off to the far recesses of the yard, and hide in the bushes.

This is customary.

Every yuppie in the world *will* tell you how friendly their neurotic overbred crime against evolution is, right before the pedigreed crime bites off your left nut. Then as you're lying in a puddle of your own blood trying to discreetly tuck your dangling vas deferens back into your breached nut sack the yuppie *will* shriek that you've provoked the purebred into chewing on your ball, and that it's your fault, your fault, always your fault!

Beware.

Please note the aforementioned *neurotic overbred crime against evolution* applies to the yuppie's children as well.

The coming of Abercrombie & Fitch is feted fetidly. As I look on, hidden behind the shrubs, the help arrives. Mr. and Mrs. America had asked the help to stop doing whatever menial labor it is that Mexicans do and go out and acquire things. Because sometimes so many things need to be acquired that even professionals such as Mr. and Mrs. America need help from the help.

So much consuming, so little time...

The Mexican menial laborers had returned with a cornucopia of items made by Chinese menial laborers. The Peek-A-Boo Gopher plush toy, Mr. Tangerine Squeaky Head, Lil' Mailman chew thing, Footlong Rubber Bone for the missus, Nipple Wax for all.

The whole shebang.

Naturally, there is a plastic tennis-ball thrower. A plastic tennis-ball thrower is a piece of plastic made in China that is a stick with a cup at the end. The cup grips a tennis ball. With a quick flick of the stick, any yuppie in charge can send a tennis ball flying. And for just $14.95, you too can throw a tennis ball.

Mr. America scoops up the tennis ball and flicks it through the air. Abercrombie remains faithfully at Mr. America's feet, mystified. Fitch runs, in the opposite direction of the ball.

"It's over there! Go on, boys! Go get it!" he implores to no avail.

It just so happens the ball has landed a dozen feet away from my position in the bushes. I need that ball. It's shaped exactly like the one hanging southwest of the HR director's big black cock. Fucking affirmative action.

But I wait. Then Fitch bulldozes Abercrombie and goes for his brother's throat. Abercrombie's cries, Mrs. America's screams, and Mr. America's grunting attempt to separate the two give me the diversion I need. I burst from the shrubbery, making a beeline for the ball. I adroitly snatch it into my mouth because I haven't earned the money necessary to buy a plastic cup and stick made by Chinese forced laborers. My original plan called for me to immediately turn around and race back to the safety of the bushes. And the plan would have worked too. Mr. and Mrs. America had no idea I'd grabbed the ball, being preoccupied with their lovely purebreds and all. But at the last second something goes haywire. I know. It's inexplicable. But I decide to change plans. I still can't explain it. The best I can figure is that I wanted to show them I could do something the perfect

ones couldn't. I wanted to show them I was worth a damn. I guess I just wanted them to love me. So with prize in mouth, I alter my trajectory and head straight for Mr. and Mrs. America, dropping the ball at their feet. Then I'm shot in the head with antibacterial cleaner and slink back to the bushes.

By way of plastic stick, an irate Mr. America again grabs and flicks the ball across the yard. "Abercrombie, Fitch—go get it!" he commands. Abercrombie scratches himself with much enthusiasm. Fitch attacks Mr. America's stick. Abercrombie one-ups his brother by remaining in a sitting position on the grass and shitting, impacting the turd all over his ass.

Enough. Take this, you bastards. I dart from the bushes, seize the ball, race towards them, flip the ball to their feet, successfully dodging antibacterial flak as I fly by.

Mr. America—his face red, moist, and engorged, giving it the look of a fine clitoris—is so incensed that he grabs the pre-slobbered ball with his hand, forgetting about the stick. An appalled Mrs. America has no choice but to fire upon him. Through the chemical haze he winds up and hurls the ball as hard as he can at my head. But I'm ready for it, sidestepping the projectile. I smile and give him a wink, then turn around and retrieve the ball, tossing it to their feet as I streak by them again.

"Is that bad ugly dog not letting you play?" Mrs. America says to the Goldens in inane baby voice. "Is the big ugly mutt thing that *I* never wanted in the first place not letting my *itsy bitsy witsy* little pup-pups play?" She turns to Mr. America and icily commands, "Get *it* out of my sight!" He needed little prompting. With fury blazing from behind Prada eyeglasses he again bare-hands the ball and fires it at me, again missing. A primordial groan slips past his perfectly clenched, perfectly bleached teeth as he lunges for me. Again I'm too quick. But the fellow yuppies who had been convened for the Goldens' celebratory barbecue, seeing a brother in distress, and seeing no nearby brown-skinned menial laborers to hire for pennies on

the drudgery, do what comes natural which is form a lynch mob to hunt me down.

My instincts tell me to get out of the yard and head for the street. But a regiment of Mr. America's yes-men from the Risk Management & Spurting Orifice Department, arming themselves with kabob skewers and spice shakers, blocks the driveway exit. I'm in danger of being outflanked by the soulless beasts from Mrs. America's Now Just As Incapable of Nurturing As a Man Professional Women's Association, so I bolt for the Pottery Barn's open front door. I don't see the closed screen door in front of it. But my wide, thick anvil of a head smashes on through. The impact is so sudden and devastating that the aluminum doorframe crumples and is blown off its hinges. The metal and mesh wreckage rockets into the house and nails some sniveling sycophant fifteen feet deep in the entry.

I don't even lose stride.

I pick up more speed. I am very fast. I see a second sniveling sycophant dead ahead. I am very fast, but my braking and cornering capabilities are marginal, at best. I'm strong enough to admit it. On a straightaway think of me as a smokin' drag racer without the extra twenty-first chromosome. Just don't ask me to turn or stop. Think of me as an American muscle car from days of yore. A 1972 Plymouth 'Cuda, to be exact. The second sniveling sycophant is tending to the first sycophant underneath the screen door remains. Can't turn. Can't stop. Don't need to when you've got my head. Think of me as a 1972 Plymouth 'Cuda with a battering ram protruding from my unzipped front grille. I barrel through, my battering ram glancing off the second yuppie's knee, flipping his leg out from under him, sending him crashing down on top of the screen door on top of his compatriot.

I burn straight into the kitchen. There I run out of room and try to turn. My handling is shitty enough as it is and of course Mr. and Mrs. America have installed tractionless hardwood floors throughout the house, even the kitchen. Who the fuck

puts wood floors in a room constantly exposed to water? Mr. and Mrs. America do when they get a great deal on the last of the Chinese old-growth forest timber. Mr. and Mrs. America realize that natural history museums are passé when you can exhibit now-extinct species inside the privacy of your very own floors.

Fucking Chinese. They should take better care of the planet. What are our corporations paying them twenty-three cents an hour for?

I skid clear across the kitchen and slam into the Brazilian old-growth cabinets. Luckily I hit headfirst. Luckily there's also a member of the help in between me and the cabinets to cushion my impact. The kitchen is crawling with help because Mr. and Mrs. America's exterminator is incompetent and they'd instructed the help to whip up some culinary delights to augment the yuppie barbecue experience. This is the first time the help had laid eyes upon me. Up until then, Mr. and Mrs. America had made sure I wouldn't interfere with any of their toil by locking me in the closet whenever they were scheduled to toil.

There are six Mexicans laboring in the kitchen on this day and all six begin screaming, including the one smashed into the Lazy Susan. *"¡El Diablo Blanco! ¡El Diablo Blanco!"* they serenade in abject terror. A couple of them have the composure to make the sign of the cross. You know, for protection. The rest wisely break into panic, fleeing from the kitchen. At the same time a squad of yuppies enters the house through the front door. The two groups collide in the entry. When yuppie meets exploited labor, exploited labor must take care not to make any sudden movements. Sudden movements by chattel will cause 80 percent of yuppies to fake a smile until they've had enough time to get far enough away from the chattel to safely use their cell phones to panic-call the U.S. Department of Jackboots. Unfortunately for the Mexicans, the yuppies they collide into in the entry are

part of the 20 percent who do not pay chattel the courtesy of a fake smile and immediately hit the chattel with their cell phones in self-defense. Whatever other electronic gadgets the yuppies are obsessed with can also be used. Bludgeoning-type gadgets seem to work best.

While waiting for the fog of war to clear from the entry, I trot upstairs. In one of the spare bedrooms I find more help. They're dressed as a mariachi band and were to be entertainment before hostilities broke out. They see me in the doorway and at once lunge through the windows, open or not. It's raining men in silver-studded charro outfits with wide-brimmed hats, which must be in a gay way. The 400-pound trumpeter takes part of the wall off on his way out the window. Which is nothing compared to what he does to the four yuppies he lands on.

I survey the front yard through the blown-out windows. It's sheer carnage. Most of the help lay dead, massacred in a bloodbath of cell phones, Blackberries, and iPods. Yuppie troop discipline has completely broken down. With no more help to kill, they've slipped into some sort of berserker rage, and have turned on each other. A Nintendo Game Boy-armed toady from Marketing is disemboweling a Franchise Performance Department lackey wielding a handheld GPS unit. Mr. America and Fitch are biting each other over the Chinese plastic tennis-ball thrower. Mrs. America is in the center of the yard sucking the HR director's big black cock.

And so on.

The U.S. Department of Jackboots arrives and is firing at the help's dead bodies. Flamboyantly dressed Mexican musical cowboys pockmark the lawn. More pockmarks erupt courtesy of the Jackboots' grenade-launching helicopter.

It's time to leave.

Before their demise the Mexicans sent out an infrasonic panic-call. They ripped this off from elephants who vocally emit a sound below the level of human hearing which can travel for

miles and alert other elephants to danger. The Mexican infrasonic panic-call sends all the other help within two miles fleeing, leaving many a toilet unscrubbed, many a lawn unblown. Worse yet, hundreds of yuppies in the area are caught in the mass Mexican stampede, leading to horrific bloodshed as many a cell phone is drawn in anger. The Jackboots are ordered elsewhere to shoot at the widening conflagration.

It's really time to leave.

I start down the stairs but stop midway. The fog of war has cleared, leaving the entry littered with Mexican-flavored corpses. The yuppies stammer about. Their stupor is different from usual. With their electronic gadgets ruined—smashed and strewn across the killing fields—they wander aimlessly, starved of the digital stimuli that give direction in this life.

One yuppie moans, "Ooooooooaargh." A long ooze of saliva falls from his mouth as he bites into the head of the maid, crunching his way to her nougat center. The rest of the yuppies do what comes natural which is follow the neighbor and feast on the flesh of the weak (or dead).

Once a good consumer, always a good consumer.

Only a text message and shopping spree can help them now.

I proceed down the stairs, avoid the undead, and peek out the front door. It's a straight shot through the carnage of the front yard to the street, and liberation. Then one yuppie plants himself in the middle of the lawn and blocks the way. He's staring at me. He's been waiting for me.

Armored head to toe in the Hilfiger casual line, he stands with three hounds of hell (purebreds) at his side. Three of the largest Bulldogs I've ever seen.

"This ends now!" bellows the yuppie, wearing war face, scowling right through me. "It's time you met *Buster*, *Buddy*, and *Max*, you dirty crossbreed!"

Wow. A yuppie with anger issues. That's something you sure don't see every day.

I begin to wonder if maybe finding a way out the rear might not be a more prudent exit strategy. That is until one flesh-eating futures broker tires of pancreas and starts in my direction. There's no turning back into the house. There's only one way out, and it's through Hilfigered yuppie and hellhounds.

I burst from the front door, churning my legs furiously, picking up speed as I head right at them. The yuppie drops his Bulldogs' leashes and yells, "Through the power of Lira Drabgrabton pureblood—kill the unclean!"

Buster leaps forward. With hip simultaneously exploding, he implodes into a saggy pile. He'll spend the rest of the war sloughing off his skin. Bad hips and bad skin are among the many congenital defects Bulldogs are cherished for. But Bulldog health problems are no more glamorous than those of many other breeds. In fact, of the 200 pedigree breeds, more than 150 have significant hereditary diseases. The Bernese Mountain Dog is lucky to reach seven years old because the breed is so chewed up by cancer. Same stats for the Irish Wolfhound. Your average mutt will live two or three times longer.

But mutts are inferior because they cost less. A real triumph of market forces, if not evolutionary forces. (Fuck off, Darwin. You're dead anyway.)

Buddy waddles forward and then suffocates.

Bulldogs are prone to numerous breathing problems. Humans have bred them to have such unnatural head and upper airway anatomies that breathing becomes a challenge, making the breed vulnerable to heat and living.

Max runs forward and we meet on the field of battle. At least I think we met. He just kind of came apart as we crashed into each other. An oversized jowl here, some folds of skin there. What the fuck? Dude just blew up.

Which is typical. Anything put to such extraordinary, contrived lengths to look tough is likely fortified with nothing but goo. Just like an American.

The yuppie starts crying for his mommy and his lawyer. I'm not really the vengeful type but he's in my path and you know I don't turn so well. Ramming speed!

My cinderblock head versus his kneecap. As the cliché goes, it's a real win/win situation. I win by emerging unscathed on the street. He wins by now having a knee that can bend forward and backward.

Mr. and Mrs. America's Pottery Barn is at the edge of some suburban sprawl that abuts a small tract of land with no tract homes. This patch of land is astonishingly undeveloped outside of a few dirt trails snaking through its hills. It's a good place to hide out and do some arson.

I get off the streets and onto a trail. I follow the path up to a ridgeline and then down into a small canyon. Here, a couple miles in, I see a human. He's by himself, walking the trail ahead of me. No motorized vehicle. No Chinese-made mountain bike. No nothing. Naturally I'm alarmed. I wasn't aware humans could walk anymore.

It's worse than I thought. He hears me and turns around to face me. No headphones. No cell phone. No head flooded with gibberish. Just walking, by himself, alone with his own thoughts, mind wandering free from the network, in unmolested nature. Some nerve on this one.

He looks at me and says with a smile, "Hey you."

I give him a wink. *Bing!* (the wink sound effect).

"You're a magnificent one." He wasn't lying.

He starts talking about how he's always preferred the company of animals to humans because animals are content to just *be* a part of nature. That most humans want nothing to do with nature, especially if they can't exert power over her with their roads, cars, all-terrain vehicles, motorboats, whatever. That even the few humans who enjoy nature without manhandling her by way of some machine still generally view her as something to challenge themselves by, something to conquer. Climb the

highest peak. Hike the longest trail. That kind of thing. A perverse, corrupted Nietzschean will to power, he calls it. A rabid drive propagated by modern society to dominate. Can't anyone be strong enough to sit back and receive from the world what she gives, instead of forcing nature to give what we presume she ought to?

Christ. I thought John Denver was dead somewhere.

A deafening roar blares from behind the guy. The sound is a cross between a speeding M1 Abrams battle tank and the splintering of a canyon-full of vegetation underneath an Abrams battle tank's tracks. The narrow hiking path is being vastly expanded by the tank crushing anything it can. This is progress.

The tank brakes to a halt a few yards up trail from us, aims, and fires. Instead of an explosive shell a giant net is ejaculated from the metal beast's uber-cock. We succumb to the money shot.

A roar from an M113 armored personnel carrier mixed with obligatory crushed-life-under-tracks sound comes from behind. Men in camouflage garb jump out, beat us with clubs, remove the net from over us so as to not injure the net, beat us with clubs, and throw us into the back of the APC.

The hiker and I had just joined the army.

Here was the problem: not enough of the incredibly stupid were signing up for the U.S. military. Recruitment drives failed. A free taco dinner with every tour of duty failed.

Kidnapping worked.

Not everyone was eligible to be kidnapped. Being wealthy or powerful disqualified you.

"Hey!" says the hiker.

"Whap!" says the club.

"Shut your granola hole!" says the soldier swinging the club.

"This is grotesque! You have no right to do this!" yells the hiker. Seconding this opinion are the other incarcerated dregs from the day's previous roundups.

"Yeah, yeah, yeah! Only we *do* have the right!" suggests soldier.

"But I wasn't doing anything except walking a nature trail!" says hiker.

"That's right. You weren't doing *anything*. You weren't doing *anything* to help your country! But you will," says soldier through the back hatch of the APC before sealing it shut.

This is what a grateful nation knew: America had many wars to fight and many people to kill and not enough suckers to do the killing. Americans also knew that buying something, buying anything, helped the patriotic cause because their keepers told them so. Buying kept afloat a system predicated on keeping power, wealth, and resources in elite hands by subjugating everyone else. And God knows there were a lot of resources overseas to be subjugated, or "liberated from tyranny" (your choice in viewpoint depending on just how fucking stupid you are).

Patriotic buying facilitates patriotic killing which facilitates more patriotic buying. But what should be done with those not consuming their citizenly share? Why, get them killing their citizenly share.

And so the Cash, Credit, or Kill Act; a.k.a. the Buyin' or Dyin' Act; a.k.a. the Patriots Pay One Way or Another Act became the law of the land mandating anyone caught in public not consuming something to be eligible for immediate induction/ abduction into the U.S. army.

Most Americans didn't give a shit about the new law because it didn't affect them because who the fuck goes out and doesn't buy something?

If the hiker had been a better patriot by buying some Chinese plastic thingy instead of jacking off to Henry David Thoreau then he wouldn't be destined for crew cut and lobotomy to help him fit in.

If I had put a little more heart into my role as star attraction in Mr. and Mrs. America's pitch-black hall closet then I

wouldn't be destined for castration before being forced to watch a leper masturbate to egg cytoplasm. My mistake.

SEVEN

"Hence that general is skillful in attack whose opponent does not know what to defend..."

—Sun Tzu

"Let's go balls out."

—Crenshaw Melon

Feeling spunky, we attack at midnight. The target was the dreaded stretch of I-405 between Santa Monica and Long Beach, capable of congealment at any hour. It did not disappoint. Despite the striking of the midnight hour, this twenty-five-mile patch of cruelty was jam-packed with the villainy, perversity, knavery, turpitude, and other assorted vileness one finds on the Disney Channel. We start out heading south on I-405 North. If loving you in the wrong direction is wrong, I don't want to be right. The leper is hoping that driving the wrong direction on multilane highways becomes trendy amongst the sheeple demographic, which is anyone hatin' on this book, which is everyone. Aw, shucks. They didn't appreciate the Unabomber either.

We dismantle Stealth Mode somewhere in oakless Sherman Oaks. The I-405 North on-ramp has signs telling us we're headed in the wrong direction. Given the course of the world, this is a

compliment. We seize the middle lane. Traffic is light and most people feel the need to cede the middle lane to an onrushing Oldsmobile. Only one angry driver presses the issue, not veering from the lane, engaging us in a game of chicken. Well, he was no chicken, but he was the other white meat. Ha!

The Sunset Boulevard exit emerges and with it materializes mondo congestion. A handful of vehicles at the crest of this gridlock wave are able to skitter to the side of the highway and avoid us. But this is a passing horror. The congestion worsens, eliminating the possibility of escape to unclogged lanes. They're locked in. We're locked in. Twenty-five glorious miles of penetrating penetration, in the face-to-face position, because we're gentlemen. We first meat a Mercedes-Benz G55 AMG SUV, which is kinda like a jeep except it's unsuitable for off-roading and costs $100,000. The driver was a trophy wife who will be scheduling major plastic surgeries during her forty-nine-day stay in bardo or whatever supposed afterlife she paid top dollar to a Beverly Hills goo-ru to chant at her about while fucking her in the ass to the moan of Om despite her being thoroughly insulated from anything resembling a connection of spirit with anything besides whatever could be purchased at Neiman Marcus which proved to be a lovely spackle for the cold dead pit masquerading as her inner self. Like I said, she proved things aren't as pretty on the inside. She had one of the most uncomely spleens I'd ever seen.

The stream of head-on collisions is nonstop after the Mercedes. Watching the repetitive cycle of twin headlights resembling a boyo's cheeks being spread apart by our priest's pile-driving cock resembling a snowplow-wedge got us in the mood right quick. Watching the repetitive cycle of oncoming sets of headlight beams split in two and cast one to each side is a fine catalyst to make epileptics go *whllaaaeeh*. Oh, fucklesticks. That's just what I need. For the leper to go into one of his seizures in the middle of traffic. If he thinks I'm shitting into his

mouth whilst splitting Corsairs then he's kinkier than Dad on all-leather Sundays. But the music seems to be soothing the savage black beast (redundant). Redbone's "Come and Smell Your Love" keeps the leper centered as he plows the center lane.

At 1.2 miles in we ram a tractor-trailer carrying a load of Shingles. Shingles is a disease caused by the varicella-zoster virus characterized by skin eruptions of fluid-filled blisters which crust over (like Grandpa) and pain along the course of involved sensory nerves, or a brand of potato chip. Shingles are packaged in long tubular canisters resembling tennis ball containers. Here is a Shingles container:

The Shingles canister presented problems. The canister proved too narrow to allow consumers easy access to bottom-dwelling chips. There had been news reports of the corpulent and the retarded (i.e., average consumers) getting their hands stuck in the canister, panicking, and being forced to eat their way through the canister to get at the remaining low-lying chips. But amateurs make mistakes and several hands had

been lost. A foot went missing in Omaha. The technical term for accidentally eating your own appendage is "friendly fire." So the corporation held accountable for Shingles potato chip canisters although never held accountable for the potato chips themselves created a new canister that still looked like a tennis ball container but added a diesel engine to the canister which powered a mini-elevator which transported bottom-dwelling potato chips to the top of the can which made sure no hands or feet would ever be lost in a Shingles potato chip canister again. The motto for the survivors of pre-diesel-motor Shingles cans is "Never Again." The innovation was top news story of the day until something scarier happened and was *Time* magazine's Invention of the Year, leading to internal combustion engines being mandated for packages of all heavily processed foods, for safety's sake.

Just before we hit the Shingles tractor-trailer TB presses the "D" button. A pole springs up from behind the center apex of the snowplow-wedge. On the pole flies a flag. On the flag is our coat of arms:

"Our flagpole is made of pure herculetium. Herculetium is the element the snowplow-wedge is constructed of. Herculetium is the element the U.S. army's Steel Peace Freedom Liberty Justice Democracy Sufferage-For-All Freedom Tank is constructed of. Herculetium is the strongest metal in the galaxy. In fact, it is nearly indestructible. In fact, the only way one can even work and shape the metal is by subjecting it to its only weakness."

"The herculetium flagpole shooting up from the herculetium snowplow-wedge is not really a pole but really a triangular wedge. This is necessary, like rickets. The snowplow-wedge is dandy for slicing into vehicles that are roughly the same height as the Olds. But very high vehicles, such as a Shingles tractor-trailer, require a fully elongated wedge. With our pole raised we are fully elongated."

We rush in where fools fear to tread. The Shingles tractor-trailer is gashed in two and explodes after the successful dissection of some combustible diesel-powered canisters or potato chips. Droplets of flame shower the highway like a fabulous Liberace ejaculation.

The new Shingles fat-substitute chips are highly flammable. Back in the '60s the secret ingredient had been sprayed on the Vietnamese in hopes that it would defoliate their virgins. But that was war because we needed to teach them freedom. Later, the secret ingredient was force-fed to political prisoners we torture in secret prisons around the world and was deemed safe for human consumption after the prisoners did not rupture immediately. But that was war because we needed to teach them freedom. The secret ingredient is now found in a myriad of champion products including all-purpose cleaner and virgin defoliator Agent Orange Glo, served à la carte in the Billy Joe Huckenfuchs infomercial.

The incendiary Shingles spread fire across the highway and into the neighboring Los Angeles National War Veteran

Cemetery. This is where some of the nation's top heroic murderers are dead. Sleep now in the fire.

At 2.3 miles in I yell "Banana!" and draw first blood as we slice through a yellow Nissan Xterra sandwiched between two Volvos. Yay! It's the Banana Game! Each time a player sees a yellow-colored vehicle he must be the first to yell "Banana!" and that counts as a point. But beware! If one sees a tan vehicle and yells "Banana!" that is a penalty and a point is taken away. The leper or purebred Himalayan Fusty Sheep Bugger with the most Bananas! at the end of the drive wins. This is one of the many games you can play with your kids in the car to make traveling an assload of fun.

At 5.4 miles in we cut through six Mercedes in a row. And not one of the pretentious fuckers was yellow.

At 8.7 miles in we get shot at by a couple of gang members. There's never a cop around when you need one. They're shooting from a couple lanes over until TB cranks the speaker at their gaudy SUV (redundant), hits the foghorn, and blows them two miles off course into a high-rise bank from where the capitalists rule and create ruined humanoids by the millions like the ones in the gaudy SUV hurtling through the fourteenth floor who would never have been allowed in the high-rise at any other time unless they reformed themselves by making a large and respectable amount of money preying on others.

At 8.8 miles in we get shot at by a yuppie in a gaudy SUV (two times the redundant) who knows the only way to act not so white is to act black which is to act like a gun-toting gangsta because he saw that being sold in the mass media. TB cranks and blows whitey acting like mass-media darky two miles off course into a high-rise bank from where the capitalists rule and create ruined humanoids by the millions like the yuppie in the gaudy SUV hurtling through the fourteenth floor who would have been allowed in the high-rise anytime because he worked there making a large and respectable amount of money preying on others.

At 16.7 miles in the black & white TV strapped to the dashboard farts: "We interrupt *The Late Grate Show with Carson Whitepuff* for breaking news!" Super News Friends 13's super-anchorman Black Mann informs from his bed and pajamas, "I'm Black Mann in the Super News Friends 13 News-Condominium of Justice where the news never sleeps and neither does super-anchorman Black Mann. The Super News Friends 13 Super Flying Chopper has spotted trouble. To you now, Super Flying Chopper!" The news helicopter is a machine and says nothing. This is considered award-winning reporting. The machine broadcasts a live video stream of an Oldsmobile parting the sea of traffic like Moses parted all that fine prison ass.

"We're on the TV," I notify the leper. "There's a news helicopter above us filming the festivities. This camera angle makes me look fat."

"Just one news helicopter? Just one channel?" TB leans over and changes channels. We're on all of them.

Then the traffic disappears. It literally goes from thick as Sister's smegma to zero. The stream of head-on collisions replaced by clean open road. He says through welder's mask, "Just before a tsunami smashes into land the water along the shoreline may recede dramatically, exposing areas that are normally always submerged. Prepare thyself."

Our back window explodes. The spitting of large-caliber assault weapon gunfire to our rear may be the reason.

"Nazis."

"So much for a warning shot." TB hits the "B" button. The trunk flings open. The trunk has been upgraded with a lining of herculetium, shielding us from any more incoming ordnance from the rear. This annoys the fourteen armor-plated SWAT vehicles who are trying to kill us.

"The Olds has been surgically altered in various places to achieve perfection. Like when the protagonist in the children's book *My Beautiful Mommy* educates her six-year-old daughter

that Mommy's new nose job, tit job, and massive body-wide cellulite suck did not remove the necrotized fat inside beautiful Mommy's head.

"The Olds's alterations consist of bulletproof tires and herculetium shielding throughout the car's body structure. But the Olds's windows are neither herculetium nor bulletproof. Think of this as our Achilles' heel."

The bullets that shattered the rear window and created various bonus holes in the front windshield as they whizzed through the car cabin corroborate the leper's diagnosis. I ain't too proud to be scared pissless. I curl up in a ball in the passenger's seat and put my paws over my head. I'm careful to not let the dangling cigarette drop from my mouth. That could start a fire. Safety first.

I look adorable. He never notices me anymore. Maybe if I surgically alter various places to achieve perfection... Like this:

My Beautiful Mommy

The leper cranks up the tunes. Redbone is singing about Injuns getting drunk and sticky together while one of the pursuing Gestapo SUVs (redundant) rides our rear so two of his Aryan *brothas* can try to pull alongside our port and starboard sides, box us in, and shoot the fuck out of us like a hot new turd in front of the paparazzi. Up my head peeks to spy in the side-view mirror a master-race racer with grinning teeth as white as whitey aiming his machine gun at my formidable but not bulletproof head. Things slow down when you're waiting for your brains to be blown out by the great protectors of truth, justice, and the American way. Just ask millions. Past, present, and future. Although the time between the words "Wait for it…" and the subsequent foghorn blast amplified through the speaker that annihilates an overpass sending thousands of tons of rubble raining down on us and the Nazis was less than a half second it seemed as long as a half second.

TB says, "Wait for it…" and presses the "G" button. A horrendous belch is summoned forth, amplified ten thousand times by the speaker on the roof that is pointed at a highway overpass just ahead that detonates, showering us in thousands of tons of concrete and rebar. I see the smiling Nazi behind us stop aiming his machine gun at me to accept an eleven-foot metal rod through his head. A plummeting concrete chunk the size of an E-Z Liv-In mobile home (Mt. Everest floor plan) that the metal rod is still attached to irrevocably flattens the Nazi and his carload of Nazi friends for life. Even larger samplings of destruction cascade down. The avalanche of overpass crushes the SWAT armada but rolls off our herculetium back like a Vietnamese Agent Orange victims' lawsuit off the Dow Chemical Company. Because international law pertaining to chemical warfare does not pertain to Dow or its subsidiary U.S. government. As we explode through a wall of asphalt TB says to Mr. Microphone, "Guess you could say there's no more *fly* in that *SWAT!*"

"That really put the *swat* in those *SWATzis!*"

"Well, their symbol is the *SWATstika!*"

"Uh-oh. Now there's a *pile* on their *Sieg Heil!*"

"Just before a tsunami smashes into land the water along the shoreline may recede dramatically, exposing areas that are normally always submerged. Prepare thyself." Granted, this last pun sucks. Out the front windshield I see why all the traffic has receded. Up ahead all traffic is being herded off the highway to a side-street exit. In front of the herd is a line of parked police cars stretched across the highway. The wall of cops readies, aims, and fires. At us. Ammunition from The Man's pistols, shotguns, machine guns, and automatic cannons deflect harmlessly off the snowplow-wedge. Three rockets hit us head-on, explode, and leave nothing but scuff marks on the herculetium. Mix a paste of two tablespoons baking powder and a little water. Rub the mixture into the scuff marks with a white cloth. Because white makes right when removing unsightly dark stains from the neighborhood (see Marvel Comics' issues #1 through 567 of *The Amazing Gentrification-Man* series).

My mud-person chauffeur (truism) floors the gas pedal. The g-forces pancake me against my seat as we go from 50 to 350 in two seconds. If we can cut through a deluge of collapsing overpass with no problem then can we cut through a dinky line of cop cars with no problem? Yes we can!

The cop car we speed through is slashed in half and blows up. Some napalm the cop had in the backseat that he used for some of his hobbies because he's a typical cop ignites. The napalm explodes from his split-open car like agitated yolk from a broken egg laid by the Dow Chemical Easter Bunny. Napalm splatters all over the highway. Cops are covered in the flaming jelly. Out of habit the cops line up to gang-rape the more effeminate cops not realizing that they are not in Le Snatch Lounge watching "Officer Pussy Wetter" strip-search herself in a baby pool of jelly. Then they realize they're on fire and

try to put themselves out by beating themselves to death with their batons. TB says to Mr. Microphone, "Guess that put some *heat* on the *heat!*"

"I love the smell of napalm in the morning. Smells like… victory."

"Guess victory smells like…*roast pig!*"

Behind us the queued cop cars become properly heated and start exploding as we re-engage the traffic that was due to be funneled off the highway by ignited cops. Telly Bawdhaw of Fox News reports, "I guess Detective Columbo is now Detective *Coal*-umbo! *Heehaw!*" while slapping a rubber chicken over his head. This report and this rubber chicken are being brought to you by giant food-genetics manipulator / chemical-weapons-to-tame-the-Third-World-&-your-garden provider / friend, the Man!santo Corporation, because the rubber chicken mechanically squawks *"Smells like…Man!santo!"* every time it's slapped over Telly Bawdhaw's head.

TB cranks the speaker towards the sky, lays on the horn, and blows the twenty cop helicopters out of the sky. When they crash their large supplies of fuel and weapons create pleasing fires throughout Los Angeles.

"Just another black man starting fires. Not very original," I critique. "Although those Korean convenience stores with their sweet & sour collie jerky did have it coming."

"Snap into a Slim Kim."

The gridlock is thick and the head-ons are aplenty all the way to Long Beach. Finally, at 25.0 miles in, the congestion on I-405 North wanes. I-405 South is another matter. Across the cement divider nothing's moving as rubberneckers stop and gawk at the freshly plowed lane we've sired. TB watches them watching us and wistfully observes, "Ironic that the teeming masses will pause to gape at a burning wreck on the side of the road but few, if any, will pause to notice the burning wreck of a species they're part of." He turns the steering wheel sharply

to the right and plows through the center divider. He keeps the wheel pulled to the right and is soon furrowing north on I-405 South, middle-lane style. Sharply turning direction from I-405 North (southbound) through a concrete wall onto I-405 South (northbound) is what is referred to in the common vernacular as turning a *U-ey*. A U-ey is a U-turn. Road signs will indicate the illegality of U-turns. If you do not see a sign, pulling a U-ey on a clogged highway through a cement median is allowed, and encouraged.

"Let's go home, boy," the leper says to me with a wink behind his welder's mask and a pat on my head.

"Is calling an agreeably white sentient being 'boy' your idea of irony, boy?"

We cut through the gridlock. The survivors across the median are using our cleared lane to drive at a pleasant clip. Many look over at us, smiling and waving. Expressing gratitude is basic civility and a cornerstone of any decent society so show your fellow commuter gratitude by showing him your tits. Or her. Bull dykes need love too.

"Modern-day drivers," he ponders, "partitioned off in their steel and glass cocoons."

"This baby's got isolation-tank-quality insulation to island you off from anything daring to live around you!"

"Cocooned away from *the real* just a few feet outside, but never cocooned away from the incessant digital whisper of the collective."

"This baby's got satellite radio!"

"...to keep minds entranced..."

"This baby's got satellite television!"

"...to keep minds sedated..."

"...got DVD players!"

"...to keep minds buried underneath an avalanche of external stimuli..."

"...got iPod selections!"

"...to keep minds drowned in data..."

"...*got global positioning systems with tranquil computer voice commanding instructions!*"

"...to keep minds from having to endure any quiet moments of reflection..."

"...*got built-in cell phones!*"

"...to keep minds from the fields of silence where imaginations grow..."

"...*got video screens!*"

"...to keep minds plugged into the Machine..."

"...*got 24/7 wireless Internet!*"

"...to keep minds thinking about consuming, not thinking about thinking..."

"...*got downloaded audio directions to consumables for weary mall pilgrims!*"

"...to keep you overstimulated and addicted..."

"...*got email and instant-messaging!*"

"...to keep you horrified at the prospect of sitting quietly with just yourself..."

"...*got video games!*"

"...to keep your attention span so short that your own thoughts become impossible..."

"...*got on-demand music videos!*"

"...to keep you stupefied and sucking on their mass-media tit..."

"...*got talk radio!*"

"...to keep you afraid..."

"...*got streaming TV news updates!*"

"...to keep you controlled..."

"...*got the ConStar 24-hour satellite tracking and surveillance system!*"

"...to keep you detached, yet shackled..."

"...*got surround-sound speakers with high-def lifelike realism!*"

"...to keep you dumb, narrow, greedy, and predictable..."

"...*got shiny chrome and now-extinct hardwood everywhere!*"

"...to keep you from the danger of discovering yourself..."

"...*got pay-per-view movies!*"

"...to keep you from the danger of discovering you've never developed a self..."

"...*got the techiest trendiest technological trend!*"

"...to keep you from real life."

"*Got Man!santo?*" squawks the rubber chicken being slapped over the bald head of TV's Telly Bawdhaw. Bawdhaw and the novelty-item-corporate-spokesman are bringing us real life which is happening right before our eyes in less-than-lifelike realism because we're not watching it on a high-priced high-definition television.

"The ones who made it, the ones who are alive," TB says, eyeing the drivers across the highway divide, "they're lucky to be alive. And now they *know* they're lucky to be alive. The value of their lives has been reintroduced to them."

"What about the dead ones?"

"They were dead in any meaningful way already. Now their physical states just match their psychological and spiritual ones."

"Matching is important. Especially color matching. Especially after Labor Day."

"Yes. No whiteys after Labor Day. The world would be a far better place if it acted upon that wise dictum."

"Well, *yeah.*"

"Plus, the traffic's actually moving now."

"Well, *yeah.*"

I can tell the traffic's moving because the helicopter overhead TV shot is a wide one showing moving traffic on the cleared I-405 North along with the ongoing operation to clear I-405 South. But I can only barely tell all this because I'm having to watch it all in grainy black & white disgrace.

"We really need to upgrade to a wireless flat-panel liquid crystal display unit. Nothing smaller than forty-two inches either. I mean, what does a fourteen-inch black & white bunny-eared TV say to the world about you? Remember. It's not just a TV. It's a lifestyle."

The leper offers no rebuttal. He's too busy fighting off the midget. The midget cannonballed through our front windshield, landed in the backseat, sprung up and started biting the back of the leper's head. I can tell all this because the news helicopter is now flying low, like, right beside us, and its zoom-lens camera is broadcasting the whole midget thing which I'm watching on the black & white TV. But only barely watching because the picture quality is so abysmal. I mean, for all I know, it's not really a midget at all. Maybe it's some sort of feral child or maybe even an elf.

Midgets are mythical creatures akin to fairies, pixies, and dwarves. Fairies are small beautiful creatures who fly around sprinkling magical dust. Pixies are small beautiful creatures who fly around sprinkling magical dust because of their marked lack of originality, which is quite popular nowadays. Dwarves have untrimmed beards that give off magical smells. Midgets are the most powerful of the mythical creatures because they are the most likely to show up in your grocery store aisle. Their propensity to interact in both the mythological world and the real world makes them powerful because of their ability to develop nuclear weapons. The first nuclear bombs ever produced were named Fat Man and Little Boy. Little Boy was developed by and for midgets. Little Boy was dropped on Hiroshima, Japan on August 6, 1945 and killed 140,000 Japanese midgets. Fat Man was dropped three days later on Nagasaki but incinerated only 40,000 regular-sized Japanese, a real disappointment. The death count disparity is because there are many more midgets in Japan than regular-sized folk. This is because the Japanese are a notoriously tiny people. Except for their cock size which

is gargantuan. Japanese midgets are estimated to have schlongs the size of a finely aged goiter. It is estimated midgets possess enough nuclear weapons to destroy the world only four times over, but enough to destroy a midget world eighteen times over. Having weapons that will destroy a world several times over is moral and sane because it acts as a deterrent against the dwarves' offensive beard odor. You could say nuclear midgets *dwarf* the power of beards. Ha!

The TV shows the midget gnawing on the leper's ear. This camera angle makes me look like I'm retaining water. The midget was previously televised barreling through our front windshield after the Olds sliced the midget's car in half. The midget did not barrel out of spite although maybe he did because midgets are a spiteful lot even though there's not *a lot* to them. Ha! When slamming your car head-on into other cars prepare for midgets and others crashing through windshields. Sudden impacts tend to send things flying. This is the natural way of things and thus good. Most regular-sized folk who go flying through their windshield will end up splattering against your snowplow-wedge. Midgets however are more aerodynamic and have the magical ability to roll up your wedge and through your windshield. Think of them as cannonballs, adorable cannonballs. The U.S. army did when it put together a corps of midgets to be used as ordnance in case they ever run out of ammo or just want a fun change of pace. Firing midgets is the right thing to do because children from the Third World are not as compact which negatively affects their flight trajectory.

"Help!" yells TB as the lil' fella is televised sinking its sharp pointy teeth into the back of his neck. My God. Does the midget look Chinese? I cover my bases and yell "Banana!" If he is a wee yellow one, I'm getting points.

"You're not helping me here!" screams TB.

"Banana!"

"I'm bleeding here!" screams TB.

"Banana!"

"It's really hard to drive and not get into an accident when you're being eaten," informs TB.

"Banana!"

"You don't get multiple Bananas! for one yellow midget! One Banana! per midget, please."

But is it really a midget? The TV's picture quality is such horseshit that I can't tell for sure. You try to I.D. a yellow midget using a black & white abomination. Go ahead. I defy you to do it. It would be inadmissible in a court of law. For all I know, this isn't a little angry Chinaman after all but instead some pissed-off fire hydrant. As the saying goes, Chinamen and fire hydrants all look alike even on a fifty-inch HDTV built in the traditional CRT-based rear-projection television format.

When he pinballed into the Olds, the rabid fire hydrant must have damaged the diesel generator in the backseat. The generator looks like something dredged from a depth-charged U-boat and is smoking more than usual. It's vital because it powers the TV. Luckily most of the fumes are blowing out the back of the car where the back window used to be. This impromptu smoke-screen looks great on the TV and impairs the vision of all those cops tailing us.

The midget starts biting the leper's left arm. Big mistake. It's the opportunity the leper has been waiting for and he ruthlessly seizes it, flinging the enthusiastic knee-high cannibal out the window with a flick of the wrist. The midget lands on the side of our cleared lane at the base of half a Lincoln Navigator. The cop on our tail, with vision impaired by backseat World War II relic reek, sees the midget on the side of the lane too late. He wildly turns his cruiser to hit the midget but flips the car instead. The overturned cop car clogs the cleared lane just to spite our good work. The rest of the cops, blinded by hate (truism) and generator, smash one by one into the flipped-cop roadblock, creating a lovely fifty-cop-car pileup.

A brilliant white light flashes on the hood of the Olds. It's either the ethereal light you see when you're dead or Potter and Futuro beaming in from the cuticular space-time continuum. I hear Potter whine as Futuro bites his buttocks so unfortunately I'm not dead. Potter retaliates with more whining and then the twisted combatants flash away to another time and venue.

We finish clearing our path at the Sunset Boulevard exit. Here the gridlock thins and we get off. The evil gases spewing from the generator join forces with the evil gases always present in Los Angeles. Smog plus smog equals a shitload of smog. In corporate circles this is called synergy. We don't even need to become stealthy Escalade because no one can see anything in this miasma. We feel our way home. Not in a gay way.

EIGHT

The Give Whitey Five movement is a radical splinter group of the Très Black movement, a radical French-speaking Tajikistani black-power splinter group of the T Bag movement. The Give Whitey Five movement is comprised of radical extremists comprised of *coq au vin*-eating darkies within the Golden Chancre region of what used to be Tajikistan before U.S. forces freed the shit out of that hellhole with exploding 15,000-pound bombs and midgets.

This reported in today's *New York Times*.

What these baguette-wielding mud people want besides savory duck confit is unclear and unimportant. They are evil and bent on destroying the American way of life always so conspicuously displayed in Los Angeles, according to reliable sources according to the *Times*.

This latest news provoked a healthy national debate on how best to kill dark-skinned boogeymen and save whitey (including whether white folk donning blackface would fly under the radar of dark-skinned boogeymen and thereby be immune to annihilation).

Various experts debated just how white whitey had to be before being anthropometrically classified as whitey. Once a whitey shade of white was agreed upon, various TV news outlets ran a banner of the white across the bottom of the screen

that viewers could match their skin against. If the viewer's skin proved to be darker than the white banner, the viewer was not whitey. If the viewer's skin matched the color or was even paler, that viewer was whitey and instructed to panic-buy their way to safety.

Now don't get me wrong. Whitey should always be a target for murderous blood-snorting terrorists hot from the Pamir Mountains. But a point of clarification needs to be made: Being whitey is not determined by your skin color. Being whitey is determined by the degree you make the skin crawl.

Being whitey is being the corporate hack, the swindling banker, the illegitimate landlord, the savior politician, the presiding judge, the agenda-setting newsman, the beguiling ad man, the indoctrinating teacher, the guiding clergyman, the lapdog cop, the lapdog soldier, and everything in between. Being whitey is being the power that feeds the power structure. Being whitey is being the system's mandarin, the system's defender, the system's slaver. Being whitey is being a groveling toe licker and an imperious dominator, depending on the situation. Being whitey is gladly playing the role of chewing maggot infesting the mangled necrotizing remains of Mother Earth. Being whitey is striving to become a bigger and better maggot. Being whitey is never imagining or ever wanting to imagine anything different. Being whitey is you, no?

Give whitey five.

Somehow the omniscient news media got it all wrong. Giving whitey five isn't about reverse racism. Humans should never be hated for their skin color. Humans should just be hated. Regardless of skin color. Period.

The smell of burning oxygen/acetylene mixture combined with the dead-meat slapping sound of skin on metal would

remind anyone of the after-hours dungeon at the Southern Baptist Convention. Concentrating on the issues of the day set forth in the *Times* is no longer possible. I raise my head from the newspaper and ask the leper, "What the fuck?"

The leper is busy welding a human head to the Olds's wheel and answers incorrectly.

The leper is concerned about how close the SWATzis came to successfully pulling alongside our ride and shooting us full of lead which is an element that damages the nervous system and causes blood and brain disorders. This is a health issue. This is where human heads come in.

"Adding human heads to your vehicle's wheels is easy, inexpensive, and fun. Alls you need to do is weld a two-foot metal spike so it protrudes out from the center of each wheel. Then stick the back of the human head against the sharp spike and slide it down to the base of the wheel. You can even line it up so the sharp end of the spike pokes out of the human head's mouth. This is a neat look because it looks like the human head on the wheel is poking its tongue out at you. Except it's not a tongue. It's a two-foot metal spike. This is funny and amuses children."

"I got my human heads on eBay."

"A dozen Third World human heads will cost you less than a dozen free-range chicken eggs. But, no. These human heads were not free-range. I'm afraid the industry is still in its infancy which lends itself to barbarism."

"If you buy your human heads by the dozen, you'll have extras. Unless you drive an 18-wheeler."

"A human head impaled on a two-foot metal spike spinning from your wheel can be used to blow out the tires of any car friendly enough to venture alongside you."

"Shiny foil sandwich wrappers from Arby's should then be glued to the human heads to make your wheels sparkly which the kids demand nowadays."

"Form and function."

"Yes, buy God."

"Used to be only merciless Zulu pimps from some bombed-out hole in Detroit could pull off the pimpmobile look. But now, even the pettiest bourgeois wants tire rims that flash like a hooker's platinum-plated twat."

"Remember: it's not just the Indians who see the value of shiny trinkets. Trade your shiny trinkets to the nearest petit bourgeois for his land, money, and freedom and do throw in some smallpox-infested blankets for him, just for over-his-head historical giggles."

"Hey! You're not the only one deft at manipulating hot spewing gases. The governor's on TV! Come. Let us gather round the telly."

California Governor Adrenal Wartzenfegger is a movie action hero. He holds the office of governor so the movie studio can trial-balloon saucy one-liners. The winning zingers appear in next summer's blockbusters.

"I have called this emergency press conference to address the horror of the Give Whitey Five movement," the governor slurs in his thick un-American accent. Lowered by invisible wires from the stage rafters is a mannequin dressed in green spandex overalls and welder's mask with matching dog stuffed animal (made in China). I'm a bit unnerved because the dog stuffed animal is as white as the white whitey banner running at the bottom of the screen of this shitty black & white TV. Time to go panic-buy a high-def big screen.

The governor poses, flexing muscles. His designer business suit rips in half, on cue, leaving only bulging oiled perfection, and a thong. The thong has the California state seal on it. *Eureka!*

The gov is 270 glorious pounds of tanned brawn and political will. He points at the mannequin, never missing a flex, and issues new policy: "I will show you through my 270 glorious pounds of tanned brawn that *TB* stands for *Terminated Bozo!*"

The line is met by laughter and applause from the press corps in attendance.

Offstage, the lieutenant governor retorts in his best terrorist (Arabic) accent, "You will not stop me, beefy hero of the people!"

"This is what I will do to you, Give Whitey Five scum," belches the gov in alleged English. He unholsters his trusty power drill and bores into the dummy's chest. "I say, *screw you*, TB!" Unholstering a battle-ax, the governor chops off the mannequin's arm and says, "Now don't get *hacked off*, TB!"

The lieutenant governor screams, "You very-well-put-together political strongman! Drop dead!"

"I don't do requests," says the gov. (Canned laughter.)

Several aides wheel in a storage tank of hot water. The governor punches through a nearby wall and tears out of it a large pipe, twirls towards the mannequin slumped up against the tank, and throws the pipe through the mannequin. Steam shoots from the breached boiler, through the pipe, through the mannequin as the governor exclaims, "Let off some steam, TB!"

The gov charges the mannequin and bites off its head, welder's mask and all. Blood comes pumping from the dummy's neck, on cue. The gov says, "Now I know! *TB* stands for *Tasty Blood!* Which you will see this summer in my next blockbuster: *Steroidula!* The story of what would happen if Dracula got on performance-enhancing substances. And remember, kids— don't do drugs!" He says this while flexing massive oiled muscles while looking straight into the camera while reading the teleprompter. A consummate professional.

The heat from the steam coursing through the mannequin causes the made-in-China stuffed animal dog to break down molecularly and release green smoke from its synthetic fibers. Luckily the asbestos in it prevents a large-scale fire.

The back wall of the press conference room explodes as a monster truck drives through. It stops by the governor's podium

and blows its horn specially modified to play Billy Ray Waylon Scurry's classic "If God Didn't Bless the USA Then How Come the USA and Jesus Kick So Much Ass!" that can be heard seventeen miles away.

It's that lovable rascal, Toughie Skabbsbull.

Toughie Skabbsbull—or "The Incredible Skabbs" to decent god-fearing folk—was the first person regularly outsmarted by phlegm to attend college. This has since become the norm amongst collegians.

During his years of higher education the Skabbs played football and majored in steroids. The Skabbs earned acclaim for intimidating his football opponents by marking his territory the way an incoherent wino marks his own lederhosen. You know, like you've seen on those nature shows.

The Skabbs marked everything—sections of the field, cheerleaders, and fans alike, making him a real fan favorite. Marking the footballs made handling them a slippery and vile proposition. Just like handling the Skabbs. He was fired from college football after fellating an underage keg of Natural Light, and swallowing; the union consummated by the Skabbs passing out in a puddle of his own precious bodily fluid 'n secret weapon. The Skabbs pleaded out and did several public service announcements on the horrors of urine and Natural Light. The controversy led to a lucrative book deal. It was a *New York Times* bestseller. It had scratch-and-sniff footnotes. The Skabbs signed a lucrative professional football deal with the Naugatuck Numbats and then royally fucked them over by being the most inadequate player in the history of inadequacy. This inadequacy happened because the Skabbs had lost his ability to piss on balls after steroids caused his own balls to shrivel up and disappear from the universe. The Skabbs underwent numerous surgeries to replace his testicles with two genuine leather medicine balls, each weighing thirty pounds. The Skabbs rented a wheelbarrow and wheelbarrowed his monster-truck balls around town and Hollywood took notice, signing him to a lucrative movie deal. The

films that followed were seminal: *One Manly Hardass with Huge Balls*; *One Man's Hardass Justice and His Huge Balls*; *One Hardass's Huge Man-Balls of Justice*; *One Man, Two Balls* (a romantic comedy); *Air Force One, Mach Two Huge Balls* (misspelled *"Mock Two Huge Balls"* on the straight-to-video cassette cover); and *A Head Full of Fist*, his breakout role from the balls genre.

The monster truck's tires are twenty feet high so the Skabbs does not use the escalator built into the side of the monster truck and instead swallows a handful of steroids and leaps out the driver's window, lands on his balls, and bounces to his feet.

The gov wraps his meat hook around the Skabbs and announces, "I think we all know that this gentleman needs no introduction!" The press corps whoops and throws their hats into the air which is supplemented by canned applause.

The Skabbs boasts two beady eyes barely visible under a cruelly immense brow jutting up from a wall that is less a forehead and more a wall. Such a "human" head has never been seen before, combining features dating back to Homo habilis with features of a possible future human species ruined by radioactive waste, industrial pollution, and Natural Light. Eighty Nobel laureates have signed a letter imploring the Skabbs to donate his head to science, the sooner the better. It remains unclear how the situation will be resolved or if the Skabbs was able to find someone to read him the letter.

The Skabbs has a carefully cultivated image tailored by a PR firm and anabolic steroids. His six-foot frame carries 400 pounds of muscle. It also carries 200 pounds of fluid retained in the skin which creates a slightly puffy, nay, a horrifically distended appearance. To alleviate this the Skabbs has tens of thousands of tiny plastic shunts sticking out of his skin which reduce the water retention by constantly dripping. The Skabbs has acne on every inch of skin except for his balls which are genuine leather. The Skabbs has worn a Mohawk since his movie *Mohawk Mo' Balls* only all his hair has since fallen out except for the twenty-

eight hairs on the back of his head that he's grown down past his buttocks. The Skabbs still wears a Mohawk to show support for vanquished Native American cultures based on communal sustainability, not shortsighted greed. Or to show support for the punk movement and its rebellion against a bourgeois value system. Or none of the above because it's really just a mullet. And the Skabbs shows he's a rebel by buying leather biker outfits which is one of the things you buy to show you're a rebel.

The Skabbs pulls out the M16 assault rifle snuggled between his balls and opens fire on the hacked mannequin and fuming stuffed animal dog. The water tank takes some friendly fire, spraying scalding steam all over the lieutenant governor who stays in character till the very end with shrieks in his best Arabic (terrorist) accent. More press corps hats are a-flying. The leper and I leap to our feet and cheer. There's canned laughter. The Skabbs gets all choked up and his balls swell with pride. They look magnificent and really stretch his leather biker chaps which make him look like a mad cow with tumid testicles which the chaps were originally made from. And certainly not in a gay way.

"Thank you, the Skabbs," thanks the gov. "I have invited the Skabbs here today to introduce my one-man task force. And that one-man task force is: the Skabbs."

Applause.

"No one is more qualified to be a one-man task force. The Skabbs has much experience being a one-man neighborhood-home-prices depreciator and he has huge balls. I can think of no one better to hunt down and destroy the TB menace. What do you think, the Skabbs?"

The Skabbs doesn't think.

"The Skabbs doesn't think. And in dangerous times such as these and all the others, this is an asset." The gov continues, "The Skabbs hasn't worked in a while. His last gig was five years ago as an extra in a used-meat commercial. So I could obviously get him on the cheap which will save the taxpayers a bundle."

The Skabbs responds with some drool.

"So you see, the Skabbs is the right man for the job. In all of his movies and infomercials he's played the role of the rebel who mindlessly smashes trite boilerplate depictions of criminals, terrorists, gangsters, convicts, outsiders, malcontents, noncon- formists, ne'er-do-wells, Pennsylvania Dutch, the homeless, stutterers, and all other enemies of the State. Because he who upholds the law and order of the State while consuming leather biker outfits and other rebel accoutrements is a rebel."

The gov says to the Skabbs, "The Skabbs: Just like in all your movies and puerile fantasies, you are a rebel with a cause. What will you do after you recklessly track down TB?"

The Skabbs replies by shoving steroid chewing gum into his mouth. He chews the gum in the over-the-top violent way you'd expect. He looks blankly at the governor. An uncomfortable minute passes. Then the Skabbs remembers to reach into his pants and turn on the tape player between his balls. The voice of the professional announcer comes streaming from the Skabbs's balls and says, "What will I do after I recklessly track down TB? I will recklessly *wreck* him!" The pre-recorded voice, coupled with the Skabbs's violent gum chewing, gives the illusion that the Skabbs can muster speech of his own. Of course this is a metaphorical representation of the way most humans "speak."

Hurrah. More hats in the air.

The Skabbs puffs out his chest and balls. Ah, the power of pride. He ejaculates a guttural belch and wildly fires his assault rifle, killing the hats. The governor slowly backpedals to his po- dium to announce, "Members of the press, please remain calm. You are only in danger if you move. This concludes today's press conference."

The TV cuts back to Telly Bawdhaw in the Fox News studio. "I guess when TB runs into the Skabbs it'll be *road* rage versus *'roid* rage! *Heehaw!*"

NINE

The next day we decide to burn down Malibu.

According to her interview in *The Moneyed Yogi* magazine, Venus Weathers-Cumming is a money-life coach. As a money-life coach, Venus teaches a metaphysical approach to money. And as with any metaphysical outlook, Venus teaches that money reflects your inner core values and has the power to reveal the real you. She can do this while levitating, for an added fee.

Venus educates: "The more we live into our fullest life's mission, the more we take. The more we take, the more we have. Thus, Wealthy & Successful people™ comprehend: the more we have, ultimately, the more we have to give." Venus puts this doctrine into practice by purchasing Tommy Hilfiger wallets for the Tommy Hilfiger wallet-sweatshop laborers every Christmas.

"As each one of us awakens to our fullest potential, the world raises [*sic*] to it's [*sic*] fullest potential [*sic*]. It moves from hopelessness to hope, from lovelessness to love, and from lack to lack of lack for all," Venus enlightens from the mountaintop superimposed on the studio greenscreen behind her.

Venus Weathers-Cumming is a rising star, or a raising star, on the national cable "news" show circuit where she can be found waxing transcendental on the melding of Buddhist spiritualism with Western materialism. Two great tastes, together at last.

Call it *spiriterialism*. Call it all the rage. Call Venus Weathers-Cumming very popular in L.A.

So I say to the leper, "Leper, today Venus Weathers-Cumming is holding a, *quote*, 'money-life coaching workshop intensive.'"

"Oh, really? Where would this money-life coaching workshop intensive be taking place?"

"Why, it would be taking place in Malibu. Naturally."

"Why, naturally."

"Admission is exorbitant to keep the spiritually impoverished halfwits with money (Americans) in, and the riffraff out. That's also a quote."

"Well, how much money do we have in the piggy bank?"

"We have exactly one piece of lint."

"More than enough to cover expenses. To the Olds!"

Fortress Malibu. Where authoritarianism is always in fine style. Naturally. The cops are everywhere and under orders to shoot first and not ask questions later upon seeing a 1994 Oldsmobile Cutlass or any vehicle not tinseled and valued under $40,000, just to be safe. Since much of the help who worked in Malibu and certainly did not live in Malibu were not decent enough to drive tinseled vehicles worth over $40,000 they were "let go" in a hail of police gunfire. But the country is at war and sacrifices needed to be made. Naturally. Since the purge of the browns, Malibu yards have browned. The country is at war and sacrifices needed to be made but how much can we be expected to endure? Then, a breakthrough. In a gesture of good will, the oil corporations agreed to allow any not-shot help to cling to the sides of the deep-water oil rigs off the Southern California coast, *rent-free*. The help's commute to work is now as simple as an invigorating twenty-five-mile oceanic swim, one way. Mexicans are naturally suited to such an arrangement, being *wetbacks* and all. Ha! Malibu yards have turned green again. The help swims to work, a green form of transportation. The oil keeps pumping, the tinseled SUVs worth over $40,000 keep

pumping, for Malibu is helping the country win the war *and* save the environment.

And the Malibu neoliberals remark to themselves it is all thanks to a kindly gesture by their old nemesis, Big Oil. Ah, the irony.

But they made a mistake. Their mistake was allowing another Escalade to pass into the city limits and not immediately opening fire on the nigger driving it. Judging people not on their race but on their showy displays of wealth may be egalitarian and all but sometimes you still gotta put the darkies in their place. That's a quote.

Venus Weathers-Cumming is hosting her money-life coaching workshop intensive at Taj Mahal II, the sequel. We drive up to the admission booth. *"Namaste,"* greets the cashier, slightly bowing with hands pressed together. He has a Buddhist monastic robe with nametag that says Phil. "It's 500 bucks per adult. Dogs get in half-price."

"Do you take credit cards?" asks the darky.

"Duh, of course." Phil rolls his eyes at such an insulting question.

The leper hands Phil the wallet that the attack-midget dropped in the backseat. "There are some cards in there. I think. Try one of them."

"Which one?"

"I don't know. Any of them. All of them."

"Uh, can I see your I.D.?" asks Phil. "You can't be too careful with identity theft."

"Indeed. See if the driver's license is in there somewhere."

Phil picks it out of the wallet and inspects it. He looks at the darky. Then back at the driver's license. "Uh, OK. Thank you, Mr. Kang Kong."

"I knew that midget was a Chinaman!" I think to the darky. "I get double-points for him!"

"The fuck you say!" yells the darky.

"What?" asks Phil.

"Oh, not you. I mean, 'The fuck you say,' is Chinese for... something ethnic," covers the darky.

"You don't look very Chinese," says Phil, squinting at the driver's license. He adds, "You don't look two-foot-four."

"Since I got that license I've taken a lot of vitamins."

"Say! Nice rims!" Phil blurts, his attention suddenly focused on our wheels with human heads with glued-on Arby's shiny foil wrappers.

"You damn straight they are, Phil."

Phil runs one of the credit cards and it works. Stupid midget hasn't cancelled it yet. Because he's under fifty cop cars.

The darky signs the receipt with some smiling penises (Chinese sinographs). Phil hands us our Unity of Consciousness media packet and waves us through. We drive the Escalade past the main gateway of fine white marble into the fine white marbled Taj Mahal II grand hall.

Venus Weathers-Cumming teaches us that people are at their best when they're at their wealthiest. This means that people are really really at their best when in a luxury automobile. That is why Venus Weathers-Cumming teaches all money-life coaching workshop intensives from inside luxury automobiles.

We park the Escalade in the front row. Behind us the lanes are rapidly filling with believers in BMWs, the proselytes of Porsche, a blissful convergence of ethereal Range Rover SUVs, the Lexus congregation, seers in Mercedes-Benzes, Acura apostles of all beautiful backgrounds, and, of course, a fundamentalist cult of Cadillac Escalades.

"Half of Malibu is parking behind us," I inform. "Glad we got here early and got a spot up front."

"Well, that's what Kang Kong paid for."

"I love it when you talk dirty in the third person."

Vendors walk between the rows of cars selling Buddhism and refreshments. The uncompromisingly augmented woman

in the Hummer to the right of us purchases a *How to Live in the Moment* instructional DVD and a Dalai Lama-flavored kefir. The Range Rover behind the Hummer buys a Compassion Burger and an Interconnectedness of Life wireless phone plan for himself and the speedboat he towed in.

The car to our left boasts comedienne, TV celebrity, lesbian, your friend and mine, Ellen DeGeneres. The leper waves and gets her attention. "Hi, Ellen. I just wanted to say I really enjoyed your work on that credit card commercial where you're shown in deep yoga meditation thinking about how secure you feel purchasing socks with American Express because of their outstanding consumer protection services."

Ellen responds, "Thank you. Here's another lil' something something you'll recognize and enjoy from my stand-up routine: I was in yoga the other day. I was in full lotus position. My chakras were all aligned. My mind is cleared of all clatter and I'm looking out of my third eye and everything that I'm supposed to be doing. It's amazing what comes up, when you sit in that silence. *'Mama keeps whites bright like the sunlight, Mama's got the magic of Clorox 2.'* "

"How funny. And true. Deep spiritual meditation really does mean reflecting upon all the wonderful goods and services available."

A vile disturbance erupts four lanes over between neighboring Lexus owners arguing whether the plural of Lexus is Lexus or Lexi. It reaches the boiling point when one of them drops their Starbucks in anger. Thankfully each left their private security muscle at home or there would have been rent-a-violence.

The crowd was getting nasty. Bloodshed should have broken out at any second. Instead, hundreds of lawsuits broke out. Naturally. And then...

Dim the grand-hall lights. Train the spotlight on the stage ahead. Cue the two oiled musclemen in loincloths who should be governor someday beside the giant bronze gong. Up swells

Handel's *Messiah*, the "Hallelujah" chorus. And in drives a Lexus GX luxury behemoth SUV *and* a Lexus LX luxury *très* behemoth SUV. The Lexus GX looks like a Nazi pillbox fortification on four wheels with some spare AMC Pacer windows thrown in for aesthetics. The Lexus LX is somehow worse.

The two SUVS take center stage. Bolted to the roofs of each SUV, linking them side by side, is a golden bridge. On the bridge, dressed in sharkskin Ann Taylor business suit, armed with profound come-hither look, is a lithe, comely young thing. This is Venus Weathers-Cumming.

Hallelujah!

The music ceases and the oiled musclemen gong their gong. The legions of spiriterialists put away their cell phones, iPods, laptops, and other electronic gadgets they had been meditating on.

On the bridge between SUVs, Venus Weathers-Cumming is in the Prasarita Padottanasana yoga pose. That is: standing with feet wide apart, upper torso bent down between spread legs, hands and head on the ground between legs. A person in the Prasarita Padottanasana position looks like a triangle—the triangle's base consisting of spread feet, hands, and upside-down head; the triangle's top being an arched spread ass.

Venus Weathers-Cumming teaches money-life coaching workshop intensives entirely in the upside-down-head-under-spread-ass position. Because she's a professional. The leper gets caught up in the mystical moment and beats his meat. As does Ellen DeGeneres.

Venus Weathers-Cumming begins, "Buddha once said, 'The secret of happiness lies in the mind's release from worldly ties.' That is why we do not wear ties here." Several embarrassed men parked in attendance remove their neckties. "Remember: Being super casual is more than just California cool—it's a moral stand. Speaking of making a stand—assume the position." Her disciples comply and triangulate

themselves into the Prasarita Padottanasana position in the front seats of their luxury automobiles. The amount of room required to perform the Prasarita Padottanasana stand is substantial and this is why the deeply spiritual generally purchase luxury SUVs.

The money-life guru cracks a smile underneath her arched crack. It's time to share who she is. It's time to get real. "My first yoga swami, a singularly authentic and clean-shaven man, bestowed unto *moi* one of the greatest lessons I have learned when he revealed: 'There is no *yoga* in *Yugo*.'" Her smile widens at such a delightful yet insightful anecdote. She brings it home: "His mavericky approach will always resonate with me in the most powerfully simplistic [*sic*] way."

"Well, at least she admits to being powerfully simplistic."

"Albeit unwittingly," whacks back the leper.

"Because using inflated words in your malapropisms is a surefire way to get published."

"That's because Venus Weathers-Cumming's book *What Would Buddha Do? (with all that cash!)* was a bestseller. That's because she has a readership and you do not. That's because the world has raised to it's fullest potential [*sic*]," grunts the cruel rub-monkey.

Venus Weathers-Cumming's teachings continue to caw from the grand hall's speakers: "When we say yes to seizing our fullest money potential, we also say yes to seizing our fullest life potential. For we are here not to be just who we are, but to be more of who we are." The capidoltists would nod blankly in appreciation of the sublimely profound if they weren't standing on their heads with asses bulging out of sunroof.

"Prior to my immersion into yoga, my spiritual evolution was left quaking in the dark, alongside the many other areas of my life that quaked in the darkness of dark. And I must confess, one of the largest areas of my life that I neglected was my relationship with money." That sad old story. But no matter

how badly you neglect your relationship with money, money is still loving enough to always take you back. "What I did not realize—before exposing myself in yoga, before consciously choosing to be more of who I am, and before choosing to live at my fullest money potential, and thus, fullest life potential—was that the pursuit of money is a spiritual odyssey!" Upside-down capidoltists hug their checkbooks and stacks of cash in large denominations. They are now one. And thus, it is one of those money-life affirming moments.

"I have since awakened to see that each one of us has our own singular programming for financial results. In order to productively upgrade my own money programming, I began by admitting that I was my biggest obstacle—that how I perceived capital, fixed income, offshore accounts—that how I perceived my own money potential had to change. In essence, my money programming was a four on a scale of ten." I calculate my own money programming level using a fun quiz found in the Unity of Consciousness media packet and am horrified to learn that I am legally dead.

"I believe that when the pupil is ready the sage appears. How can you know if you are ready?"

"*Oh!* I'm *ready* to shoot hot Jesus-loving spermatozoon all over her nice round ova! Zygote, here I come!"

"How can you know if you are ready? You are ready when you act in spite of your fright because you have reached a place in your own spiriterial evolution where your old results with money are no longer satisfactory. Once you arrive here, you have begun to adopt the crucial practice that many rich and flourishing people live by: the W.I.T. (Whatever It Takes) approach, a full and utter commitment to realizing your fullest money potential, and thus fullest life potential." Yes. Whatever It Takes to get my Lockheed Martin stocks up. A smallish nuclear war would boost Lockheed Martin nuclear-weapon sales, boost my money potential, and thus life potential.

"Money reflects your inner core values and has the power to reveal the real you. The more money you have, the more positive choices you have." The less money you have, the less positive choices you have. If you have no money, you have no positive choices. People with no money are soulless ditches, devoid of that divine spark evident in the wealthy, or at least the upwardly mobile. That is why the billions of soulless ditches on Earth do not spend their time living life to the fullest by investing in Lockheed Martin stock and instead laze about in Tommy Hilfiger wallet sweatshops. She can use that in her next book.

"Your centered, self-motivated, self-centered movement toward wealth enlightenment will be profound and sublime. My journey has taught me that the more we have, the more we have to give. By choosing to say yes to living to my fullest money potential, and thus my fullest life potential—" And thus I vomit. And thus the leper jizzes all over the thought of Venus Weathers-Cumming's haploid reproductive cells. And thus the leper cleans up and presses the "E" button on the steering wheel. And thus out the tailpipe our Escalade jizzes black goo with phosphorescent green streaks, splattering all over the Escalade behind us. "I'm guessing the folks around here will enjoy this *money* shot!"

"You mean this *money-life* shot," I correct.

Our Escalade keeps squirting. The bukkake-lovin' Escalade to our rear is slathered in black and green ooze which begins to pool and spread throughout the Taj Mahal II grand hall.

"Smells like teen spirit."

"Yes. The ejaculate is redolent of toxic industrial waste on a bright summer morn. Maybe because it is toxic industrial waste. A small sampling of the hundreds of millions of pounds of toxic waste that have been *invested* in this great nation's low-income and minority neighborhoods."

"The smart investing of toxic waste in low-income neighborhoods (where the soulless ditches live) helps keep my corporate stocks up, boosting my money potential, and thus life potential."

"When the news story broke that Dow Chemical had agreed to spend money to clean up its toxins left from a pesticide-plant accident in Bhopal, India, horrified investors *dumped* (ha!) Dow's stock. The corporation's share price fell 4.24 percent in just 23 minutes, wiping $2 billion off its market value."

"There is nothing that shakes investor confidence more than a company that agrees to clean up its poisons that killed 20,000 people."

"That's a lot of soulless ditches."

"But not enough to justify the cost of a cleanup."

"Thankfully the cleanup news story was revealed to be a hoax in time to restore investor confidence. Saved was Dow's stock and not Bhopal."

"It is the W.I.T. (Whatever It Takes) approach, a full and utter commitment to realizing your fullest money potential, and thus fullest life potential."

"Why, there are over a hundred toxic waste sites in South Central L.A. alone! Mutagenic acid alkyl sludge is Watts' most valuable resource, as listed in *Forbes* magazine. Since Malibu has no toxic waste sites to boast, I'm bringing a bit of the 'hood to the country club."

"Oh, just like when whitey goes to the mall to buy a corporate-label gangsta rap CD sung by a carefully manufactured black millionaire and then blares this genuine street music from the speakers of his luxury SUV in his neighborhood of uniform, cheaply vulgar, shoddily constructed suburban Taj Mahals before triangulating himself into the Prasarita Padottanasana position in the Taj Mahal II."

"Yes. That is an authentic expression of bringing the 'hood to the country club."

"You always were an unruly porch monkey."

The whitey in the luxury SUV being doused in gangsta sludge is irate. He just paid a bunch of spics next to nothing to detail his Escalade because he is here not just to be who he is, but to be more of who he is: "Which is a leprotic weeping pustule on the body humanity. No offense."

"None taken," says the leper as he plays with his meat puppet.

The yuppie in the Escalade cannot get out of the Escalade to properly bitch for fear of sullying his Bruno Maglis in the growing mire so he starts honking his horn. This disturbs the Lexus owners who resume shouting at each other and filing lawsuits. But Venus Weathers-Cumming rules with an iron fist and reminds all warring factions of the Zen of the yen, especially considering today's exchange rate. This fails to pacify one of the Lexus owners who has flown into a rage and is urinating on his archenemy's windshield. Venus Weathers-Cumming: "Please, gentle upscale souls, please! The Lexus GX and Lexus LX are still family even though the GX retails for $46,000 while the LX goes for $67,000 which means the LX is a 31 percent more positive choice, if you do the math. But Lexus GX owners can reduce this positive-choice gap by purchasing the many positive-choice options available, such as custom floor mats. Another way to bridge this gap is to customize your Lexus GX with the purchase of a Lexus LX and then join them with a bridge. That is why I come to you on a bridge between a Lexus GX and a Lexus LX. For this bridge is a symbol—a symbol of the bridge connecting the Lexus GX and LX, and thus, us all."

The one Lexus owner finishes draining his bladder onto the offending Lexus and yells, "I'll piss on every single one of your *Lexi*, you dirty little faggot!"

"The plural of Lexus is *Lexus*, motherfucker!" yells back the gentle lad in the pissed-on Lexus as he throws a custom chrome-

plated Lexus floor mat out the window at his adversary, missing laughably.

Venus Weathers-Cumming pleads for harmony. "Please, paying friends! Remember: Buddha said that 'virtuous deeds are a shelter.' And there is nothing more virtuous than finding a good tax shelter. As explained in my new book *Walking the Noble Eightfold Path to Junk-Bond Investing*. On sale now at fine book chains and your nearest Compassion Burger vendors."

The spiriterialist in the Escalade is screaming, honking, and flashing his lights. The spiriterialist on the Lexus is squatting and shitting on the car's hood. Venus Weathers-Cumming is chanting, "You must be the change you wish to see in the world. You must be the change you wish to see in the world," while jingling the change in her Coach purse.

Touched, TB hits the "E" button. Our Escalade stops spewing mephitic pollution but Venus Weathers-Cumming does not. TB counters by announcing into Mr. Microphone: "Yoga in Mayfair or Fifth Avenue, or in any other place which is on the telephone, is a spiritual fake." Then he lays on the horn, amplified ten thousand times through the speaker. The blast wave launches Venus Weathers-Cumming and her interconnected SUVs through the back wall of the Taj Mahal II and twenty-five miles out to sea. There they hit an oil rig. This is considered ham-handed irony. "An inflated consciousness is always egocentric and conscious of nothing but its own existence. It is incapable of learning from the past, incapable of understanding contemporary events, and incapable of drawing right conclusions about the future. It is hypnotized by itself and therefore cannot be argued with. It inevitably dooms itself to calamities that must strike it dead." TB opens his trench coat revealing green spandex overalls while tossing on welder's mask. Up swells Handel's *Messiah*. He floors the gas pedal, plows through the stage, and out yet another newly created hole in the back of the Taj Mahal II. "Resistance to the organized mass can be effected only by the man who is as well

organized in his individuality as the mass itself." Smoldering dollar bills inside the dollar-bill incense burners onstage topple into the black and green sludge we've graciously left behind. "I guess the black and green sludge is volatile," TB says while watching the Taj Mahal II's marble dome blast off in his rear-view mirror. "It is the individual's task to differentiate himself from all the others and stand on his own feet. All collective identities…interfere with the fulfillment of this task. Such collective identities are crutches for the lame, shields for the timid, beds for the lazy, nurseries for the irresponsible…" He slides "Synchronicity II" into the 8-track tape player.

"Now that's what I call being an angry *Jung* man!" Pun-believable!

"Now that's what I call being *Jung* at heart!" Pun-stoppable!

"Go West, *Jung* man!"

We go west. Behind us the Taj Mahal II is spitting flaming black and green lava out of where its top used to be. Also being ejected are flaming boulders resembling flaming luxury automobiles. The rain of burning industrial waste and Audis sets the countryside on fire, the countryside being mansions, boutiques, and mansions. Panic! Pandemonium! Our Lord and God Pan hath returned, dear Nietzsche!

We really had the bourgeois on the run. A hysterical woman drove the family SUV up her driveway and over her husband, using the car's four-wheel drive for the first-ever time. The bourgeois never use their SUV's four-wheel drive, but it's reassuring to know they *could* (in order to off-road the spouse). Why this hysterical woman in SUV was not attending Venus Weathers-Cumming's money-life coaching workshop intensive remains an inscrutable mystery of life. Then the Taj Mahal II's domed top lands on Dr. Hoffman's Haus of Liposuction and a desperate situation gets worse.

TB slides "5 Million Ways to Kill a CEO" into the 8-track tape player.

The rain of fire and luxury brimstones burns up most everything, including our tarp. Not being an Escalade in Malibu is a dicey proposition and the cops not afire open fire on us and the help, just to be safe, but our herculetium defenses serve us well. We speed through a wall of cop cars and emerge on the Pacific Coast Highway. TB cranks the speaker back towards the hills overlooking Malibu and blows the horn. The blast wave triggers a series of landslides, burying any mansions and cops still capable of antisocial behavior, just to be safe.

With Malibu safely behind us and sliding into the sea, we continue west on the PCH. It's a four-lane deal, two lanes in each direction, making it imperative for cars to stay right and cede the left lane to those wishing to pass, which never happens. "Cars that coagulate in the left lane are the seeds of gridlock. And *God damn* the seeds of gridlock!" he screams through Mr. Microphone while slicing through a Toyota Land Cruiser SUV puttering in the left lane. A few hundred yards straight ahead is the duplicate vision of another Toyota Land Cruiser big'un mindlessly adrift in the left lane. "The filthy bastards will learn," mutters the leper. "I will teach them." He floors the gas and rear-ends the offending monstrosity with such speed, precision, and vengeance that the two SUV halves continue to roll a quarter-mile up the road before fully incinerating. After another dozen of these left-lane tutorials we find a Toyota Flyspeck miraculously driving in the right lane. "Carry on," TB announces while passing. The subcompact's driver gives us a courteous nod.

And then, the mother lode. Twenty-five Harley-Davidson motorcyclists glutting the highway like a bunch of fleshy, middle-aged, numbingly ignorant, cretinously conforming fuckwits riding overpriced, underperforming pieces of tinseled buffoonery glutting a highway. 'Tis simile magic.

"The Harley-Davidson is the great social-class unifier of our time. Coveted by corporation overlords down to lawyers

and doctors down to your average septic tank pumper—the highest whitey to the lowest buys into this figment of a lack of imagination."

"The image fabricated by the Harley-Davidson Corporation of society's rebel—the lone individual making his own way on the open road on *their* corporate-produced motorcycle—is well thought of by the thoroughly leashed haute bourgeois, petit bourgeois, and prole alike."

"After all, what better way to be the rugged individual than purchase the same symbol of rebellion that your dentist neighbor rides on his weekends."

"That plaque-picking rogue!"

"What better way to rebel than dress in a standardized Harley outfit consisting of leather and American flags while riding the same motorcycle used by thousands of police departments nationwide."

"Well, I defy you to find a dictionary that defines 'rebel' (intransitive verb) as:

1. To refuse allegiance to and oppose by force an established government or ruling authority.
2. To resist or defy an authority or a generally accepted convention."

TB cranks the speaker at the last bike in the herd and taps the horn. The abbreviated sound blast is enough to propel the flagpole on the back of the motorcycle forward and through the rider. An American flag impaled in a Harley biker's throat is one of the better ways to fly the flag.

"Guess the American flag got that patriot all *choked* up."

"They're all flag-suckers, which must make him their *deep throat*."

TB cranks the speaker at another Harley and taps the horn. The sound blip causes the bike's shiny metal gewgaws stuck everywhere possible to vibrate and shoot off. Anything within the fifteen-foot blast radius is gored by chrome shrapnel.

"Remember: a standardly decorated Harley-Davidson makes a great garish grenade, when properly jiggled."

"Guess he did more than blow a gasket!"

"Remember: every rebellion of the individual begins and ends with conforming to the day's popular motorcycle aesthetic in order to gain acceptance from the other individuals as you all group-hump your uniformly overblown tailpipes in the Wal-Mart parking lot."

TB accelerates and cuts in half that Harley model with the many shimmering tin cans glued to it.

"The Harley motorcycle started out largely as the domain of working-class toughs. But I'm afraid that market is *so* limited. So, add shimmering tin cans and market it to the more affluent bourgeoisie, and, ta-da! Now it's largely been co-opted by large yuppies yearning to humorously portray themselves as working-class toughs as a pastime."

"In olden times the aristocracy had their sophistication, the intellectuals had their ideas, the poor had their dirt. This gave the poor the only form of authenticity around and menacing body odor. The bourgeoisie had specious imitations of all above traits. Fast forward to present-day America. Gone is the culture of the rich, the adroitness of the intellectual, the earthiness of the poor. All that remains is an all-devouring bourgeoisie and their simulacra of culture, knowledge, and authenticity they watch nightly on the TV."

"Yeah, and we're on the TV!" I exclaim.

"The Harley rider shows an uncanny knack for knowing absolutely nothing outside the narrow confines of: his job, pop culture, and the top five catchphrases the mass-media sphincter is currently excreting."

"This grinding ignorance coupled with the usual amount of laziness and complacency leaves a society of cretins who honestly believe the pursuit of cliquish bauble is a valid 'lifestyle.'" TB weaves back and forth, knocking the lifestyle out of the Harley

herd. The TV news helicopter above us zooms in their camera on the shiny heads on our wheels. Telly Bawdhaw reports, "Now that's what I call getting some *head!*"

"Bawdhaw hit the nail on the *head* with that one."

"It's actually a *spike* through the head," corrects the leper as he steers the head spikes into the Harley beside us, shredding the bike's custom wheels, sending the leather-clad chunk of dolt hurtling headfirst fifty feet without the aid of his ride.

"Guess that guy is falling *head over heels* for us!"

"*Heads* will *roll* for this!" publicly announces the leper as he head spikes that Harley model with the chrome faux buzzsaws mounted on the handlebars.

"Now that's using your *head!*" I say.

"Full steam a*head!*" he says.

"Looks like TB should have given that Harley a *heads*-up!" Bawdhaw says. Then: "Looks like TB is going to *head* them off at the pass." Then: "Looks like real journalism would be way over my *head*. Not to mention the average viewer." I look at the leper. The leper looks at me. Pun-omenal!

The leper spikes that Harley model resembling Liberace's piano on two wheels.

I retort, "But in defense of the average Harley rider, he's almost always fat as fuck."

"Conceded," he concedes.

Only one lone Harley remains. But without his herd to follow, the rugged individual panics and flops off his bike. His Harley model with the sequined bust of John Wayne goes skidding down the road. The nonconformist goes skidding behind it. He's a 250 pounder, not including all the leather and American flags, so he's skinnier than the average Harley rider so TB decides to just run him over. That is the morally wrong thing to do because 250 pounds of advertised all-American beef is in reality all-American fat which explodes and gets into the hardest-to-clean places when run over. Tires covered in all-American corpulence have

no traction which is undesirable at 110 miles per hour. The leper hits the brakes, the Olds slides sideways and flips. I'm not sure how many times we roll over. Telly Bawdhaw lost count after one. Naturally. We eventually stop rolling with the Olds beached on its passenger side. "Lovely view," I say looking out my window at the pavement. TB blowtorches another cigarette, his seatbelt keeping him suspended above me. "What now, power leper?"

"Uh, I dunno. Watch TV?"

"Is that all you can come up with?"

"Pretty much."

"You flip the car on its side and don't even think to ask if the TV is all right. You're an insensitive lout."

"I'm sorry. Is the TV all right?"

"Yes, no thanks to you! Crazy leprous Negro (redundant), rolling the Olds again and again until Telly Bawdhaw lost count after one."

Telly Bawdhaw remains strapped to the sideways dashboard and reports: "Guess TB needs to learn to *roll* with the punches! *Heehaw!* Or, when he runs over Harley riders: *roll* with the *paunches! Heehaw!*"

The Fox News helicopter fires a Hellfire missile at us. But this is no ordinary Hellfire missile. Because on it is a mini camera that gives the audience at home a bird's-eye view of the missile and its flight towards a target. Even better, Fox News viewers are invited to log on to the Fox News website for their chance to actually guide the missile to a target. It's all part of the Fox News promise: "We discharge, you decide."

Whichever lunatic Fox News watcher (truism) is controlling this missile proves himself to be a real ace at playing with his joystick while staring at the computer screen. Because he guides that baby straight down into the Olds's exposed undercarriage. The blast flips us into the air, spinning the car several more times than the news can count. We land in the scrub off the highway on all four wheels. The missile explosion ignites the flammable

Harley fat all over the road. It also burns the fat off our tires, allowing them to regain traction. We drive off.

"The TV shows yet another Hellfire missile launched at us."

"Well, as you've witnessed, that won't be able to penetrate our herculetium."

"What if it flies in our window?" I worry. "I mean, the corresponding fireball may not harm the car proper but I'll be damned if I want to end up with a complexion as black and heathen as yours. No offense."

The backward darky says nothing because he knows I'm white and right as he eyes the TV to get an idea of the missile's position, hand cranks the speaker in that direction, blasts the horn, and shatters the missile in midair.

The Get Some Action Now 9, Red Alert 11, Super News Friends 13, and Boing Boing 69 News helicopters arrive and launch their Hellfire missiles. They're a little pissy for getting scooped by the Fox News Hellfire missiles. The leper is in a surly mood and yanks the hand crank, spinning the speaker round and round while rudely blaring the horn. Any missile in the air is obliterated. Any news helicopter in the air is obliterated. "Great. There goes our TV coverage. I hope you're happy with yourself."

The leper doesn't apologize, being the remorseless leper that he is. The news channels panic without Hellfire missile video and threaten to go to reruns of *I Love Lucy*. Super News Friends 13 salvages their telecast by having an artist draw what TB could be doing. Red Alert 11 one-ups Super News Friends 13 by playing scenes from a demolition derby video game. Get Some Action Now 9's Jizzette Hernandezbaum shows all the things she can do with her tongue. Then more breaking news from Thousand Oaks saves the ratings day. A band of bitchy eco-terrorists is threatening one of the city's many fine parking lots.

"It just so happens that Thousand Oaks is less than twenty miles from what used to be the Malibu area," the leper says.

"How dare these bitchy eco-terrorists grab our breaking news. How dare they threaten one of Thousand Oaks' many fine parking lots. Have they no shame?"

"Let's ride."

We drive recklessly up the back roads of the Santa Monica Mountains. On the other side of the mountains are the valley, more sprawl, and Thousand Oaks where Captain Biodegradable and his infamous Low-Flow Plumbing Fixtures Posse are holding a tree hostage and getting live TV coverage.

Some background: Thousand Oaks is a city of over 100,000 ultra-white humans. To the uninitiated and the sighted, Thousand Oaks appears to be a pestiferous tumor of aggressively spreading suburbia. As such, there is no real downtown although residents proudly assert the Janss Marketplace Mall and The Oaks Mall constitute a mecca for congregation and culture. And indeed, having two malls as your mecca sums up a lot.

Thousand Oaks residents boast that theirs is a "master planned city." For more on this concept, see the chapter "Lebensraum and the Master Race Planned City" in *Mein Kampf.*

Thousand Oaks, a master planned city, was created by a corporation in the mid-1950s. Which sums up a lot. Naturally.

Thousand Oaks city officials are quick to tell you of their extensive efforts to save the oak trees of the area from development. This is done by carefully pouring the cement all around the trees instead of directly over them. (Anything other than oaks claiming to be natural gets the directly-over treatment, in order to maintain that natural, master planned look.) City officials also point out that for every unfortunate oak tree steamrolled by sprawl, three more are planted elsewhere. The elsewhere possibly being on the over thirty golf courses within twenty miles of the Thousand Oaks city center. Because enjoying trees is best done by those wise enough to pay for country club memberships. The rest of the plants and animals displaced

by golf are welcome to enjoy the trees if they pay to play eighteen holes which includes one free drink in the clubhouse. Unless the displaced animals are the Mexican help and then they are welcome to get their asses back to work spraying toxic chemicals on the fairways to keep them weed-free and natural. And master planned. Naturally.

Captain Biodegradable and his infamous Low-Flow Plumbing Fixtures Posse are televised disrupting the construction of a new Thousand Oaks parking lot for a new Thousand Oaks golf course. They struck with sudden fury and abandonment, leaping out of their eco-van made of 100 percent peat moss and chaining themselves to several low-flow toilets which they chained to a tree set for steamrolling. "Hell no, we won't flow!" they chant.

Telly Bawdhaw reports, "Guess these terrorists figure this stunt will leave them *flush* with success!"

Some cops we hadn't gotten around to killing are about to arrest the terrorists until the cops realize there's no room back at the Thousand Oaks jail because it's full of all the surplus trees they couldn't replant on golf courses; and minorities. So the cops have no choice but to Taser the terrorists until they convulse and then pour asphalt over them and the tree.

According to the United Nations Convention on Biological Diversity, humans are responsible for the worst spate of extinctions since the dinosaurs vanished 65 million years ago. A bloated human population of around 7 billion (and counting) is destroying the environment for animals and plants via expanding cities, deforestation, introduction of invasive species, pollution, and global warming. The U.N. report goes on to estimate the current pace of extinctions is 1,000 times faster than historical rates. This mass wipeout of planetary life has benefits. As creatures of all stripes rapidly blink off the Endangered Species List and out of existence forever, lots of new space opens up on the List, which allowed the Bush administration to list parking

lots as an endangered species, providing them much-needed federal protection.

The feds arrive and arrest the terrorists and low-flow toilets for violations punishable by all forms of torture deemed not to be torture by whichever plutocrat is now taking their turn running the Land Of Liberty (LOL). The feds and the cops slap each other's backs in some good-natured ribbing over the 100 percent peat mossmobile and how this proves the eco-terrorists are a bunch of fags that deserve the stomping they're gonna get. They're less jocular about the terrorists in the Oldsmobile springing off the mountain road and landing on top of them. Those who aren't crushed run like star-spangled pus from a gurgling sore. TB guns the engine and gives chase. It turns out that heads with spikes coming out of their mouths mounted on wheels are adept at goring feds and cops running like the modern lifestyles detailed monthly in *Pustulant Oozing Sores*, the magazine, a Condé Nast jewel. Remember: *living* a *life* is passé. Now there is *acquiring* a life*style*.

"One really can't go wrong in choosing the *Haughtiness of Novelty Intellectualism to Mask a Dominating Inferiority Complex with Typical Modern Sense of Alienation* lifestyle," I tell the leper while pawing through *The New Yorker*.

"I've always been partial to its familial *Haughtiness of Flatulent Nouveau Riche Usually Suburban/Always Dumb Fuck* lifestyle. Preferably in an ecru," he says while not paging through the *Robb Report, GQ, Vile Illustrated*, etc.

"Indeed. With a complementary dash of the *I've Augmented Everything Except My Hideously Plastic Soul Plastic Surgery* lifestyle."

"Any life*style* worth its own magazine and corresponding accessories *will* have a solid plastic cornerstone."

Having a typical modern and trendy short attention span, the leper tires of spiking cops and feds. Get it? *Tires* of spiking? Ha! After he tires of spiking the cops and feds (subscribers to *Maxim*

and *Baton Those Bitches* magazines (pleasant enough publications for the *Uber SS Crypto-Gay* lifestyle)) he snowplow-wedges through the cops' and feds' cars. Cop cars are easy as ever. The feds' all-black Gestapo-inspired/inspiring SUVs are softer than a newborn yuppie's head. But the feds' tank is a tough nut to orally stimulate. The leper warns, "We don't have enough velocity. Hold on!" as we smash into the front of the tank. Uh-oh. Explosive reactive armor. Explosive reactive armor is composed of a layer of high explosive in between two metal plates called the reactive elements. Upon being struck by a penetrating weapon, the explosive detonates, forcibly driving the metal plates apart to repel and damage the penetrator. Unless that suave penetrator is sporting a herculetium prophylactic, ribbed for her pleasure.

"All Chinamen are so short that they are zoologically classified as midgets."

"The Japanese are natural midgets (well chronicled). The Chinese are unnatural midgets. The Chinese have mutated into a race of mutant supermidgets (many of them angry—beware) after generously turning their environment into mutagenic acid alkyl sludge in order to make an elite class of avarassholes (avaricious + asshole = good capitalist) (the vast majority of whom live far, far away from China's poisoned mutagenic acid alkyl sludge landscape) enough money to be the all-devouring plague of locusts riding hilariously unintentionally self-parodying Harley-Davidson motorcycles that their God, country, and life*styles* demand."

"So the Chinese are a kindly race as long as they stay in those fucking mines and sweatshops."

The tank's explosive reactive armor explosion cannot pierce our herculetium cock sock but can propel us up and over the tank. Not before we're able to thrust the head of our snowplow-wedge into her heady armored folds. Granted, it's not full penetration, but it is a man-sized gash (redundant), a slit running up the front all the way to her gender-bedeviling erect cannon,

which we slice right off. A tank with a slit in the front topped by a cut-off phallus is like another raging 280-pound clitorally circumcised Young Republican, poetically speaking. The gash is large enough to disrupt the tank's interior stock of ammunition, sending explosive shells shooting from her lovingly torn cleft down onto the nearby golf course.

Fore!

The few remaining feds and cops not laid to waste by rolling heads with Arby's wrappers mix with shell-shocked duffers in a madcap retreat broadcast by the new news helicopters. Several of the news helicopters fire off ratings-starved Hellfire missiles, but the viewers at home, in an improbable display of intelligence, steer the missiles out of our direction and into the golf cart brimming with whiteys on Hole 13.

"How's that?" stammers a stunned leper.

"*Either* the viewers at home have learned they can't steer their missiles through our sonic defenses and have gone looking for other quarry to explode *or* we've got some degenerate converts out there."

Another Hellfire missile lands thirty yards in front of us, courteously annihilating the feds' RV and its towed howitzer. The leper looks at me and raises an eyebrow.

"So, what's to do in Thousand Oaks?"

"Besides having over thirty golf courses within twenty miles of the Thousand Oaks city center, including ten golf courses within only five miles of the heart of darkness, there's a strip mall for every occasion," I say as we crash through a strip mall.

"Golf and shopping, eh?"

"The solid framework for any valid life*style*."

"In that same vein, did you know Thousand Oaks boasts the largest auto mall on the planet?"

"Glory be."

"We could sneak a peek at the latest discontinued Oldsmobiles."

"Let's go auto shopping!"

We crash back out of the strip mall and onto the road heading north. "May the wind from the massive fireball currently ripping through the diminishing-to-our-rear strip mall from the multiple Hellfire missile explosions be always at your back."

"*Erin go Bragh*, you foul ebony brute."

"Having a *ball*, TB? Well then have *two* of them! Two massive *man-balls* of justice!" goes the professional pre-recorded voice-over broadcasting from the monster truck parked in front of the auto mall.

So anyway, we turn the corner and slam on the brakes and marvel at the world's largest auto mall stretched grandiosely before us with a monster truck parked in front of it braying canned catchphrases promising to smother us in the most massive balls available in the leather sporting goods market today. The various TV news channels squawk breaking-news alarms with graphics promising the ultimate showdown between terrorism and testicles is finally at hand.

The best breakdown of the showdown is on Fox News's *Best Damn News Show, Period!*. Arnoldo Glom, star of the popular sitcom *Goiters!* and its popular spinoff Fox News program *Goiters!*, flexes his news-analyst muscle by elucidating the difference between a 1994 Oldsmobile Cutlass Supreme and the Skabbs's monster truck.

Arnoldo Glom: "The Skabbs's monster truck is hot!" (Subhuman hooting from the *Best Damn News Show, Period!* in-studio audience.) "Dude! Yes! The Skabbs's monster truck is hot! The Skabbs's monster truck has huge twenty-foot tires that look like huge, round, bouncing—" (a *boing!* sound bleeps out the word *jugglies!* followed by subhuman hooting from the *Best Damn News Show, Period!* in-studio audience). "Dude! The Skabbs pursues all things overblown, driven by a twisted will to power fecklessly masking chasmal insecurities, because he's an American." (Subhuman hooting.) "More

FYI: The monster truck wasn't born a truck at all, but originated as a school bus. This is because the Skabbs requires an engine laughably large enough to mask chasmal feelings of inferiority. What, am I stuttering? Who's been writing this teleprompter script? Alfred Adler? Just gimme jugglies forever!" (Subhuman hooting from Arnoldo Glom.) "The Skabbs has had his school bus specially modified, shortening it in length, in order to take him back to his childhood school days. But, as we all know, the heart of the Skabbs's monster short bus dangles between its tires. There, swinging underneath the undercarriage, hang two huge death-dealing wrecking balls! Now that's an accessory an Oldsmobile can only dream about!"

Fellow *Best Damn News Show, Period!* news analyst Telly Bawdhaw rebuts Arnoldo Glom's nuanced thesis by hitting Arnoldo Glom over the head with a rubber chicken. Arnoldo Glom rebuts the rebuttal by unsheathing a twelve-inch rubber dildo and engaging the rubber chicken in a *Cock v. Cock* fencing duel. *Boing!* sound effects induce the desired in-studio subhuman laughter in the mighty-imbecilic range.

Christian Guildenstern is the *Best Damn News Show, Period!* moderator. Christian Guildenstern is a Jew named Christian so as to not appear so Jewy. Christian Guildenstern wears blackface makeup so as to not appear so Jewy. Christian Guildenstern nasally whines, "Telly Bawdhaw and Arnoldo Glom, thank you for that illuminating report. *Fo' shizzle*, guys!" Christian Guildenstern throws out last year's expired street jargon so as to not appear so Jewy which makes him look even Jewier than ever thought possible. The powers that be could hire a real live black to replace Christian Guildenstern in blackface to save on makeup costs but are thwarted by Christian Guildenstern's superhero power of crawling on hands and knees while asskissing the powers that be (while in blackface)—the mark of any quality corporate-media journalist. *"Fo' shizzle! Fo' shizzle!"*

shrieks Christian Guildenstern who looks hurt nobody's patted him on his yarmulke for the genuinely urban effort.

The sound of metal striking metal pings from our snowplow-wedge which is now awash in a magical yellow liquid. More evil elixir explodes on the herculetium-shielded roof speaker. Still another liquid bomb detonates on the hood, covering the Olds in yellow fluid that's…

"…redolent of urine," I finish.

"We're being shelled," concludes the leper.

Erectly pointed at us, rising between the two huge death-dealing wrecking balls hanging underneath the Skabbs's monster short bus, is the cannon which is squirting shells which detonate in a spray of aerosolized jaundice.

"Ye gods! He's pissing on us!" I fret.

"No. It's worse than piss," the leper frets. "It's Natural Light."

The dead canary we keep in the glove compartment to warn us of chemical and biological weapons attack was still dead. By the time the leper has fastened the gas mask over my oversized head, the Olds is lost in a death-dealing haze of popularly priced beer. The red bud of the lit cigarette poking through welder's mask glows hot as the leper takes a life-affirming drag, protecting his lungs from the Natural Light effluvium. He floors the gas pedal, blindly accelerating through the near-premium beer fog of war. Desperately he mashes the steering wheel "A" button, deploying hydraulic jacks, springing us up from the clutches of the yellow miasma and into the clutches of the brown miasma perpetually blanketing Southern California.

We fly a couple hundred feet and land in another strip mall. "What a darling little boutique!" the leper acknowledges, keeping the gas pedal flat to the floor as we hurtle over racks of $200 ratty-chic t-shirts. *Haute Vermin*, to be pronounced in affected French accent, has many trendy upscale slaved-in-China faux-homelesswear accessories that explode in fire as the strip mall

absorbs repeated Hellfire missile hits. Not before the darling boutique's back wall is properly crashed through.

We tear through another parking lot and skid to a stop in another parking lot. The leper cranks the roof speaker, aiming it at the monster short bus fifty yards in front of us, and announces into Mr. Microphone, "The Skabbs, your man-balls of justice must *listen* to me." A horrendous blast of foghorn is sent merrily on its way. It should have blown that fucker's balls back to the Sport Chalet from whence they were rang up. But intact his balls remain. In fact, the fucker didn't even twitch. "Come again?" wonders the leper as he blares the horn again. Again, nothing. A burst of light radiates from on top of our car hood. Potter materializes from the cuticular space-time continuum, interlocked with Futuro in perfunctory desperate wrestling match. Potter, the consummate news professional, reports: "The carbon-based life form augmented with testicular implements of noted physical therapeutic value, coarsely delineated as 'the Skabbs' and 'man-balls,' but more eloquently defined as carbon-based life form augmented with testicular implements of noted physical therapeutic value, currently located at a position efficaciously described as latitude 34.16252836853424, longitude -118.83147239685059, is operating a mechanized vehicle disproportionately augmented to mask chasmal feelings of inferiority. The aforesaid monster short bus utilizes an advanced computer system far beyond the Skabbs's understanding, which says very little. This super advanced supercomputer—developed by the military-industrial complex, which is nothing more than the gigantor state-subsidized R & D infrastructure created for private corporate economic interests—is required to operate the monster short bus's high-powered sound detection and cancellation apparatus (see military-industrial complex for corporate profit thingy)."

The leper looks at me and asks, "So what is he saying? That the Skabbs's monster short bus has a computer that detects

incoming destructive sound waves and somehow counteracts them?"

"Beats me. He lost me at the molecular weight of man-balls."

"That can't be possible," stumbles the leper.

"That is not only possible," reports Potter, "but inevitable. Active noise cancellation will now be defined using the following rudimentary linguistic codification: Active noise cancellation is consummated via use of a computer that anatomizes the waveform of the background aural or nonaural noise, consequently generating a polarization reversed waveform to nullify it via interference. The aforestated waveform has duplicate or directly congruent amplitude to the waveform of the original sonance yet its polarity is reversed, creating destructive interference that reduces the amplitude of the perceived sonance. In crude layman's terms."

"I understand all that," bitches the leper in testy mood. "A computer detects incoming sound and counters it by producing sound at the same frequency 180 degrees out of phase to cancel the original sound. But to defeat our massively ridiculously powerful foghorn belch the Skabbs's monster short bus would need its own massively ridiculous sound-producing device."

Potter would raise an eyebrow if he had one.

"The Skabbs simply can't be as loud as us!"

Potter reports, "Your supposition is un*sound*. Pun-tastic."

"Yeah," I chime in. "Anyone going to such lengths to mask chasmal feelings of inferiority *will* be as loud as a Harley-Davidson."

Futuro sticks most of his hand into Potter's nose as Potter reports, "The Skabbs's monster short bus horn is the Loudest Damn Air Raid Siren, Period, the loudest air raid siren ever built in all the cuticular space-time continuum. The Loudest Damn Air Raid Siren, Period uses a portable coal factory to power a siren weighing 50,543 pounds. The really loud air raid siren was

originally placed in the geodetic center of the United States as part of the great nation's project to build one convenient, centrally located air raid siren that would service the whole nation when it reasoned that nuclear weapons needed to be exploded. Until Armageddon, the air raid siren was used to play really loud commercials. After the downfall of communism, in a gesture of good will, the United States did not dismantle its nuclear weapons built to destroy all life on the planet and instead dismantled the air raid siren built to warn all life that it was to be destroyed. Then the Skabbs purchased the air raid siren on eBay. Consequently, the Skabbs's monster short bus horn has just enough power to negate foghorn belches amplified ten thousand times." Potter removes his club-like cock from the confines of his brown polyester suit and clubs Futuro with it. A flash of light blinks the combatants to another fabulous destination on the cuticular space-time continuum.

The leper hits the foghorn again, just to be sure. The effort is once again blunted by the Skabbs's horn. "Aw, shucks," laments the leper as he floors the accelerator, presses the "A" button, and springs us into the air at the Skabbs.

We land wedge first on the monster short bus's hood. A colossal electric crack sparks from the point of impact. Uh-oh. Electric reactive armor. Electric reactive armor is composed of two conductive plates sandwiching insulating material, creating a potently powered capacitor. In use, a high-voltage energy source, like your standard portable coal factory that's capable of powering a huge air raid siren, electrifies the armor. As an incoming projectile penetrates the plates, the circuit is closed to discharge the capacitor, funneling a massive amount of energy into the penetrator which may vaporize it or even turn it into a plasma, significantly diffusing the attack.

We are not vaporized or even turned into a plasma. Unfortunately. This is because the electricity is routed through the Olds's herculetium-augmented framework, sequestering it away

from the carbon-based life forms in the cabin. The energy conducted through the skeleton of the car is released in the form of a lightning bolt shooting out of our tailpipe towards some local golfers. Fore. However, we do not escape unblemished. The charged pulse fries the fuse for our turn signal, making it impossible for us to drive in a safe manner. Also, the electrical blast repels the Olds before it can penetrate the Skabbs's monster short bus. The explosion launches us 450 feet off target into a strip mall.

So we crash-land in another strip mall. The Olds stops rolling, coming to rest on the roof/speaker. "Being upside down is distasteful," the leper says.

"Being in an Oldsmobile is distasteful," I clarify.

The back wall of the strip mall explodes. In charges a monster short bus with twenty-foot tires. The Skabbs bull rushes us. His left front tire digs into our side. He's climbing over us.

Yes. We've been mounted.

All the windows in the Olds shatter under the immense weight. Of course they would have shattered way back when we flipped the Olds outside of Malibu if the storywriter didn't lick balls. And the only reason your grandfather can lick his balls is because they hang to his knees. So fuck off with your boastful family pictures. A paroxysm of flying glass tears through the cabin. My left ear is punctured by a shard. Another gashes my muzzle, just inches below my right eye. The Skabbs's rear tire follows its predecessor and steamrollers over us. The car groans under the pressure but our herculetium defenses hold; the Oldsmobile does not implode. Unfortunately.

The monster short bus bounces over and past us. Its high speed and high center of gravity leave it teetering on the edge of rolling over, but the swinging wrecking balls in the undercarriage act as a counterbalance, steadying the behemoth, preventing a tip-over though not preventing momentum from carrying it through the one wall of the strip mall still standing.

"Do you think he'll be back?"

"I'm bleeding here, leper. So forgive me if I don't engage you in witty colloquy. Which would be a first for this book. Are we going to die?"

"You mean in an existential sense?"

At this point I would have bitten that infernal leper if the Olds hadn't been punted airborne again.

The Skabbs had blitzed us anew. But he doesn't lay a tire on us this time. Instead he uses the monster short bus's twenty-foot clearance to pass completely over the Olds, then slams on his brakes. The sudden shift in inertia swings the wrecking balls at the back of the undercarriage forward, straight into us. The force of impact, enhanced by another electric shock that blows the fuse for our windshield wipers and shoots more lightning out of our ass onto a neighboring golf course, hammers us into the air. We crash on some electrocuted golfers on a neighboring golf course.

The leper moans in pain. A metal rod has broken off the diesel generator strapped in the back. The pole is sticking straight through the driver's seat, and straight through his shoulder. I watch him as he screams, pulling himself forward along the spike, leaving a coat of blood across the metal. He stops a moment, girding himself, then finishes the deed, sliding off the rod's jagged end and collapsing with his chest on the steering wheel.

The welder's mask has fallen from his head. He's crying.

"Are you all right?" I ask him.

He winces. "I can drive with one arm. How are you, boy?"

"Bruises and cuts, yes. Broken beyond repair, no," I say, giving him a small crooked smile. I don't have to tell him about the deep gash across my forehead trickling blood into my eyes. But I choose not to tell him that I'm not ready to die.

"Getting a *charge* out of my man-balls, TB?" goes the professional pre-recorded voice-over broadcasting from the monster short bus roaring towards us. The only good thing being, on this occasion, we've landed on all four wheels. TB presses the accelerator pedal. The Olds's tires spin in the turf, gaining traction

just in time to lurch out of the path of the Skabbs. Cornering is not a strength of a monster short bus with twenty-foot tires. By the time he's able to fully turn around we're off the green and on the street.

"What do we do?" I ask.

"We get to Thousand Oaks and hit the freeway. I think we can outrun him from there."

"And if we can't outrun him?"

"Our horn is useless against his air raid siren defense system. We snowplow-wedge him again and we'll be shocked into something uglier than the Texas 'justice' system. Another knock from the bastard's electric wrecking balls will leave us battered and fried. If we can't outrun him..."

Behind us the golf course spontaneously combusts. *When Golf Courses Spontaneously Combust!* is a popular Fox News program. It is also what happens when the Skabbs turns on his monster short bus flamethrower.

Car flamethrowers were first developed in South Africa to deal with that country's nigger pedestrian problem. Here's the report:

Flamethrower a hot new option on S. African cars

December 25, 1998

JOHANNESBURG, South Africa -- Crime-crazed South Africans have enlisted a powerful new ally in the war on crime: the car flamethrower.

Shooting a man-high fireball, reportedly with no damage to the paint, the Master's Blaster has been installed on 25 South African vehicles since a fabulous debut last month.

At less than the cost of a set of used white walls, this inexpensive defense promises to leave carjackers hot under the collar.

Carjacking the Skabbs's monster short bus is impossible unless the perpetrator is armed with a twenty-foot ladder. But just to be safe, the vehicle's sides are equipped with flamethrowers that shoot a wall of fire twenty feet down, plus another hundred feet along the course of the ground, just to be safe. An additional flamethrower deters a carjacking from anyone a hundred feet to the rear. One more on the roof deters low-flying birds and aircraft.

The monster short bus thunders from incinerated Hole 18 onto the road behind us. The arc of fire shooting around the vehicle engulfs the strip malls to each side of the road.

Eyeing the rear-view mirror nervously, the leper keeps his foot on the gas. "I think the Skabbs is driving us," he says.

"Driving us?"

"He's torching everything around him. There's no escape to the rear now. He's driving us forward."

"Driving us forward to *where*?"

"Or to *what*?"

We arrive at the answer. Curdling in every sprawling nook and cranny, festering in every properly paved recess of Thousand Oaks, are Harley-Davidson motorcycle enthusiasts.

According to hysterical TV reports (redundant), one million Harley riders from across the nation have converged upon Thousand Oaks to assist the hero of the infirm of mind in his effort to purge the world of the scourge of terrorism perpetrated by Oldsmobiles.

In unison, one million of the dimmest of the dim start their Harley motors, each one specially designed to be earsplitting. The noise is cataclysmic. It's as if Thousand Oaks were the world's asshole ripping a planet-sized fart. Oh, wait...

"Comically adorned motorcycles modified to be deafening. Such is the natural order of things when one considers that illuminating human species paradox: Those who have the least to say will invariably say the most, and loudly so. And those

completely bereft of imagination will make loud noises mechanically," Potter should have elucidated somewhere along the cuticular space-time continuum.

According to hysterical TV reports: "These one million largely large, doughy societal sycophants have cut off all avenues of escape. A *wide* net has been laid, or lard. (Rubber chicken slapping over head.)"

"According to Telly Bawdhaw," I relay to the leper, "where there's sprawl, there's a Harley (truism). Congealing in Calabasas to the east, Newbury Park to the west, and Seamy Valley to the north are hordes of Harley-Davidson nonconformists. They're also pressing in from the remains of Malibu to the south, a sampling of whom we ran into and over earlier in this abysmally never-ending chapter. A wide net has been laid, or lard. Oh, and you know about the steroidal psychopath chasing us straight into this gigantic noose. We're trapped."

The Harleys closing in on us from Route 23 (officially named the *Military Intelligence Memorial Freeway* because Americans are a peace-loving lot, just ask them) open the attack with motorcyclists from the lowest Harley socioeconomic stratum throwing Molotov cocktails made from Natural Light. The upper-enders have class and throw alit imported bottled water from pure glacial sources.

TB swerves onto a side street with the horde pouring in behind us. That's no good. Ahead the avenue is blocked by a horde. An especially surly leather-clad lump pulls alongside us and throws his Molotov Starbucks through our back window. The diesel generator takes a direct hit and bursts into flames bigger than the ones previously bursting from it. The leper turns around, pulls the metal bar piercing his seat from its resting place like Arthur yanking his Excalibur, and throws the rod back to the perturbed generator wherefrom it originally came. This somehow does nothing to appease the generator or the fire so the leper blowtorches a ring of flame around the

generator. The charred firebreak hems the inferno in. Unable to leap the boundary, and with no more Oldsmobile upholstery to burn, it shrinks to an irritated smolder.

TB jerks a hard right, hops the curb, and crashes through a strip mall. The horde pursues us. Some stop to shop. Some withstand the natural urge to consume and go with the urge to throw burning objects at pariahs. Our trunk takes several hits and is aflame. The ones that miss burn down the Phun 'n Phallic Phonez kiosk.

We drive into the T.G.I. Comatoast chain restaurant. At the center of the good-times American eatery is the bar built to withstand impact speeds of 10 miles per hour; but not 70. Beer kegs and old-growth timber detonate as the bar is cleaved via snowplow-wedge. A *ding!* happily rings from the good-times bell that's rung when the bartender collects a tip. Several errantly thrown Molotovs light up the bartender.

We nose through a wall decorated with bibelots signifying good times and are birthed to the other side. Now gutting the adjoining Burns & Chernobyl chain bookstore I notice they're having a buy one intellectually pretentious item, get another intellectually counterfeit item free sale, which I inform the leper of as he's crashing through a passel of Starbucks-addled yuppies, the *How To Become A Wise Person In Just Two Minutes A Day* audiobook display, and the back wall. TB slams on the brakes and skids to a stop in the parking lot. "I have an idea," he says.

"Is it just so crazy that it just might work?"

He turns the wheel and floors the gas. The Olds spins around and leaps back into the Burns & Chernobyl all-media super-fortress. The Negroid fails to signal, turns left into the music department, rudely skids the car to a halt, and cranks the speaker at the Harley horde funneling towards us through the T.G.I. Comatoast puncture wound. The foghorn blast blows the vanguard horde members back into the innards of the ruined

strip mall. TB opens his car door, walks over to the life-size cardboard cutout of a warbling fantastical beast in satin dress, and picks up an 8-track tape. "Céline Dion is your idea?" I ask as he buckles his seatbelt and stomps the accelerator.

We rocket through another wall into a parking lot where we're greeted by the crack of cannon fire. A can of Natural Light detonates on our roof. "It's the Skabbs!" I cleverly deduce.

"That's what I'm banking on," declares the leper as he steers us onto a grassy knoll that has had the grass paved over. The Skabbs pursues us with hordes of Harleys filing in to his sides and rear. Those filing within a hundred feet are flamethrowered before they might ladder their way to a monster short bus car-jacking. The leper accelerates up the knoll and smashes through a guardrail onto Highway 101 East. The eardrum-eradicating sounds of short bus engine augmented by portable coal factory plus half a million purposeless Harleys roar behind us as they give chase. Ahead Highway 101 looks strangely free of traffic. According to hysterical TV reports, the contingent of Harleys to our east in Calabasas got off to a late start after being sidetracked at an all-you-can-eat buffet that doubles as a giant trough where voracious marauding pigs crowd against one another in a glori-ous fight to see who can get the most dross into their slavering drool-begetting snouts. According to hysterical TV reports, we have only minutes before we run head-on into the other half million of these bloated purposeless "hogs."

TB leans on the accelerator, going from 90 mph to 390. After opening up some distance between us and the Skabbs plus en-tourage, the leper mashes the brakes. The Olds skids to a halt in the center of the highway, in the center of the enemy ring that's collapsing in on us.

"Well, if your master strategy was to place us in the inescap-able bull's-eye of a million and one murderous retards, then I'd say you've succeeded. Gold star for you!"

"Wait for it…"

The Skabbs appears on the horizon to the west. Hellish black smoke billows from monster short bus as engine and portable coal factory thunder at top speed. Behind him the freeway is covered in an unceasing wave of lobotomized leather and chrome. To our east an identical dark stain of motorized malignancy materializes and surges towards us.

"Wait for it…"

Like a spit of an island trapped between two onrushing tsunamis…

"Wait for it…"

Like an overripe melon pinned inside a tightening vise…

"Wait for it…"

Ten seconds to the oncoming philistines, with Molotovs lit…

"Wait for it…"

Five seconds to the Skabbs, with speeding death-dealing wrecking balls a-hanging…

"Wait for it…"

Four…three…two…brace for doom…

"Now!"

TB thumbs something on the steering wheel. It's the dreaded "F" button! An electronic pulse transmits from the Oldsmobile. This pulse corrupts the signal received by all Global Positioning System devices for fifteen miles in all directions. Instead of relaying reliable information as to location and directions, all GPS units from Calabasas to Camarillo, from Seamy Valley to the late Malibu, now relay only one thing: "TURN AN IMMEDIATE RIGHT!"

This is not a problem for those not hooked into GPS or for those who do not blindly follow directions dictated by GPS. But for Americans, who by nature follow blindly (especially the dictates of electronic gadgetry), this proves a problem.

One million rugged individuals on Harley-Davidson motorcycles equipped with every shining beeping novelty known

to man turn an immediate right. Not being told to slow down, they crash full speed into highway retaining walls and ditches. The smashed remains of inflated whiteys on inflated machines collect thirty feet deep in some places. The wreckage is so mountainous that it completely covers the omnipresent litter for which the sides of Southern California freeways are known worldwide. And this is to say nothing of the hundreds of thousands unfortunate enough to crash straight into strip malls.

Where there's sprawl, there's Harley horror.

Oh, the Skabbs. The great coveter of all things exerting power over nature is less than fifty yards from speeding into us upon receiving orders to turn right. He wrenches his steering wheel as immediately and violently as one would expect, flipping the monster short bus. Electric reactive armor tumbles into highway asphalt, rendering an explosion powerful enough to launch the monster short bus clear over us and hundreds of feet into the air. The two wrecking balls furiously spin around the soaring colossus like a pair of moons orbiting a particularly disagreeable planet. Gravity eventually pulls the twisting projectile back down. The crash generates a rich and full-bodied shock wave.

We drive by the impact crater a quarter mile up the highway. The wrecking balls which once so proudly dangled between rear tires have been castrated from the undercarriage, completely ripped off. They now lay lodged in a nearby strip mall. The hull of the monster short bus is equally in ruin, torn in half. And there, prostrate amongst the rubble, is the Skabbs. With neck so broken his tiny head flops against his back in the breeze; and where his tiny head used to sit is now wedged: one man-ball of justice. Where the other man-ball got off to, no man can say.

Driving is a joy. All highways and roads in the area are in a pristine state, having been cleared of traffic by order of GPS. After passing Calabasas the leper cranks the speaker back

towards our handiwork. He turns up the volume to maximum blow and then inserts the 8-track entitled *Céline Dion: Smoother Than Chemo.*

An opera singer's piercing voice can shatter glass. Céline Dion's warbling in falsetto is far more destructive.

"Wait for it…"

Amplified ten thousand times through our speaker, the yodeling vibrates one million standardly garish Harley-Davidsons. Everywhere: shiny metal gewgaws quiver wildly and explode. One million gaudy land mines, detonating simultaneously. Worse: one million white, fleshy, largely gelatinous Harley enthusiasts are as equally susceptible to jiggling as their crass motorcycle embellishments. Everywhere: carcasses o' lard asses quiver wildly and explode. One million pigs in blankets of leather, detonating simultaneously.

Exploded-Harley-enthusiast blubber drips from sea to shining strip mall until dropped Molotovs, the Skabbs's overturned monster short bus still-aflame flamethrowers, and crashing TV news and cop helicopters that TB foghorn belches out of the sky ignite the highly incendiary lipids. From Calabasas to Seamy Valley to Thousand Oaks to the reaches of Oxnard, all sprawl is cauterized from the landscape by the righteous branding iron of sizzling American corpulence.

Mission accomplished. Big thumbs-up. If only there were an aircraft carrier for us to photo-op on.

TEN

The next day I take time to (cliché) lick my wounds. Because I'm a fucking dog. Andean Savory Goat Ball Pointer. Purebred.

The leper tries in vain to lick himself then throws a couple of band-aids over the entry and exit holes in his shoulder then settles down to a good book. *'Twas the Twat Before Christmas* is a classic for a reason.

After wiping off he fires up his other blowtorch and begins installing blinds on all the Olds's windows. "The look is timeless and elegant: window blinds over smashed-out windows," I congratulate.

"This is form *and* function," he says. "These always stylish Venetian blinds are made of herculetium. They're penetration-proof. I lifted them off an army general's Winnebago."

"Yes. Thank you for not installing them *before* we got shot at, Molotoved, and testicularly manhandled by man-balls of justice."

"You're welcome. Pulling down herculetium blinds over your car windows means you won't be able to see anything out your windows. This is challenging when driving on highways at high speeds so please pull blinds down over your car windows at speeds under 85 mph only in neighborhoods when trying this at home. We'll need herculetium blinds now that we have eliminated the local police state's helicopters. The world's police state

will now feel obligated to ratchet it up by using their satellites to guide their missiles fired thousands of miles away by their warplanes and (coming soon!) space-based weapon systems that pinpoint targets anywhere in the world and, with absolutely no warning, murder them. There is no defense against unseen missiles raining down from the heavens to crater innocent lepers and pups driving on the highway except for professionally installed herculetium Levolors."

"I know. I've seen the masterpiece *Syriana*. And actually understood the film. Because I'm a Significantly Brighter Than the Supremely Arrogant in His Own Stupidity Mass-Man. Purebred."

While laid up healing my various wounds I catch up on some invaluable TV watching. On the news, a somber scene, as the networks respectfully cover the tearful funeral of the world's largest auto mall. It's being sold as the world's largest funeral and is being brought to you with only minimal commercial interruption. One such commercial is that one from Carl's Jr. showing a bottle of Coke repeatedly penetrating two buns. Oh, it's won awards.

Elsewhere, Billy Joe Huckenfuchs has a new infomercial. This time he's selling Third World human heads stuck on car wheels. They're all the rage since a dazzling debut in fabulous Malibu in the sea.

Here's a TV news report on vultures being seen circling over the L.A. area for the first time ever. The vulture's digestive tract is a marvel of nature. They can ingest and withstand virtually anything. Except L.A. air. "L.A. residents not already rotting are in danger of being killed by falling poisoned vultures!" according to hysterical TV news reports and "You could say poisoned vultures are *dropping like flies!*" according to Telly Bawdhaw.

Back to Billy Joe Huckenfuchs shouting from TV land: "Pimp your ride with human remains! *Bling bling* has met *brain brain!* Flashy! Stylish! The carcasses that get you noticed! These

heads you see here spinning on my Lexus LX and GX wheels are the finest quality Third World heads money can buy! Shamzam! These are the poorest heads on the planet, harvested direct to you from the 50 percent of the world's population that owns less than 1 percent of the world's wealth! But now, thanks to you, they have jobs! Good jobs! There's no other way these impoverished heads would ever be riding a Range Rover!"

The New York Times Channel is reporting that several grassroots groups have popped up to petition TB to come and clean up their traffic messes. This, in addition to booming sales of heads on wheels and other TB-related knickknacks, proves the soundness of the TB brand and capitalism. Such is the probing insight cornered by *The New York Times.*

Billy Joe Huckenfuchs: "Human heads turn any old Oldsmobile into a pussy magnet! (Pictorial aid proves this beyond doubt.) Keeping up with the Joneses has never been so affordable! Because human heads are a dime a dozen! Literally! You get twelve of the finest heads the global economy has to offer for the *low low low* price of ten cents! Plus shipping and handling. It's the magic of the human overpopulation explosion working to give you the best deal capitalism can *buy buy buy!* And since *The New York Times* isn't reporting that to you, it must not be news! Shamzam!"

But *The New York Times* Channel worries: "How can this nascent groundswell of support for TB, a person so depraved that he has failed to accept the influx of global capital while driving an Oldsmobile, be remedied? How can our System in which the top 2 percent of the global population owns over 50 percent of all global wealth and the top 10 percent owns almost all wealth (with the gap between haves and have-nots continuing to widen rapidly) continue to effectively dupe the billions upon billions of socioeconomic untouchables so they never become aware of real alternatives? How can the billions upon billions of socioeconomic dead-ends continue to

be brainwashed into not seizing the fruits of their own labor? Continue to defraud local communities into ceding their resources to outsiders? Continue to insist that capitalism's corporate darlings not pay for the full economic value of the resources, including air and water, they consume or degrade? Continue to manipulate through price fixing, collusion, special deals, hidden subsidies, tax breaks, etc., etc. a market that is anything but free, but continue to call it the '*free market*' while snickering because the billions and billions are too dim to look beyond our spurious definitions anyway? Continue to conceal the possibility of a society in which the economy is organized around *real* free market exchange between producers, and production is carried out mainly by self-employed artisans and farmers, small producers' cooperatives, worker-controlled large enterprises, and consumers' cooperatives? Continue to sucker the propertyless billions and billions into not insisting that *occupancy and use* be the only legitimate standard for establishing ownership of land (the homes and businesses on that land included)? Continue to endorse overorganization, gigantism, and homogenization over local independence? In sum: How can we continue to keep control of the world in the short, while ensuring the destruction of the world in the long?

"We at *The New York Times* see only one way to continue accomplishing all this: Keep them reading *The New York Times*."

My mistake. I offer a complete retraction and apology. *The New York Times* did not report any of that. So none of that is news and certainly not up for discussion.

The Learning Channel [*sic*] has on a show about midgets. Then a show about tattoos. Then a show about brummagem motorcycles. Then a show about a couple of prolifically stupid humans who improved the world by spawning a litter. Then another show about still more prolifically stupid prolific breeders sullying the gene pool and what a delight this is. Then a show

about human heads stuck on brummagem motorcycle wheels (the correlation between the devaluation of human (head) life and humans who single-handedly overpopulate the planet is surprisingly not recognized by The Learning Channel).

I shit you not.

Learning has never felt so good.

The squeals of swine and banjos screech from the Olds's speaker. "*Aye carumba!* We're under nuclear attack!" I yell.

The leper pops his head out of the driver's window. "No. It's my 8-track tape featuring the Hydra Triguplets Ol' Timey Country Chorus."

The Hydra Triguplets were America's first multiple-birth pregnancy yielding thirty offspring. A miracle. A blessing from God and one of His supranational corporations that lays golden fertility drugs. Lerna Hydra was the mother who did not live in a pothole although she thought like one. Lerna Hydra had money, a husband with sperm, and a suburban tract home brimming with processed foods which America applauded as the rightful qualifications for uncontrolled breeding. And all other life on the planet wept. So America cheered and made Lerna and her husband with sperm and their thirty lovelies celebrities by demanding they get their own show on The Learning Channel stocked with processed everything because supranational corporations know the value of corporate-product placement in corporate-media-generated circus stories and because every life is sacred so a litter of thirty is thirty times sacred. The thirty babies grew up to be fine upstanding two-foot-tall humanoids resembling pigs. Obviously a show-biz career would be their calling. Thus the thirty-member Hydra Triguplets Ol' Timey Country Chorus was formed. And incorporated.

The sounds emitted from singing pig-people are not to be toyed with. This "music" temporarily alters the structure of herculetium at the subatomic level, changing the hardest metal

in the universe to goo in just a yodel. This is virtually identical to how Céline Dion's shrill cries explode fat Harley bikers and shows a marked lack of imagination. Thus herculetium can be shaped and molded with the right chords, and destroyed with the wrong ones.

"Turn that shit down. I'm trying to watch the TV," I shout.

"That shit is necessary in order to properly install herculetium blinds on a herculetium Olds," he retaliates. Fucker.

"Fucker."

"Don't 'fucker' me. I'll be done soon. And it's not like you're missing anything on the TV anyway."

"Wrong. The Learning Channel has on a show about the Hydra Triguplets Ol' Timey Country Chorus. Did you know pig-people are now referred to as *pigple*? And that most Americans now fall under that definition? All hail capitalism. No, you didn't know that. Because you're un*Learn*ed. So how come the police state hasn't blasted Hydra Triguplet squeals at us, turning our herculetium defenses into goo, then nuke us?"

"Hydra Triguplet squeals do not turn herculetium into goo. You should change that in the book unless you just don't give a fuck which you obviously don't, judging by your book. Hydra Triguplet squeals only slightly alter herculetium, making it only slightly malleable. And even under those conditions the element is still the strongest in the universe and can only be worked using special tools also made of herculetium. It still can't be exploded, melted, burned, combusted, conflagrated, incinerated, smoked, torched, or flambéed."

"Then why in the beginning of the chapter did it say you were using your blowtorch on it?"

"Likely it's more shitty writing."

This horrific excuse for witty raillery comes crashing to a halt like the book did on page one. The back door to the Batcave flies open. In walks Jack.

Fucker.

Jack delivers in patented sneer: "Well, what have we here?"

"Another Shriners orgy?" I guess.

"They do love the children," interjects the leper.

"Especially burned ones. But who doesn't enjoy a little charred prepubescent ass while donning a fez?" Jack skillfully argues. "Now that we've been introduced, you boys are trespassing on my property."

"One could contend that you clearly don't need and use this land, and that by actually living here we are the rightful owners," the leper says from behind newly installed driver's window Levelors.

Jack smirks. "'Property is theft'? Is that right, *Monsieur Proudhon*? Well, I'm not so sure the moneyed oligarchs controlling the State which issues ersatz titles of land ownership to moneyed oligarchs agree with you. Besides, I *do* use this land." Jack unzips his trousers, pulls out several *Anger Management* DVDs, tosses them on the immoral remains of Adam Sandler, and shits all over them. "Those DVDs were rounded up in East Timor. Christ! It's harder to rid that place of that movie than it is to eradicate 200,000 East Timorese (more than a third of the country's population) by way of a U.S.-backed genocide from 1975 to 1999," Jack laments.

We all take a moment to admire the excrement on Adam Sandler. The leper finally breaks the solemn silence: "Well, I will give you that it's traditional for good capidoltists to 'use' their illegitimately held land as a dumping ground for their toxic waste from their toxic industries."

Jack: "But thanks to today's global economy it's now even cheaper to ship your toxic waste from your toxic industries overseas. That's why God made the Third World."

Guano: "Consider just the *electronic waste* portion of it: 50 to 80 percent of the United States' e-waste—that is collected to be recycled—actually gets shipped out of the country to dump sites like Guiyu, China where the synergy of capitalism

and the human overpopulation explosion pays thousands of men, women, and children $1.50 per day to burn, smash, and pick apart the electronic waste for the precious metals inside, exposing these throwaway people and the environment to countless toxic hazards. Correspondingly, their ground water is so polluted that drinking water has to be trucked in. A river sample from the area had 190 times the pollution levels allowed under World Health Organization guidelines."

Leper: "As a side note: way back in 1992, the Basel Convention went into force. The Basel Convention is the United Nations treaty designed to prevent the transfer of hazardous waste from developed to less developed countries. Charmingly, the United States is the only developed country in the world that has not ratified the treaty."

Jack: "Because that treaty is bad for business."

Leper: "And whose business would that be?"

Jack: "The 1 percent of the population who own 40 percent of the world's wealth."

Leper: "Not a fair assessment. The 2 percent of the population who own over 50 percent of the world's wealth have a right to make a profit on human misery and environmental destruction."

Jack: "Hear, hear! And they say the American Dream is dead."

Guano: "Of course Guiyu, China is just one example. India and Pakistan are appreciated far and wide (in corporate circles) for their attractive dumps."

Leper: "For hundreds of years, slave labor and natural resources have been extracted out of Africa. Now, Africa is being filled with the world's most sickening refuse. One open dump in Nairobi alone absorbs 2,000 tons of the First World's garbage *every day*. You see, whitey *is* capable of giving something back to Africa."

"Hey now! What about Central and South America? Mexico? Haiti, for God's sake? So many items for consumers to consume,

so many toxic by-products, so many Third World dumps, so little time," I thoughtfully appreciate.

Jack: "I like your style, boys. Instead of just whining about being enslaved you're actually doing something about it; and with an Oldsmobile. Impressive. Not like that slimy pussy, John Mired."

Leper and Guano in unison: *"John Mired!"*

Jack: "John Mired. Slimy pussy."

Guano: "Yes. He sure is dreamy."

Leper: "A golden nugget dangling from the corporate mass media's pop-music end of the alimentary canal who is to be held responsible for what the music-critics branch of the corporate mass media saluted as a modern chef-d'oeuvre: 'Waiting on the World to Sex Change: Your Body Is a Surgically Altered Wonderland.' Hark!"

Justice™ Department: "Due to imperious copyright laws designed to stifle creativity while bolstering corporate-media greed and lawsuits, song lyrics cannot be reprinted here. So instead we'll paraphrase, even though that too represents a legal risk since we'll be using the English language without permission from its inventors, writers, or copywriters, you fucking sheep."

It is contended in "Let's Laze About and Wait on the World to Change, Bro" that the Mired young generation is unfairly seen as standing for nothing.

Leper: "But his generation *does* stand for something. In a recent Pew poll, 81 percent of the 18- to 25-year-olds surveyed said their generation's most-important or second-most-important life goal is to get rich."

Guano: "Yes, but you're failing to report that 51 percent of the 18- to 25-year-olds said their generation's most-important or second-most-important life goal is to be famous."

Jack: "Conceded. So as slimy pussy suggests, all his dudes and dudettes *do* stand for something."

It is contended in "Waiting on the World to Regime Change" that the Mired young generation cares about the ills of the world caused by those in power, including the plight of troops overseas who miss Christmas to fight war.

Leper: "More than lyrics soppier than a slimy pussy's vaginal sponge, this is marketed as a daring antiwar message. His generation cares about making money, not the conquest of foreign peoples to create new capitalist markets where labor can be exploited and profited off of. His generation craves the mass consumables made so affordable by the stealing of foreign natural resources like oil, not killing Iraqis. His generation wants gasoline for their sweet pimped-out rides that have peace-sign bumper stickers, not the enslaving of whole peoples in the Middle East by U.S.-backed dictatorships for the benefit of supranational oil corporations who bless us with gasoline. Can't we all just get along? War wouldn't happen if his generation ran the world."

It is contended and sold in "Waiting on the World to Change Channels" that another evil is the system's control and manipulation of information using television.

Jack: "Ah, yes. The system is using your television to brainwash you. But not your major-corporate-label music. *Trust slimy pussy. Slimy pussy is your friend.*"

The system: "So, you're just a tad brighter than the average huminion? You've become dubious? Cynical? You don't trust the government, the corporations, and their mass media anymore? Well, we are perfectly happy to parody ourselves, to insult ourselves, even to explain all of our ugly intentions and evil doings in detail—*as long as it keeps your attention.* We have television shows, news programs, newspaper articles, umpteen genres of music, books, advertisements, comic strips, purchasable symbols, et al. that have been carefully designed for those of you who don't have confidence in us anymore. Anything to keep you *plugged in.* Anything to keep you *buying.*

"We play on your cynicism, cashing in on it, encouraging it. You may know better to have any faith in us, but as long as we keep you captivated with our irony and self-deprecation, you won't be able to conceive of any alternatives. Rather than having the imagination and idealism to strike out against the status quo, you'll join the ranks of the *Daily Show* disciples, still playing your part in the system, just buying the cynical broadcast of it."

Guano: "Yeah! We're not bitter hack writers who can't get published by the System, we're revolutionary heroes taking a noble stand!"

But "Waiting on the World to Change Oligarchs" promises that sometime in the future the Mired generation will rule the people.

Jack: "Like hell. These pussies don't have the balls."

Leper: "Good to see they yearn to rule over their fellow man. I'd say their feelings for *real* democracy fit right in with current policy."

Guano: "Well, you can't get rich and famous unless you do a little ruling over the people."

Leper: "Thankfully, ruling over your fellow man never requires war. Because their generation hates war. Just look at all of them taking their hatred of war to the streets while they listen to tough antiwar songs like 'Waiting on My Cynically Chic Complacence to Change' programmed into their recently purchased iPods which were slaved in China. As long as the filthy poor of the world keep giving us consumables, resources, and labor on the cheap then there's no need to go in and kill them and make our military killers miss holidays. That's why war is so frustrating and we hate it. Really. My iPod says so."

Song refrain: Until they are handed power, because they sure as fuck aren't taking it by taking action, Mired and his generation seem content to do nothing except repeating ad nauseam that they are waiting.

Leper: "Because waiting for someone else to do it for us is the only thing we know."

Guano: "Just hire some Mexicans. For a buck an hour they'll do anything."

Jack, Leper, Guano: "What a slimy pussy!"

"Like I said, boys, I like your style," goes Jack. "You've got balls."

"Technically, I don't. Fucker."

"Now normally I'd be a good capidoltist and use my illegitimate land titles to charge the peasantry illegitimate rent, or just have your asses illegitimately evicted. But it's comforting to know you're here amongst my feces, feces-esque movie, and cured Adam Sandler remains."

"Normally we'd just run you over," the leper reciprocates.

"So I propose you continue doing your thing: keeping the roads clear, annihilating vast swaths of suburban sprawl, you know, staying out of trouble," Jack suggests. "In return, I won't cause you any trouble."

"We might be amenable to all that," says the leper.

"But," Jack counters, "I will ask one small favor."

"Here it comes," the leper grumbles.

"I want you boys to chauffeur me to the Academy Awards presentation."

"Can't afford a stretched Hummer limo or something equally classily overcompensating?"

"I can't afford not to be seen rollin' with Arby's wrappers glued to heads on wheels. Slimy pussy's generation of spineless pussies, like all the rest of the lackeys out there, can't consume this latest frivolity fast enough."

"Shamzam! You're nobody if you're not getting the heads that are turning heads!" screams Billy Joe Huckenfuchs.

"You could say this fad is the best thing since sliced *head. Heehaw!*" reports Telly Bawdhaw.

The leper reasons, "Every Hummer owner, being what they

are, will by now have complied with adding human heads jazzed up with shiny foil refuse to their wheels."

Jack warmly assures, "I don't want a Hummer. I don't want a limo. Daddy likes his Cutlass."

"Well, it is a Cutlass *Supreme*."

I interject, "The Academy Awards are always a big TV ratings draw. We *could* stand a little face time."

"Well," the leper slowly says while scratching his head through his giant afro, "if you don't mind sharing the backseat with a suffocating diesel generator, then I guess you've got your ride."

"That's fine, boys. It's a pleasure to be on board. Now if you'll excuse me, I'm going to have sex."

Jack leaves and I tell the leper, "Did you notice how during the course of that dialogue there was very little real distinction between me, you, and even Jack?"

"More fine writing, me boyo. More fine writing."

ELEVEN

Not resting on previous shenanigans, we continue our fabulous, all-expenses-paid terror campaign. In the days that follow, I-5, I-605, I-105, I-210, I-710, the 110, the 91, the 60, and that guy's driveway all fall to the snowplow-wedge.

Plowing highways clogged full of traffic is like painting your house: necessary, but lacking in artistic expression. The artistic expression comes in when you graffiti on the front of your freshly painted house "My next door neighbor's vagina smells like a Dow Chemical factory."

Our broad brush strokes clear enough traffic from the roads to allow us the space to create. With the herd thinned, one can concentrate on the details that make art, art. These details are best brought to life, and death, by way of hunt-and-destroy forays.

Charge: Lexus LS, with the left passing lane clear, chooses to pass vehicles on the right. Verdict: Guilty. Sentence: Lexus LS driver passed, through his colon.

Roads free of gridlock allow one to better hunt the tailgaters, the reckless speeders, the cell phone zombies…

Charge: BMW 550i riding the asses of other cars. Verdict: Guilty. Sentence: BMW 550i loses ass.

…the litter throwers, the rubberneckers, the single-driver-in-carpool-lane cheaters…

Charge: Asian driver. Verdict: Guilty. Sentence: Chop suey-ed. Ha!

…the red-light runners…

Acura RL weaving in and out of traffic. Only the hair weave remains.

… the passing-lane pluggers…

Ford Explorer tosses cigarette butt out window. Cigarette and Ford still smoldering.

…the road-rage amateurs…

Driver of a Hummer who paid extra money for a California specialty license plate with a cute whale tale on it in which at least thirty-four cents from the specialty plate goes to protecting the environment—because the Hummer driver can't afford not to care—gutted for being too dim to enjoy over-the-top irony.

…and cops too. After a solid month of this profoundly soul-redeeming antisocial behavior we'd killed a lot of cops. I think, like, all of them.

Three percent of the population thrives when liberated from authoritarianism. Three percent of the population will form new economies built on mutualism, fairness, sustainability, and justice. Three percent will live peaceably with themselves and nature. Three percent will live in a way that ensures the survival of humanity and the world. Then the 97 percent will burn the 3 percent's co-ops to the fucking ground. Ninety-seven percent of the population has been so ruined by the present system that it needs a fascist foot up its ass to keep the 97 percent from ass-fucking themselves with semi-automatic weapons to oblivion. Institutionalized inequities, pathological hypocrisy, herd-numbing stupidity, and good old-fashioned greed & violence systematized over centuries yield you a 97 percent ruined-humanoids profit (a great return on all your capidoltist investments by any standard).

No more cops, no more control of the Southern California run-on megalopolis. A locally autonomous kibbutz springs up

in the middle of South Central. Community resources are restored to their rightful owners (i.e., the community) and shared. Individuals claim ownership of the homes and businesses they use and occupy. The fruit of his labor goes to that laborer. Decision-making is decentralized, left to freely associating individuals. And the 97 percent burn it all to the fucking ground.

Well-armed street thugs rampage at the first sign of an authority vacuum. Demented by lifetimes of injustice and oppression, they indulge in binges of murder in order to feel empowered for the first time in their wasted existences. Like millions of clustered hand grenades, they wind up destroying everything and everyone around them, including themselves.

The other end of the gangrenous 97 percent is left to pick up—or buy up—the pieces. These are the opportunists; those who feel no compunction about profiting off the misfortune of others as part of a larger ongoing strategy to exploit the shit out of the weak and the environment. In the common vernacular, they are known as yuppies.

Between putrescent yuppies and thugs is the middle portion of our putrescent 97 percent: the multitude too timid or dumb to make effectual parasites or gangsters. Throw these peons an occasional bone and they become fine lapdogs for their yuppie lords, acting as a buffer between the controlling criminal capitalists and the corroded criminal commoners always spawned by this ruinous way.

The newly freed federation of South Central cooperatives comes under immediate attack from the newly uncaged street hoods. It's really amazing to see what the 97 percent's most psychologically pathological can do when properly motivated. Although I'm sure the yuppies will object to being classified as less psychologically pathological than your average impoverished goon, and they have a point. Please accept my apology.

Semantics aside, 3 percent of the wise are way too outnumbered and will be disemboweled by the 97 percent's most

psychologically pathological this side of yuppies. But just before being massacred in a barrage of bullets, the mutualists break out the TB-Signal. The TB-Signal is a specially modified Klieg searchlight with a stylized symbol of the Give Whitey Five black fist o' ass-kicking attached to the light so that it projects a large black fist emblem on the sky. It is a blatant rip-off of Batman's Bat-Signal. The TB-Signal is used by the co-opers as a method of contacting and summoning TB to their assistance in the event of a serious crisis. Unfortunately L.A.'s omnipresent smog has precluded anyone from seeing the sky since the 1940s so the TB-Signal goes completely unnoticed.

Most of South Central and the region's many other poverty-decimated communities find themselves burning. Which the mass-media experts rule to be an improvement.

But the thugs get uppity and begin despoiling areas outside those exhibiting the always chic urban-blight motif. The yuppies of Bel Air are threatened before they can fully invest in a wide variety of corporate weapon-maker stocks to thereby make the best of an unfortunate situation.

Then the great nation's *el presidente* restores order to the situation by revoking all civil rights until it is realized that civil rights had been revoked sometime long, long ago. Plus, 97 percent of the public don't care about civil rights especially if these civil rights thingies interfere with watching something on TV. So civil rights remain a figment of the national mythology. Instead, 97 percent of the population are in favor of developing a big red button that when pushed will make all problems disappear.

Sometime before this latest national crisis, sometime in the middle of those halcyon days known as the Bush presidency when any American was still free to either go with God or go to Guantanamo, I sent this to *The New York Times* to not publish as usual:

Dear Habeas Corpus,

Happy birthday! Wow. Today you are 792 years old! Enjoy it when your Guantanamo guards celebrate by sending 792 volts of electricity through your testicles via a birthday set of jumper cables. That'll get ya glowing hotter than any cake candles! And now the birthday boy won't ever have to worry about a lawyer. Because legal defense makes for a shitty present anyway.

Warmly yours,

Guano (because you can't spell Guantanamo *without a little* Guano! *Ha!)*

But those were simpler times before we as a great nation learned that it was far more tasteful to keep our network of worldwide secret torture prisons *secret.*

With no LAPD attack helicopters left in the cupboard (you're fucking welcome!) the army buys more shitloads of attack helicopters, sending corporate weapon-maker stocks through the roof, making the best of an unfortunate situation. The army sends in their attack helicopters to shoot a shitload of Hellfire missiles at marauding thugs. Marauding thugs need to learn their place, which is apparently not in Bel Air. The army invites viewers to log on at home and guide Hellfire missiles to their proper ghetto location. Making war on the poor into a video game is a fun way to train America's poor to kill the foreign poor which is often referred to (with a snicker) as *serving one's country in the military* so America can win her (more snickering) *war on terror, wars of liberation,* and *war on childhood obesity.* Besides being a wonderful military recruitment tool targeting the younger generation whose love for video games trumps their deep hatred of war, it was all a wonderful TV ratings success.

Back to the L.A. diatribe. What you have remaining are a few feudal estates where the lords rule, the serfs toil, and the very poorest figuratively and literally burn—the justification for this being the threat of military weapons.

So things were exactly the same as always.

Armed military occupiers placed on every street corner look just like armed police occupiers on every street corner. So with things back to normal and even better than normal now that those 3 percenters aren't around to drag everybody down everybody can settle in for some quality TV time.

Time for the Academy Awards.

Jack enters the Batcave dressed in tuxedo. It makes him look fat. "Hi, Jack. You look fat. And I don't mean *fat* as in: *wow, Annie's pussy sho is fat* as in *delightful and the best thing since sliced head*. No. I mean *fat* as in: *swollen distended Harley-biker fat*." I add, "You fucking tub."

Jack says, "I'm, like, a hundred fucking years old by now. The metabolism and schlong ain't what they used to be." He shoves a moon pie into his mouth.

"Enough tomfoolery," TB says in his finest Ebonics. "Let's go."

We pile in the Olds, tear out of the Batcave, and hit the streets. We are wearing our backup tarp and disguised as an Escalade, which had become a federal crime after the Cadillac Corporation got pissy over unsavory elements using tarps to upgrade their pieces of shit into Escalades. New laws are created in America when the Cadillac Corporation properly orders its employees in Congress and the White House to properly pass legislation that makes wearing a tarp a federal offense punishable by a prison term of forever which is considered light sentencing by today's standards in the Land Of The Free with purchase of second item of equal or greater value.

After a few miles TB pulls over into some asshole's McMansion driveway and plows through their front door. "Knock knock," he

says. Being a Negro, he parks in their living room. The stunned yuppies on the Italian leather furniture watch as he gets out, removes the tarp off the car, courteously tips his welder's mask towards his hosts, gets back in, and speeds off through the back door. "Wait for it…"

Behind us the McMansion explodes in a huge fireball.

I explain to Jack: "You see, that's a little joke we like to play on the bourgeois neighbors. The State's spy satellites that spy on us and everybody else don't look twice at an *Escalade* driving around these oh-so-decent parts. But when they detect an *Oldsmobile* careening out of some gaudy, sterile, mass-produced yuppie tract palace, they think they've spied where TB lives and automatically destroy the tract palace by firing down their missiles from in-flight warplanes or space-based weapon systems. Do it enough and it adds up. This week we cratered half The Valley with this prank."

"It's kind of like taking the old flaming-bag-of-dogshit-on-the-front-step gag to the next level," adds TB.

"And I don't mind telling you, it was *my* idea," I can't help but to boast.

From the backseat Jack leans forward and pats me on the head. "You know, boy, you're smarter than most humans."

"*Smarter than most humans?* How kind. That's like complimenting someone for eating less people than Idi Amin."

The leper pulls down the herculetium blinds before the next missile rains down on our roof. The warplane-launched or space-launched projectile fails at penetrating our defenses but does make a fifty-foot pothole in the road.

TB keeps his foot on the accelerator as the Olds crawls out of the crater. Jack bitches, "I don't mean to bitch, but if they keep hitting us with missiles all the way to the Oscars it's going to be a really bumpy ride and I've got my hemorrhoids to consider."

"Don't worry," says TB. "They'll always stop their missile attacks once you get on the highways."

"That's valuable information for those trying this at home."

The leper continues: "You see, the State is loath to destroy its own highways. Because that would make its corporate partners very angry."

"You see," I continue, "corporations look to externalize as many of their costs as possible to increase their profits. And it tends to be more profitable to make other people pay their bills for their impact on society. Economists have a word for this: *externalities.*"

TB: "So, for instance, corporations say, 'Let's let somebody else supply the military power to the Middle East to protect the oil at its source. Let's let somebody else build the roads so we can freely ship our goods and bring consumers to our door. Let's let somebody else pay the cost to solve our problems.'"

Guano: "So many externalities, so little time."

TB: "Corporations are externalizing machines. They will externalize any cost that the unwary or uncaring public will allow them to externalize."

Guano: "We ripped off most of the above shit about how you're being ripped off by the corporations from *The Corporation*, an illuminating documentary. For other illuminating shit we haven't gotten around to plagiarizing yet, check out *The Corporation.*"

TB: "More. Environmental destruction is yet another neato corporate externality. A corporation, let's say in Love Canal or Bhopal or China, creates deadly pollutants. The communities there get sick from the fouled air, water, etc. Massive cleanups are required. The corporation has created market externalities. What the corporation has done is it has shifted part of the cost of production onto its neighbors. In an efficient and *truly free* market, all the costs of production would be borne by the producer. But corporations don't want a *truly free* market because they would never want to bear the full costs of their production. So they use the State to deflect the costs onto the public to maximize their own corporate profits."

Guano: "In modern-day capitalism, the line between the State and Big Private Business Interests is blurred to the point of irrelevance."

TB: "Hand in hand."

Guano: "Tongue in ass."

TB: "Together forever."

Guano: "Joanie Loves Chachi."

TB: "Kill 'em all and let God sort 'em out."

Guano: "God is dead, you black heathen Übermensch."

As dead as the armada of tanks blocking the Highway 101 on-ramp. The Olds cuts through 'em. The sounds of disjoining metal and bone snap to the beat of exploding munitions interlaced with the shrieks of mutilated little boys playing soldier in their dying death machines: our melody of righteous vengeance. This terrible anthem is one these soldiers know. They're just accustomed to being in the audience, not in the orchestra.

With the blinds down, we can't see dick. Luckily the ubiquitous TV news helicopters are broadcasting us live. Guided by the dashboard light of trusty black & white, bunny-ear-antennaed co-pilot, the leper uses the televised aerial shots to steer.

"Driving at high speeds with blinds down steering to the electronically simulated image of you radiating from your TV is like playing a video game."

"Bullshit," the leper rebuts. "If this were a video game I'd get double points for this!" as he maneuvers the Olds through the last of the tanks and into the tanks' refueling truck.

"I'll bet that slimy pussy John Mired plays video games when he's not playing with himself," mutters Jack.

The overhead TV shot shows us proceeding beyond the highway on-ramp littered with tank remnants blistering in a spreading pool of fire.

"Need a *light*?" broadcasts TB from the rooftop speaker.

"Guess you could say those tanks are *out* like a *light*," broadcasts Telly Bawdhaw from the TV.

"Fucking slimy pussy," broadcasts Jack from the backseat.

"How the hell am I supposed to drive with this split screen shit!" explodes the leper.

"Slimy pussy!"

"This split screen shit offers something for every mass-man," I assuage. "On the left side of the TV screen, viewers and lepers stay entranced with the latest helicopter media frenzy. On the right side of the TV screen, stay entranced with the latest meretricious dross leaking from the Academy Awards show."

"You mean to tell me we're forced to share airtime with a flatulently meaningless awards show because a flatulently meaningless awards show is as newsworthy as the latest helicopter media frenzy?"

"Sorry, brother. You're old news. This clearing the roads of traffic to demonstrate the twin evils of *overcentralization*— particularly in the form of capitalism but to a lesser extent nationalism and religion as well—and human *overpopulation* is tired. And it's a real downer. Nobody cares that overpopulation and overcentralization (byproducts of your modern technology) are the root causes creating the cancerous psychopathic society around us. Nobody understands what the fuck you've been trying to say from the beginning. Remember: short attention spans demand something somehow even more ridiculous than the last ridiculous stunt used to mesmerize the masses with short attention spans. So keep it light; and fun! Try adding some newborn babies, midgets, electronic gadgets, and big ol' titties to your routine. Maybe that'll get you some *buzz*."

"How about monkeys dressed up as humans? I hear they're a hoot."

"Good as gold as long as the monkeys are restricted to making funny faces and rubbing themselves. Anything beyond that may intellectually intimidate your audience."

"There's that slimy pussy!" Jack screams, pointing at the right split screen. John Mired is this year's Academy Awards

musical guest. He's sharing the stage with this year's fellow musical guests The Black Eyed Peas. John Mired is performing his Grammy Award winner "Pusillanimously Waiting on the World to Change and Wondering Like the Ignoramus That I Am Why It Never Does Change" because it gives voice to the young generation. The Black Eyed Peas are performing their Grammy Award winner "My Humps" because the young generation made this song the most downloaded song in the country, which speaks volumes of their voice.

Jack stops waiting on the world to change and takes direct action by humping the generator in the backseat. He declares, "Boys, step on it. I wouldn't want to be late. I'm scheduled to present the Best Picture award right after slimy pussy finishes oozing onstage."

"Oh, yeah? Who's gonna win?" I ask.

"Wait. Consider: if the likes of slimy pussy can win a Grammy Award for the likes of 'Waiting on the World to Change My Tampon' and The Black Eyed Peas can win a Grammy Award for the seminal work 'My Humps,' what does that tell you about the relevancy of awards in general?"

"Yeah. Because if associations of abject experts and dullards didn't hand out awards, how would we know what was good?"

"And knowing what you know about the mass-man's fondness for awards given by associations of abject experts and dullards, who can you count on to win this year's Oscar for Best Picture?"

"*Crash!*" the leper and I shout in unison. "Hooray!"

"For those not in the know, *Crash* is a self-aggrandizing dolt-ish heap of maggoty rot leaking ridiculously superficial artificial bromidic stereotypes onto the movie screen in what has been applauded as an importantly flatulent Hollywood edict on race relations. Put another way, watching *Crash* is the intellectual and moral equivalent to watching a steaming pile of shit. No, seriously. It's true. That statement has been vetted by a panel of experts and dullards."

"But in *Crash's* defense it's not only completely devoid of intelligence, but humor too."

"Wrong. It's actually a very funny movie; albeit unintentionally."

"I like a movie that pantomimes formulaic racial boilerplates while never addressing the real issue underlying race relations—that being the topic of *class*—because focusing on the inequities of capitalism and its hierarchal stratification of society won't get you Best Picture nominations from rich stereotypical Hollywood types mouthing their liberal false blather on equality for all as long as equality doesn't translate into equal sharing of resources and the abolishment of class in a society that has served the class of rich stereotypical Hollywood types so well."

"Likening *Crash* to a steaming pile isn't fair to steaming piles."

The leper takes the exit towards Highland Avenue, knifes through the tanks and armored limousines, turns down the red carpet, through the Kodak Theatre front doors, down the main aisle, and up onto stage. Jack steps out of the Olds and walks to the podium. His tuxedo is only slightly ruffled and he looks fat. He puts on his eyeglasses and picks up the envelope from the podium. "Ladies and gentlemen," he says into the microphone, "any organization that would exalt a movie like *Crash* is an organization full of pussies. *Slimy pussies.*" Jack rips open his tuxedo jacket. Underneath is another jacket: one tailored from the highest quality C-4 plastic explosive. "Say, that's why he looked so fat in the tux!" I exclaim.

"Here's Johnny!" exclaims Jack, jumping into the front row of the audience, into the waiting arms of John Mired.

The detonation craters slimy pussy and the Kodak Theatre as efficiently as any Terror State's space-based weapon system could. Luckily we kept the blinds down and watched the explosion on TV. Then a tractor-trailer comes careening through the one wall still standing.

It's Governor Adrenal Wartzenfegger. Hooray!

The gov is driving an 18-wheeler covered in corporate sponsor logos. The trailer is a working Starbucks store. The director of the film crew nailed to the top of the trailer barks instructions through his cone thingy megaphone as the camera rolls.

On the TV it shows the gov's semi ram into us. The TV-news radar gun clocks him going 125 in a 25. Dick.

The force of collision sends us hurtling airborne. The feet of the film crew's gaffer remain nailed to the trailer roof but the rest of him tears loose. He and we crash into a chain movie theater two blocks away. *Crash* is playing. *"Heehaw!"* says Telly Bawdhaw. We're knocked unconscious by the crash and the intellectual bludgeoning from Best Picture.

TWELVE

"Where are we?"

"Don't know. Brain hurts."

"That fucking movie."

"At least it's stopped playing. Sandra Bullock is a national treasure. Which sums up the nation."

The Olds is nowhere to be found. We're lying on some synthetic grass. I get up on all fours, squat, and piss. I piss like a girl. You would too if they snipped off your balls before adulthood. Oh wait, they did: it's called the American education system.

The leper starts to yell because he doesn't like being squatted over and urinated on even though watching the same thing online will cost you $12.95 per month on Sandra-Bullock-Showering-In-A-Steaming-Stream-Of-Animal-Husbandry.com which is always showing that climactic scene from *Crash* when the uncircumcised donkey pisses into Sandra's open mouth. Which is Sandra's one talent.

So I finish up on the synthetic grass which elicits a thick un-American accent to boom: "Do not piss on the Astroturf! OK to piss on the black man. Lots of precedent there."

It's Governor Adrenal Wartzenfegger. Hooray!

The fearless governor of California is standing on a raised platform. He's in a stylish business suit that rips off revealing flexed oiled muscles. The gov bulges in various poses for several

minutes as the film crew, unnailed from the tractor-trailer, rolls the camera. Various angles of the gov's thong are chronicled.

The political strongman lights a cigar, taking care not to ignite his well-oiled muscles. He puffs out his line: "TB, I will *smoke* you!"

"Cut!" yells the director through his megaphone. He hops off the folding chair to gesticulate something into the governor's ear, hops back on the folding chair and yells "Action!"

The gov puffs out his line: "TB, I will smoke *you!*"

"Cut! That's a wrap!" yells the director, bouncing to the governor's side to congratulate him.

"Am I supposed to respond to that horseshit line with my own horseshit line?" the leper asks.

"No," I tell him. "Black men should be seen, not heard."

"Especially those playing straw boss in high office."

We're sitting in the middle of a rectangular plot of artificial turf, 120 yards long, 160 feet wide. The area has been marked with lines of chalk.

We're sitting on a football field.

Just beyond the field's out-of-bounds markers are vertical walls made of canvas that stretch from the synthetic grass up thirty feet, then slant in to form a roof.

We're sitting on a football field inside a giant tent.

The governor's platform rises ten feet above the turf at the back of the end zone. He's getting makeup done. Another crew sprays oil onto/into every convexity and cranny. A third team recharges the neon on the California state seal on the thong. "What do you think of my personal smoking tent, TB?" the governor asks, not bothering to look at us.

"If you want me to engage in a speaking part in this horseshit production then I want my own trailer. And a fluffer."

"Only if you're a SAG member," the gov chuckles. "But I'm afraid not even SAG can save you now."

"Are you sure? You forget, I'm not going by your script."

"Oh, you're going by our script. Everyone does. And you've played your role well as 'terrorist,' 'public enemy,' 'the next Hitler,' et cetera, et cetera. But now the script calls for corralling the latest and greatest villain in, which we have. And now that you are *in*, you'll play the role of captive audience. Like all the rest." The gov puffs on his cigar, and finally looks at us. "And I'm sorry to say, this role does not end well for you. Or your mutt."

"I don't even know this leper," I explain to the gov. "He just picked me up because I'm one of those sexy hitchhikers with cut-off Daisy Dukes riding up my ass that he likes to masturbate to while thinking about ova."

The gov continues, "This place is more than just a stately pleasure dome where I issue decrees. This is also where your sad sordid tale of individualism and rebellion will come to an end."

"I'm just a Mexican itinerant farm worker he abducted from my happy home at the Man!santo genetically modified rubber-chicken field. *Hola*. See? *Sí*."

Says the gov, "Now I will admit you have caused your share of hardships for us. You've killed a lot of people; a thinned herd is a healthier herd, and harder for us to control."

"How about a quick-witted itinerant farm worker named George and his hulking, slow-witted friend Lennie whose love of soft things and simplemindedness with his brutal strength often lands him in trouble?"

Gov: "It's a basic cornerstone of capitalism: Keep a large surplus of labor around to exploit. The teeming masses require only enough resources to prevent them from revolting; and this is far less than their equitable share, I assure you. The weight of their crushing numbers along with persuasive conditioning from cradle to grave keeps them ignorant and passive. *Passive* to their masters anyway; *patriotic* when it comes to killin' any 'foreign' 'foe' we masters whip up on a routine basis for the

nationalistic dupes. *Bwahaha!* and other sound effects to indicate evil scheming."

"No, really. He masturbates to eggs. The pervert can't get enough of that sweet sweet oosphere. I'll testify."

Gov: "But of course you've also destroyed a lot of our capital. Which is a hell of a lot more offensive than eliminating a few million dullards. After all, dullards will always make more dullards."

TB: "Yeah. Sorry about ass-fucking so much of your accumulated capital. Sometimes I can't help myself."

Gov: "Ah! He graces us with speech!"

TB: "I do more than speak, motherfucker."

Gov: "Not for long."

TB: "We'll see. Why don't you come on down here from your little pedestal and we'll discuss it."

Gov: "You make me laugh, girlie man. I am twice your size. I am well-oiled. I am in a thong. I would pound you."

TB: "Just like you do to the rest of the boys."

Guano: "And not at all in a gay way."

Gov: "You tempt me. But I will refrain from personally removing your limbs from their sockets until the confession scene has been shot."

TB: "You're the consummate professional. What am I supposed to confess?"

Gov: "That you've been a naughty boy. And that you regret helping to detonate every Hollywood star."

TB: "Got 'em all, eh?"

Gov: "All but Academy Awards host Stew John."

TB: "Stew John? Who also greasily hosts a nightly TV-news spoof known for favoring the puppet on the left over the puppet on the right but most of all favoring The Man holding both puppets? To paraphrase the Gospel of Bill Hicks."

Gov: "Yes. *That* Stew John. Greasy perpetrator of edgy political commentary assured to have the veneer of incisiveness

without being so incisive as to disturb the status quo/Stew John's advertisers."

TB: "Damn. How'd we miss that greasy System shill?"

Gov: "Shrapnel just slid off the grease."

TB: "Well I'll be."

Gov: "Thankfully, network TV's darling huckster most favored by the latte liberal is still alive and keeping 'em plugged in, channeling audience anger into nothing but advertising dollars."

TB: "I've always appreciated his skill in mocking those obtuse enough to exhibit a gleeful acceptance of the Machine by showing us how much more urbane and intellectual it is to instead exhibit a cynical acceptance of the Machine."

Gov: "He is a valuable tool, albeit a greasy one. And lucky for you he's still crossing picket lines to broadcast how we must all stand in solidarity against the money-grubbing media lords."

TB: "It's a great message. A real ratings winner for media lords."

Gov: "If you'd offed him, *The New York Times* would be even more pissed."

TB: "Oh, no. Bad press?"

Gov: "You've offended the great 'left'-leaning sensibilities of the Gray Lady."

TB: "The Gray Lady is a whore."

Gov: "And a valuable whore. No one sets the 'news' agenda better than the flagship for the legion of money-grubbing newspapers, magazines, websites, baseball teams, paper mills, and TV & radio stations owned in the past, present, and future by The New York Times Company (NYSE: NYT)."

TB: "All the news that's fit to print dollar bills."

Gov: "What are you, some profit-hating commie?"

TB: "State communism is even more pernicious than State capitalism. Although, thanks to mergers, a handful of mega-corporations consolidating their control over the market have

made the difference between State communism and capitalism negligible."

Gov: "Sweet Jesus, man! Is there any other game in town?"

TB: "There could be many different games in many different towns. Let the individuals in all the different towns decide what different economic models work best for their different situations."

Gov: "Too complex."

TB: "Not really. For the individual, the presence of multiple currency paradigms would be akin to having various subscriptions or club memberships; and it would be no more complex than the current capitalist system in which the average American consumer uses several credit cards with various debts, owes mortgages, car payments, et cetera. More economic models mean more choice. A single monolithic one-size-fits-all system is a clumsily inefficient—and tyrannical—way to facilitate the exchange of all goods, services, and resources."

"But the springing forth of organic economies at the local level and the overlapping of such systems would have to be predicated upon the reduction of the State and the removal of the corporations," the gov says with a smirk.

TB: "Of course. 'Tis true. And to eliminate the corporations all one has to do is change the definition of property. Easy."

Gov: "And how would you redefine property?"

TB: "By making property ownership solely based on use and occupancy."

The gov scoffs, "And no other title of ownership is valid? You already went over this earlier in the book," the gov scoffs.

TB: "*Jawohl, mein Führer*. It goes like this: If you respectfully use the land you occupy, it's yours. If you live in the house on that land, it's yours. If you work in the business on that land, that business and what it produces are yours. If you don't use and occupy it, it's not yours. Of course, as in life, these rules

aren't without qualifications. For example, a person using land in such a way that it unfairly pollutes the community, or usurps more than an equitable share of community resources, is not legitimately using the land and therefore is not entitled to it. Individual communities can work out their own standards and details, but the principle is simple and just."

Gov: "Does that mean while my car is parked and I'm not using it someone else could just take it? What about my television? If I leave my thong with incandescent California state seal on the bathroom floor, could one of those weasels from the State Board of Equalization claim it?"

TB: "Ah, a feeble attempt at *reductio ad absurdum*. All those things are personal possessions, not property. Personal, movable possessions, like a hammer or a refrigerator or a thong, are obviously yours to keep whether you use them or not. *Property* refers to the land, along with the homes and businesses connected to that land."

Gov: "More *reductio ad absurdum*. If I go away on vacation, someone will claim my house!"

TB: "You've got the common touch of common imbecility. You can go away on vacation and keep your home. Only if you abandon it to live elsewhere do you lose privilege to it."

Gov: "Say I use and occupy my home. Then I decide I want to sell it. Can I?"

TB: "Yes, of course. I would think selling a home you no longer want to be in is a very good idea. However, the sale of your home does not confer property ownership to the buyer; that buyer must after the sale use and occupy that house for it to be his. If he abandons it or tries to rent it to someone else, he loses the right to call that property his own."

Gov: "What if I want to build a house on my bit of land that I'm using and occupying? Can I pay someone to build the house for me?"

TB: "Sure. It's a free market."

Gov: "What if I don't have the resources/money to pay the house builder?"

TB: "Different communities would have different approaches on issuing ultra-low-interest or no-interest credit to their citizens. One obvious solution could be democratically run, not-for-profit banks (like credit unions)—organizations beholden to helping members of their community instead of helping themselves to profits."

Gov: "What if I go to your local credit union, get a close-to-interest-free home loan because your credit union issues those because they're not-for-profit, build my home, live in my home, then refuse to pay the loan back? I'm using and occupying the home, so it's mine, right? In your system, they have no right to kick me out of something I'm using and occupying!"

TB: "No strategy is infallible and universal. Hell, *nothing in life* (except death) *is universal.* No rule or theory or law should ever be so venerated to compel a person to march in lockstep to it without *thinking.* If after thinking about the situation the person reasons that the rule is worth following, great, then follow it. If not, fuck the rule and think of a better way of doing what needs to be done. But alas, the automatons are all so terrified of change."

Gov: "That's because the automatons are terrified at having to think for themselves. They love prepackaged orders, good or bad ones. Doesn't matter to them. But back to the question at hand: Is your convoluted condemnation of brainlessly adhering to a system your way of admitting that your property system based on use and occupancy can be bilked by individuals who choose to not repay their home loans?"

TB: "Come on. Clearly if you do not pay back your home loan you are in violation of the spirit of fair use and occupancy. If you can't or won't pay back the loan, eviction may still be an outcome. But there is evidence to suggest that nonprofit, community-controlled banks have a much lower bad-debt rate than

conventional banks because these financial co-ops are based on solidarity, and failing to repay a loan from a free-banking initiative is culturally equivalent to stealing from your friends.

"Now, this is no utopia I'm proposing—this is merely a *more just, more equitable* way for humans to live with each other. Misfortunes will still happen. And some people will still try to take advantage of others. As always. But a community based on economic mutualism would work very hard to help its fellow citizens meet their agreed-upon commitments and responsibilities because there's no incentive to want to see them fail. Unlike in capitalism: where the prospect of making a profit by foreclosing on your distressed neighbor brings out the worst in people. And you wonder why your society can't produce more decent folk.

"Economic mutualism is only one possible solution. Decentralized syndicalism is another. There's no reason these methods, and others, can't exist side by side. Let the individuals decide for themselves what works best for them and their communities."

"Property ownership through use and occupancy means I can't own any vacation home I don't actually live in," the gov laughs. "It means I can't own any investment property I don't physically occupy. It means I don't own the resources from the land unless I'm physically cultivating or extracting them myself; and in a sustainable fashion to boot! It means I can't own a share of any corporation that I don't physically work at; and that means *no corporations*! Good god! No more buying stock and expecting a piece of what someone else has produced. No more obscene amounts of accumulated capital. Now where's the fun in that?"

TB: "I grant you it would be a drag to have to endure a just dispersal of resources. Fuck. What could be worse than every person being entitled to the bit of land they live on, giving them a stake in their own community. What could be worse than the

laborer getting the full fruits of his labor. If he works with others, he and his fellow workers democratically decide how to fairly share what's produced. The harder and longer he works, the more he's likely to earn; but thanks to the use-and-occupy rule, he can't accumulate the capital necessary to divorce any other producer from the means of production. As Benjamin Tucker saw it: 'the natural wage of labor is its product; this wage, or product, is the only just source of income (leaving out, of course, gift, inheritance, etc.); all who derive income from any other source abstract it directly or indirectly from the natural and just wage of labor…' This abstracting process generally takes one of two forms—interest and rent; these two constitute usury and are simply different methods of levying tribute for the use of capital; capital simply being stored-up labor which has already received its pay in full, its use ought to be gratuitous; the lender of capital is entitled to its return intact and nothing more; the only reason why the banker, the stockholder, the landlord, the manufacturer, and the merchant are able to exact usury from labor lies in the fact that they are backed by legal privilege."

Gov: "Then who would invest in enterprises if they're not entitled to profit off it?"

TB: "Individuals would clearly invest in their own businesses since they would be the ones to benefit from it. Same goes for groups of workers banding together in collective business endeavors. The community itself could invest in various local enterprises that will benefit the community. Investments of labor, time, money, and other resources would still be made. Just no longer by parasites expecting to profit from an endeavor they themselves are not going to labor for."

Gov: "According to your warped little outlook, can profits ever be ethical?"

TB: "Are you using Adam Smith's technical definition of profit? Smith said: 'The *profit* or *gain of capital* is altogether different from the *wages of labor.*' Earnings made by laborers in

full control of all they produce who are freely exchanging with other such laborers—all completely uncoerced—are legitimate. Everything outside of these wages of labor (except gifts, inheritance, etc.) is unethical."

Gov: "You're calling the profiting off of quasi-slave labor unethical? That's un-American."

TB: "Conceded."

Gov: "Damn it! Slave labor has always been the backbone of any strong economy! Look at your history, man! You want some pyramids built? Then you'd better have legions of dirt-poor Egyptians! Or at least a Chevy full of Mexicans."

TB: "Recent evidence suggests the pyramids were not built by slaves. But I grant you that slaves certainly did help build the Roman Empire; and continue to help build the American Empire."

Gov: "Right! Flash forward to modern times. If all those Chinese zipperheads and the rest of the billions of poor slobs everywhere else weren't slaving away making corporations A through Z healthy profits, you'd have to build thousands of giant arenas to stick all the poor slobs in, oil them up in loincloths, and fight them to the death in spectacular gladiator contests with homosexual undertones. And how would you build all those arenas in the first place without corporations exploiting quasi-slave labor? Do you see what a vicious circle that is?"

TB: "It's not just Chinese slave laborers who are deprived the fruits of their labor. It's all workers worldwide. The alienation of the laborer from what he produces is a keystone of capitalism. Capitalists steal the laborers' products like so: Those with accumulated capital (capitalists) use their capital to extort profits (accumulated capital) from exploited labor who have little or no accumulated capital; the more profits (accumulated capital) those with accumulated capital (capitalists) make, the more they can exploit labor to make more accumulated capital (profits) for those with accumulated capital. Perhaps you've heard: the rich

get richer and the poor get poorer. Do you care what a vicious circle that is?"

Guano: "I've always been partial to 'the rich get richer and the poor get—babies!'"

Gov: "No, no, no. That's not what *The New York Times* says."

TB: "You don't say."

Gov: "*The New York Times* says TB has validated his worth in the global economy as an incorporable transnational entity and yet has rebuffed the inflow of private capital offered at a generous stock price (along with rudely declining various buyout packages). The *Times* admits that TB is the latest shameful terrorist threatening the Global Corporate State from the periphery of its own global financial system and needs to be murdered, as the reactionary 'right' says. But the famously 'left'-leaning newspaper also sees the need for a deeper reform-minded program that placates the untouchables enough to keep them catatonic, out of death-dealing Oldsmobiles, and economically/democratically feckless. Yes, our great pseudo-nation within the Global Corporate State must now expend valuable capital to kill recalcitrant terrorists who refuse to sell their carefully crafted brand name. But the *Times* has vision, an eye for the long term, and harshly rebukes the Corporate State for not providing its own leprous road-cleansing icon with scrumptiously adorable canine sidekick (direct quote) for the masses to worship. 'Where is the Corporate State's TB?' critically asks *The New York Times.* 'How have we as a great pseudo-nation in the Global Corporate State allowed this to happen?' *Times* reporter Thomas L. Friedman has dispatched his mustache, the womb broom of capitalism, to find out."

TB: "Hmm. 'Death to the agitated but shame on the bosses for letting them get agitated.' That old 'liberal' tune."

Gov: "You're lucky. You'll only be dead. Those 'left'-leaning

media bastards want me politically castrated."

TB: "The 'left-right' spectrum of mainstream American politics is a wonderful way to delineate the difference between the reactionary statist capitalists of the 'liberal' 'left' and the uber-reactionary statist capitalists of the 'conservative' 'right.'"

Gov: "Indeed. God forbid the masses should get their hands on an honest way to model political positions. It wouldn't do anyone any good to have the less stultified ones notice how alike America's political 'left' and 'right' really are. It might prompt them to seek genuine alternatives. Then again, probably not. Most of them are so hopelessly lazy and dull that they would never want to be troubled with *real* freedom. They *want* to be directed and controlled. The multitude seeks and follows the few who are strong enough to take the burden of freedom from them."

Guano: "Dostoevsky's Grand Inquisitor declares that under him all mankind will live and die gladly in ignorance. Though he leads them only to 'death and destruction' they will be content along the way. The Grand Inquisitor is a self-martyr, devoting his life to keeping choice from humanity."

TB: "Whether it be the Grand Inquisitor using the institution of organized religion to prevent the masses from being burdened with trying to know God in an authentic and personal way, or the Grand Governor Inquisitor using governmental and business/media institutions to prevent the masses from being burdened with the freedom to live according to their own will, it's enslavement all the same."

Gov: "The last thing the masses want is the *responsibility of choice* in any avenue of life. So we choose for them. And they are grateful."

Guano: "Best yet: tell all the suckers that they're free, and they'll actually believe it, because they're suckers. Ho ho!"

TB: "As if they're free to self-govern without State interference. As if they're free to form their own local economies without State intervention. As if they're free to ask nothing from the

State and be left alone in return. As if they're free to opt out of the State and live independently."

Guano: "Said Goethe, 'None are more hopelessly enslaved than those who falsely believe they are free.'"

The Grand Inquisitor: "But let me tell Thee that now, today, people are more persuaded than ever that they have perfect freedom, yet they have brought their freedom to us and laid it humbly at our feet.

"They will become timid and will look to us and huddle close to us in fear, as chicks to the hen. They will marvel at us and will be awe-stricken before us, and will be proud at our being so powerful and clever that we have been able to subdue such a turbulent flock of thousands of millions. They will tremble impotently before our wrath, their minds will grow fearful, they will be quick to shed tears like women and children, but they will be just as ready at a sign from us to pass to laughter and rejoicing, to happy mirth and childish song. Yes, we shall set them to work, but in their leisure hours we shall make their life like a child's game, with children's songs and innocent dance. Oh, we shall allow them even sin, they are weak and helpless, and they will love us like children because we allow them to sin. We shall tell them that every sin will be expiated, if it is done with our permission, that we allow them to sin because we love them, and the punishment for these sins we take upon ourselves. And we shall take it upon ourselves, and they will adore us as their saviors who have taken on themselves their sins before God. And they will have no secrets from us."

Guano: "Thanks to the Patriot Act."

The Grand Inquisitor: "The most painful secrets of their conscience, all, all they will bring to us, and we shall have an answer for all. And they will be glad to believe our answer, for it will save them from the great anxiety and terrible agony they endure at present in making a free decision for themselves. And all will be happy, all the millions (now billions) of creatures except the hundred thousand who rule over them. For only we,

we who guard the mystery, shall be unhappy."

Nietzsche: "The mystery being that there is no one true god's-eye perspective from which to view life. Your modern Western values are fraudulent. And while I'm at it: your God is dead."

The Grand Inquisitor: "Existentialism is dead. We're talking zero ratings."

Dostoevsky & Nietzsche: "As dead as we are! *Ha-cha-cha-cha-cha!*" (Both soft-shoe it off the stage while twirling canes and top hats.)

TB: "Yeah. It must really suck to be the ruling elite."

Gov: "My kind, we the select few, do carry a great weight: shielding the rabble from freedom while constantly telling them how free they are on their prime-time television programming (and all the rest of their programming) so the question of true freedom will never infringe upon their freedom to mindlessly absorb whatever's being peddled to them on their prime-time television programming (and all the rest of their programming). Remember: 95 percent of the people in the world need to be told what to do and how to behave."

TB: "Uh, that's actually 97 percent."

Guano: "And the other 3 percent are now dead."

Gov: "Right. So, technically, it's now 100 percent who need to be told what to do and how to behave. Makes my job easier. Which brings us back to here. I'm sorry you've awakened to the realities of the Matrix and had the bad taste to try to awaken others. That's what this place is for."

TB: "A giant smoking tent with artificial turf?"

Guano: "I love what you've done to the place."

Gov: "It's the necessary location for the penultimate scene of our movie. The storyline goes like this: A young poor leprotic Negroid—one of the customary billions of capitalism's casualties—decides to not delude himself with our prefabricated pipe dreams of making lots of bling bling through a career in

pro sports, music, or drug sales and instead strikes back at the disease of the System and human overpopulation by using an Oldsmobile Cutlass with herculetium snowplow-wedge to cut through traffic, the System, and human overpopulation. With the help of his well-hung Bernese Mountain Queef Wrangler, purebred, this menace to society destroys much of Los Angeles, the city leading the way in greed, shortsightedness, and general meretricious stupidity."

Guano: "You had me at leprotic Negroid."

Gov: "But just when it appears the villainous villeins are on the verge of bringing the slavers down and all is lost, our hero, the glistening and hard master of California, captures the evildoers and takes them to his smoking tent in the desert. For it is here, on a moonlit night, to the cheers of the adoring masses, that our bulging hero emperor not only extracts a full and legal confession from the terrorists but also converts them to the side of good/goods."

TB: "Two problems. One: there are no cheering adoring masses here."

Gov: "Ah. They'll be superimposed in during editing. It's not like the masses have any idea what's real and what's not."

TB: "Two: I'm not into confessions and there's no way you're getting a conversion."

Gov: "*You* don't need to convert. Your look-alike replacement will play the role admirably in our final triumphant scene. We're casting for the role as we speak."

TB: "Then you'd better get his ass in here right now, because I ain't giving you the satisfaction of a confession either."

Gov: "Oh, you will. You will."

Guano: "I'll confess right now if it'll save on pain and dismemberment."

Gov: "In all my other violence-laden summer blockbusters, conversion of the archenemy is never needed. Because blowing up their head with an exploding harpoon is far more audience-

friendly. But, as *The New York Times* bitched, the Corporate State needs its very own TB to awe the great unwashed. Blowing up your head like a singing humpback whale performing for a boatful of spear-chucking Japs, although personally very satisfying, would leave a certain segment of our moviegoers unfulfilled."

TB: "They have reason to feel unfulfilled."

Gov: "Yes, but the reason movies such as mine are made is to distract the masses from the underlying reasons why they feel unfulfilled. And to make assloads of box-office cash off the dupes, of course."

Guano: "Of course"

TB: "Naturally."

Gov: "We conduct audience research before a movie project is undertaken to discern what will best sell. This is called the art of moviemaking. Our audience research indicates that among the 2 percent who own over 50 percent of the world's everything, TB's popularity is running between 0 and 0 percent. For these 2 percent, an exploding harpoon in your head would make a lovely ending. Then there's the 48 percent group who own varying degrees of nothing while the bank owns varying degrees of everything yet these poor saps have still been convinced that they are 'owners.' Among these laughable marks, TB's popularity is just a blip over zero. Again, your detonating cranium would serve us just fine. But, unfortunately, among the remaining 50 percent who own basically nothing *and are actually aware they own nothing* (unregistered non-voters) a certain sentimentality exists for TB that is alarmingly over just a blip. And it is for this reason that the TB brand has validated its worth in the global economy and must be incorporated as a transnational entity. Which means no exploding harpoon."

Guano: "Aw, shucks. I never get to see anything good."

TB: "Yeah. You'd better keep the multitude who have nothing and are aware of it well pacified with your multitude of distractions, lest those poor bastards have a minute to think about

how fucked over they're getting and decide to change things by fucking you up."

Gov: "Which is why we need to convert *you* from a possible problem to a real distracting solution."

The gov positively glows.

"It's the makeup, bronze self-tanner, precious bodily oils, and neonized thong."

His pit crews withdraw. The director seizes the megaphone and screams "Action!"

Winking at the rolling camera, the governor grandiosely delivers: "Friends, Californians, countrymen, lend me your ears! I come to bury TB, not to praise him." (Cheering masses superimposed in during the editing process.)

The gov promises: "Blood and destruction shall be so in use / And dreadful objects so familiar / That mothers shall but smile when they behold / Their infants quarter'd with the hands of war / All pity choked with custom of fell deeds!" (Young woman shaking her huge titties superimposed in during editing process.)

"And so Caesar / Yeah, call me Caesar / Ranging for revenge / With some ho named Ate by my side come hot from hell / Shall in these confines with a monarch's voice / Cry 'Havoc!' and let slip the dogs of war / That this foul deed shall smell above the earth / With carrion leper, groaning for burial / 'Cause you know what that means, y'all: We gonna get *ballin'!*" (Early 1990s footage of Arsenio Hall audience shouting "Woof! Woof! Woof!" while pumping their fists superimposed in.)

The gates underneath the gov's platform fling open. A flood of theatrical smoke pours forth. Lasers bounce off the disco ball being lowered over the fifty-yard line. Cheerleaders shaking their huge titties are superimposed in. All to the rollicking twang of Billy Ray Waylon Scurry's Grammy Award winner "Drink Like Me and You'll Piss As Much Patriotic Piss to Float the USA's Kick-Ass Battleship Named the USS *Jesus Has Come*

to Kick Your Sand-Nigger Ass! Again!"

It's the Skabbs!

"But we killed that idiot!"

"You cannot kill the man-balls of justice! You can only completely sever the man-balls' spine in four different locations causing irreversible quadriplegia." To quote the official government press release.

From the smoke emerges the Skabbs's Harley-Davidson. It boasts enough chrome and gaudy metals to have required its very own strip mine. From between the handlebars erectly protrudes forward a twelve-foot jackhammer (chrome plated). Studies suggest giant augmented jackhammers and the like are coveted by overcompensating sexually inadequate males for one very small reason. In that same vein (pun-rific!), reattached to the Skabbs's crotch are two genuine leather medicine balls which have been upgraded with chrome plating. The Skabbs's shiny new thirty-pound man-balls hang one to each side of the Harley and drag on the ground. This scuffs their chrome plating. To prevent this, each side of the Harley is equipped with a Mexican who runs alongside carrying a man-ball on his back like Atlas shouldering the weight of the Earth.

The Skabbs is completely paralyzed from the neck down. He is cerebrally paralyzed from the neck up; as always. A sip-and-puff tube runs from the Harley's handlebars into the Skabbs's mouth. He controls the Harley by blowing into the sip-and-puff tube which is chrome plated.

The motorcycle perpetually leans on the pair of chrome-plated training wheels and does not fall over.

The reason Harley exhaust pipes are so loud is to overpower any nearby intelligent conversation that Harley riders are naturally unable to partake in.

The film crew completes a wide sweeping shot of the Skabbs's pipes. These exhaust pipes are specially modified and are a hundred feet long and were once industrial smokestacks.

They are now chrome plated. Please see above concerning the very small reason for giant overblown whatever.

The Skabbs's pipes are loud enough to drown out any intelligent conversations within a five-mile radius. Also drowned out are these unintelligent movie lines which will later be dubbed in during the editing process:

Gov: "TB, I believe you know the Skabbs."

TB: "Yeah, we've met. For someone as spinelessly subservient to mass culture, I'm surprised he even had a spine for me to break."

Gov: "A spine, maybe. A brain, no. Which is what any good master wants from his adorably manageable mass-man."

Guano: "Keeps the military ranks full."

TB: "Yes, and so much more! Theodor Adorno saw how well the culture industry—which manufactures and spreads cultural commodities through the mass media—manipulates the population. Popular culture is a potent tool for creating acquiescent subjects; the facile pleasures available through consumption of popular culture make people docile and complacent, no matter how wretched their economic circumstances."

Guano: "I enjoy how the 'differences' among cultural goods make them appear different, but they are in reality just superficial variations of the same thing. Adorno conceptualized this phenomenon as *pseudo-individualization* and the *always-the-same*. He recognized this mass-produced culture as a threat to the more challenging creative works that are actually capable of providing one some insight."

TB: "Culture industries cultivate false needs; that is, needs that are conveniently manufactured and satisfied by capitalism. True needs, in contrast, are freedom, creativity, and genuine happiness. Adorno saw how well capitalism blurs the line between false and true needs."

Guano: "Well, life does take Visa."

Gov: "Oh, you're no fun. I say give the people what they

want! The same old same old freshly repackaged over and over again, glimmering in our limelight, for all to see. The masses can't get enough of it!"

Theodor Adorno: "In general they are intoxicated by the fame of mass culture, a fame which the latter knows how to manipulate; they could just as well get together in clubs for worshipping film stars or for collecting autographs. What is important to them is the sense of belonging as such, identification, without paying particular attention to its content. As girls, they have trained themselves to faint upon hearing the voice of a 'crooner.' Their applause, cued in by a light-signal, is transmitted directly on the popular radio programs they are permitted to attend. They call themselves 'jitter-bugs,' bugs which carry out reflex movements, performers of their own ecstasy. Merely to be carried away by anything at all, to have something of their own, compensates for their impoverished and barren existence."

Guano: "The kids are jitterbugging on ecstasy? Ye gods! Please spay and neuter your children!"

Gov: "As boys and girls, they've been trained to cheer upon seeing our action hero of the hour pulverize the villain and villainous cause of the hour. Their cheers, cued in by whatever catchphrase we're peddling, are easy-to-program-and-predict reflex movements. All so they can feel a part of something— anything!—that at least looks more exciting than their pallid, pathetic lives. You know, all that 'impoverished and barren existence' tripe."

The Grand Inquisitor: "Man seeks to worship what is established beyond dispute, so that all men would agree at once to worship it. For these pitiful creatures are concerned not only to find what one or the other can worship, but to find community of worship is the chief misery of every man individually and of all humanity from the beginning of time. For the sake of common worship they've slain each other with the sword. They have set up gods and challenged one another, 'Put away your

gods and come and worship ours, or we will kill you and your gods!' And so it will be to the end of the world, even when gods disappear from the earth; they will fall down before idols just the same."

Gov: "And what an idol we have for them today to follow!" The Skabbs belches into his puff tube, revving the Harley's engine, expelling exhaust gases through its hundred-foot pipes. Blood squirts from our eardrums.

The director leaps out of his folding chair and grabs the megaphone. He shouts: "All right! All right! This is the big scene where the Skabbs extracts a full and legal confession from the terrorists using full and legal torture!"

Gov: "It's not *torture*. It's *enhanced interrogation methods* or, even better, *alternate procedures*. I gotta give him credit: For a U.S. president who could barely formulate a sentence, his administration came up with the most comically genius euphemisms."

Guano: *"Clear Skies Initiative. Operation Iraqi Freedom. USA Patriot Act. Doubleplusgoodthinking joycamps."*

TB: "The president borrowed that last one from his *big brother*."

Guano: "Tre-pun-dous!"

Gov: "Awe-pun!"

Guano: "If you play *Healthy Forests Initiative* backwards on your record player you can hear a chainsaw. And that Paul McCartney is dead."

TB: "The McCartney joke was a bit obvious."

Guano: "Shit, man. So is this whole fucking book."

TB: "My favorite is *illegal enemy combatant*. As in: any poor bastard arbitrarily kidnapped by the State and sent to hellish secret prisons where they'll get the shit tortured out of them."

Guano: "You mean *evildoers detained* through use of *extraordinary rendition* who choose to *cooperate with authorities* by way of *enhanced interrogation methods* at America's network of

worldwide *black sites.*"

TB: "'Black sites' is just a euphemism for 'doubleplusgood-thinking joycamps.'"

Gov: "Come on, boys! Attributing America's fondness for torture to one recent administration alone is unfair. America's been torturing folks for generations! Flashback to 1996: the Intelligence Oversight Board under President Clinton conceded that U.S.-produced training materials condoned 'execution of guerrillas, extortion, physical abuse, coercion and false imprisonment.' In the 1950s, CIA-funded experiments on psychiatric patients and prisoners, featuring sensory deprivation and self-inflicted pain, were tested in the field by CIA agents in Vietnam as a fun part of the Phoenix Program which boasted forty interrogation centers that murdered more than 20,000 suspects and tortured thousands upon thousands more. This American know-how & can-do spirit was then used on Latin America and Asia under the guise of police training. Not to brag, but we taught many a right-wing death squad everything they know."

"Yes, but at least during the Bush years, America openly admitted to torturing the fuck out of whoever. Because openness in depriving people of their legal and human rights is the lifeblood of democracy," I say as an American flag flies proudly from my asshole.

"As opposed to today's current policy of just outsourcing our torture to friendly Third World subordinates," goes leper.

"Such is the modern global economy," I say as an American flag flies proudly from my asshole.

The director ejaculates from his folding chair and ejaculates: "Action!"

"Wait," says the leper. "What's my motivation in this scene?"

"I told you he's impossible to work with," I say.

Screams the director: "Your motivation is to shriek a full

confession in order to halt the *alternate procedures* about to be conducted on you in accordance with the American Way and not the Geneva Conventions by the Skabbs!"

"Are these alternate procedures the same as alternate life-styles? Because if so I'm going to have to buy an alternate-life-style wardrobe to indicate to others that I am living an alternate lifestyle. Which can be pretty expensive."

Gov: "You're telling me. You should see what it costs the State to dress the Skabbs in outlaw rebel biker outfits to demon-strate that he is an outlaw rebel rebelling for the State."

TB: "What am I supposed to confess?"

Gov: "That whatever it is you believe is evil and that you're really, really sorry. That you won't do it again and that you were just being a limp-wristed commie."

TB: "Baby, I'm an anarchist. Or at least a pragmatist with anarchist ideals. I see that man, in his current contemptible state, isn't responsible enough for the freedoms enjoyed in an anarchist society where all violent or coercive institutions are dissolved allowing every person to have an equal right to natu-ral resources and the tools of production. No, at this stage, man needs the supervision of some form of State. But anarchism should always be the goal. And in working to attain that goal, authoritarian structures must always be questioned; and if they cannot be justified, they must be removed. And there is little about the current power structure that is justifiable."

Noam Chomsky: "Power is always illegitimate, unless it proves itself to be legitimate. So the burden of proof is always on those who claim that some authoritarian hierarchic relation is legitimate. If it can't be proven, it should be dismantled. If I'm walking down the street with my four-year-old grand-daughter, and she starts to run into the street, and I grab her arm and pull her back, that's an exercise of power and author-ity, but I can give a justification for it, and it's obvious what the justification would be. And maybe there are other cases

where you can justify it."

TB: "At present, there is justification for *some* State power. This is because most humans nowadays are like four-year-olds. (The power structure has an interest in creating these emotionally stunted imps by the billions because they in turn ensure a need for the power structure; after all, childlike citizens require supervision!) But even in this present situation, State power can be eliminated in certain areas and reduced in others by decentralizing it and transferring some responsibilities to individuals and local communities. Where State power remains it should be focused on helping the four-year-olds grow up. By this I mean having the State legitimate what power it has by using it to: redefine property along use-and-occupancy lines and prohibit usury (interest and rent), thus ending capitalism; dismantle all nuclear weapons worldwide; teach the populace responsibility in living, sustainability in living, and ways to cultivate critical consciousness through techniques like critical pedagogy; reduce birth rates to bring humanity back into ecological balance with the rest of the planet. If the States of the world set about on *that* agenda, then maybe the generations following all these four-year-olds would mature into the healthier, better adjusted adults that need progressively less and less State supervision."

Guano: "But of course, that ain't happening. The State as we know it today has nothing resembling those policies or goals. It is a State formed for the purpose of accumulating wealth for the wealthy small minority who control it. It is a State in place to consolidate ever more power in the hands of the few who are already powerful. And the billions of four-year-olds perpetuate it by accepting it."

Noam Chomsky: "But the question that always should be asked uppermost in our mind is, 'Why should I accept it?' It's the responsibility of those who exercise power to show that somehow it's legitimate. It's not the responsibility of anyone

else to show that it's illegitimate. It's illegitimate by assumption if it's a relation of authority among human beings which places some above others. That's illegitimate by assumption. Unless you can give a strong argument to show that it's right, you've lost."

TB: "And there is no justification for the suffocating centralization of American power. The United States, with its monstrous arsenal of military weapons and technology, belligerently expanding its corporate enterprises throughout the world, stealing resources, usurping more and more power, is the single greatest threat to all life on the planet in human history."

The gov screams: "That's ridiculous! What about the Inquisition! *The Nazis*, for Christ's sake!"

Guano: "The Nazis, and a host of other historical groups, may have been more malevolent, but none comes close to endangering the entire planet like the present-day U.S. That's because the Nazis didn't wield anywhere near the power the U.S. has amassed. The Nazis couldn't control the entire globe like the U.S. They may have had the will, but they did not have the technology. Total and complete world dominion is a very recent phenomenon; and a very American one."

TB: "Modern technology demands a concentration of power. Power this concentrated imperils life and makes real freedom impossible. There is no justification for the United States of Authoritarianism. And I'm here to tear it down."

Gov: "Hmm. I see. OK. Mutilate them."

Director: "Action!"

The Skabbs slowly moves the Harley up to us at the fifty-yard line. He can only move as fast as the two Mexicans running beside him carrying his man-balls. Then the two Mexicans see me and flee in the opposite direction. They've rudely dropped the Skabbs's chrome man-balls to the ground. Now the Skabbs cannot move the Harley for fear of scratching his scrotum.

We just sit there and look at the paralyzed Skabbs on his

paralyzed Harley for lack of anything better to do. The Skabbs drools on himself. This is going to be one taut scene after they superimpose it in.

Out of the tunnel pours more theatrical smoke. We'd be able to hear the malefic droning of an all-terrain vehicle if it weren't for the Skabbs's pipes. Thank you, the Skabbs! The all-terrain vehicle, known as an *ATV* or a *quad* because of its four wheels, charges out of the smoke and skids to a stop at the side of the Skabbs who is also known as a quad. Ha! There is no one in the ATV's driver seat. Grafted onto the ATV between its handlebars is the head of a dog. The head snarls and snaps its jaws at us. It's a Pit Bull head.

Gov: "What other dog would you expect the Skabbs to have?"

Also: The Pit Bull's balls are intact and have been grafted on between the rear tires.

Gov: "Outside of the head and balls, the rest of the dog is now all machine. It's yet another exciting new technology created via the gigantor State-subsidized R & D infrastructure in place to benefit private corporate economic interests. Next week we're scheduled to transplant the Skabbs's head and balls onto his Harley; although there has been a sizeable debate as to whether we'd be better off grafting on his balls and just throwing away the head. The Skabbs is a leading proponent of throwing away the head. This technology will soon be sold to the public; quadriplegics and mental quadriplegics alike. We predict incredible demand for grafting the thing citizens care most about, their genitals, onto the thing they care second most about, popular material possessions. The thought of becoming a headless cum-spewing Cadillac Escalade or a multi-orgasmic plasma television is already what most people aspire to, and wish for their children; according to market research. So sales will be brisk."

Aldous Huxley: "It's a brave new world!"

Guano, TB, and the gov: "Yay!"

The Skabbs drools. Upon this command the all-terrain vehicular Pit Bull named Max, naturally, spins its back tires and turfs the artificial turf. The friction from whirling tires on polypropylene "grass" lubricated with silicone on a base of expanded polyethylene elicits plumes of smoke and a high-pitched whine akin to a violin on Quaaludes, but no fire. Another miracle of modern technology.

Aldous Huxley: "Yay!"

All-terrain vehicles are the vehicles of choice for the legions of nature lovers who prefer their nature bereft of natural life. ATVs turf environmentally sensitive areas creating wide swaths of ecological havoc far better than ordinary foot traffic making ATVs a fine choice for those unable to enjoy nature due to indolence and idiocy.

Many ATV enthusiasts compensate for their deep feelings of powerlessness by rolling over the habitats of smaller weaker creatures with loud polluting machines. Many ATV enthusiasts are Harley-Davidson enthusiasts.

The ATV Pit Bull's wheels dig into the turf, gain traction, and spring it forward at its target; its target being us. The leper and I scatter, tumbling out of the thing's path before it can crush us under tread like just another of Mother Earth's small fuzzy roadkill. The Skabbs joins in on the fun by slobbering into his puff tube which activates the twelve-foot chrome jackhammer bulging forward from between handlebars. The jackhammer jabs its bit harmlessly in the air serving no purpose other than to glimmer and make noise, like everything else attached to Harleys.

TB says to me, "The Skabbs can't move that ridiculous Harley (redundant) because of the lame ball-scratching joke. I'm going to take him out. Try to keep his purebred off me."

"And how would you suggest I do that? Make like a virgin meadow and let him plow me?"

"Like most things overpowered and underthought, nimble-ness is lost on an ATV. They maneuver like shit and require wide turning radiuses. Use your dexterity and cunning."

"Dexterity and cunning. Thanks. Wouldn't want to give me anything that would actually *work*, like a death ray or giant spiked dildo. Fucking leper."

TB picks himself up off the turf and bolts towards the Skabbs. The four-wheeled Pit Bull guns its engine and takes off after him. I've half a mind to let the ATV ram him. But I'm not thinking clearly because of all the overinflated-engine fumes so I run in front of the Pit Bull to divert its attention. It works. Shit. Now the fucking blasphemy against life is hunting me.

I race down the sideline towards the far end zone. My legs have never churned so furiously. I am flying. My plan is to sprint into the end zone, then make as close to a ninety-degree turn as I can. The ATV won't be able to match the maneuver. At best, if it brakes and turns too hard, it'll flip over—a charming characteristic of ATVs and an entertaining means of population control. At the very least I figure it won't be able to stop or turn before hitting the canvas wall at the back of the end zone, buy-ing me and the leper some time while it untangles itself. That was the plan anyway. The problem is the mechanized monster is bearing down on me before I can even clear the twenty-yard line. As fast and magnificent a bastard as I am, there is no land animal alive that is faster than a typical cretin's off-road vehicle. Because you always want to be able to break the highway speed limit while despoiling large tracts of unspoiled nature.

It's turn now or die. I turn. It's hardly a ninety-degree turn. I don't corner well. But it's a sharper cut than the four-wheeler can manage. I look back to see the Pit Bull motoring off in the direction I'd abandoned. By the time the ATV has stemmed its inertia and turned around, I'm thirty yards away.

Shit. I can do this all day. That maladroit purebred ain't ever gonna catch me.

Meanwhile the leper charges the Skabbs at the fifty-yard line. He leaps, dropping the hips, exploding with the legs, aiming shoulder at target, demonstrating perfect football tackling technique. The Skabbs counters by slobbering into his puff tube. Hundreds of six-foot-long needles spring out in all directions from the Harley. They are chrome. Several of them pierce TB before he can impact the Skabbs. My friend screams in agony, suspended in midair, impaled on at least a half-dozen giant spines. The Skabbs laughs and slobbers, secure in his nest of glimmering thorns.

"Cut!" shrieks the director.

From the tunnel runs in a massive whitey sweating anabolic steroids in outlaw rebel biker costume. It's the Skabbs's stunt double!

"Action!" shrieks the director.

The Skabbs's stunt double grabs TB by the back of the neck and yanks him off the Harley crucifix. The leper drops to the ground beneath the chrome needles shining red with his blood. He's wounded badly and can't defend himself. He needs me.

I run to him.

The Skabbs's stunt double reaches into his outlaw rebel biker tight leather pants, which are not at all in a gay way, and pulls out a morning star—a medieval weapon which is basically a club with a head that's a spiked ball. Those backward medieval bastards couldn't afford one that was upgraded with chrome plating though.

The Skabbs's stunt double stands over TB and raises the club in the air, preparing to strike. He doesn't see me streaking in from the flank. I sense the ATV Pit Bull is right behind me. Can't worry about that now. Going full-bore, I lower my anvil-like head, about to slam it into the side of the stunt double's knee. He swings the morning star down! Not at TB, but into me! A blast of pain shoots through my left shoulder as the heavy spiked ball knocks me off my feet. I miss his leg and tumble by helplessly.

But the ATV Pit Bull is on the same trajectory and won't be put off course. Too late to turn, too fast to stop, the thing smashes into the stunt double's side. The Skabbs's doppelganger goes down, rolling end over end alongside the Harley's smokestacks.

I get up and involuntarily yelp as I try to put weight on my bludgeoned shoulder. It feels shattered. The Pit Bull, which has skidded to a stop only a few feet away, leaks an expression more a sneer than a snarl. It knows I'm down to three legs.

The machined canine squares up to face me, taking obvious delight in the smell of my blood streaming from the puncture wounds left by the morning star's spikes. If I turn and flee, it'll easily run me down. I need to keep it in front of me with a few feet separation. When it accelerates forward, I'll try to jump to the side and dodge it.

But it doesn't accelerate forward. It just sits there, idling; sneering. I concentrate on the thing's wheels, ready to react to their slightest movement. But they remain stationary. Then a flash of fur and teeth, and more surging pain—the Pit Bull's head has shot off its ATV body and clamped down on my left foreleg! I hear the sickening crunch of bone as jaws snap down on my already crippled limb. I instinctively bite back, sinking my fangs into the monster's face. I get a solid grip and violently shake my head back and forth, feeling the attacker's skin ripping under my teeth. It releases my leg and jerks its head back. I've inflicted large gashes over its eye and a smaller cut on its muzzle. Unfortunately, the wounds look superficial. My wounds are not. My left forelimb is mangled and covered in blood. The pain is excruciating. The only good thing, which was impossible to register at the time, is that the bitten leg had already been rendered useless by the morning star blow. If the Pit Bull had instead landed the attack on my right foreleg, I would no longer be able to stand. Meaning, I'd be dead.

Through the pain I force myself to focus on the foul anathema before me. Its head is swinging back and forth like a snarling

pendulum. A six-foot extensible/contractible neck connects the head to vehicular body. Can't bite into the neck—it's steel.

Where is the thing's weakness? How can I kill it?

Like some kind of abominable accordion, the neck compresses in and expands out in conformity with the Pit Bull's panting. Suddenly the head shoots towards me again. It's aiming for my front right leg, but this time I'm ready for it, greeting its teeth with my own. Jaws collide, snapping wildly. Fang clashing fang, lips ripped and bleeding. The Pit Bull's neck contracts and the head withdraws, unable to breach my guard.

The thing switches tactics and accelerates forward. With only three good legs, I barely am able to sidestep it. As I scramble from its path, its neck stretches across its body allowing the head to take a bite at me. The fangs narrowly miss my jugular, slashing my already gored shoulder as it motors past in the opposite direction. I've earned a few seconds of grace as my clumsy foe is forced to turn around.

The Skabbs cackles. America's hero slobbers into his puff tube. Then a pumping sound. Then the hundreds of needles jutting out from the Harley squirt urine pumped from the Skabbs's urine collection bag. A chrome-plated urine collection bag.

Everything within a ten-yard circle of the Skabbs is getting pissed on. Triumphant music is edited in. The Skabbs has overcome quadriplegia and acute mindlessness to still bravely mark his territory and all those unfortunate enough to be on his territory or on any place he considers to be his territory which is everywhere else. "And what could be more American than that!" is narrated in during editing.

The camera pans across the fifty American flags that spring up on the Harley's exhaust pipes. This is called product placement.

TB wheezes under the noxious influence of America's hero's waste product. But the Skabbs's stunt double always feels rejuvenated after a long hot golden shower. With one hand he picks

up TB by the throat and carries him to the Harley's pipes. The camera zooms in. On cue, the stunt double rams TB's face into the chrome smokestack where there's a chrome plaque that reads: "Fat kick-ass hog pipes generously donated by the Dow Chemical Company."

The magic of product placement. A magical tinkling sound is edited in.

The stunt double is repeatedly smashing TB's head into the chrome smokestack and seems intent on spilling his brain all over the product placement. Fuck that guy and fuck this scene. I limp over and bite him on the ass.

My teeth easily pierce his outlaw rebel biker tight leather pants and sink into some fine steroidally marinated cheeks. The stunt double starts to cry. The Skabbs starts to cry. This cannot be superimposed out during the editing process so the director screams "Cut!" and two movie extras run in to try to separate me from the ass flaps.

The two movie extras are splendid simpletons dressed head to toe in star-spangled red, white, and blue (with chrome trim). One of them grabs me and tries to pull me off. The other takes a red, white, and blue crowbar and tries to pry me off. But I'm locked in and locked on. Then they threaten to bring in the star-spangled Jaws of Life and I decide I've had enough ass. So I shake my head violently back and forth, tearing off the left gluteus maximus and matching outlaw rebel biker tight leather pants.

The director screams "Action!" and the camera zooms in on the Skabbs's pantsless, half-assed stunt double. A stunt double is supposed to look like the actor they're replacing and the Skabbs's stunt double accurately exhibits two steroidally withered balls the size of subatomic quarks. The balls are too small to ever see but physicists have proved their existence mathematically.

The Skabbs and stunt double sport a penis the size of a hang-nail. Compared to their balls the cock is ginormous.

The Skabbs's stunt double stands pantsless beneath the smokestacks' chrome plaque that reads: "At Dow, our smokestacks are all well-enDOWed!"

Editor's note: superimpose in two giant elephant balls here. The boys down in the product-placement cubicle send many thanks.

A shiny light materializes on the fifty-yard line. Potter and Futuro emerge, locked in battle. They roll around and whine. The Skabbs is jealous of all things shiny so he drools into his puff tube. A searchlight pops up on the Harley and begins wildly spinning. It complements the Christmas lights blinking on the Harley. They complement the red, white, and blue fireworks exploding over the Harley's fifty American flags. The Skabbs looks to see if Potter and Futuro have noticed his shiny little bits and is sad to learn they are too busy rolling on each other to notice. The Skabbs begins to cry again.

The stunt double considers his hangnail penis and decides upon a catharsis which is to strangle the nearest black man.

"Uh, TB, while the life is being choked out of you, the script says you are to realize your sins and confess them, thus completing your grand conversion to typical bootlicking goose-stepping American parrot, I mean patriot," notifies the gov.

Thomas Jefferson: "The tree of liberty must be refreshed from time to time with the blood of patriots and tyrants. God forbid we should ever be twenty years without such a rebellion."

Gov: "*Oh no you didn't!* Your brands of patriot and revolution are long dead. Now there is only the System. Ever present, ever powerful, entrenched. Who cares that Thomas Jefferson would be horrified at present-day America! Lazy brainwashed sheep would rather worship icons, like Thomas Jefferson, than think about the actual ideas their icons advocated, decide if those ideas are valid for their lives, and if so, put them into action in their lives!"

Jesus Christ: "Duh. That's what the whole Jesus/Grand Inquisitor thing was about."

Gov: "Thomas Jefferson, Jesus Christ, and soon TB. All dead. Now only icons—meaningless images used for control. All dead!"

The stunt double straddling TB's chest removes his hands from the leper's throat. TB continues to choke. This amuses the stunt double. TB violently jerks, his body contorting; extremities, trunk, and head spasmodically twitching as he descends into a full-blown convulsion.

I scream, "All the shiny lights bouncing off all the chrome and the disco ball hanging over the fifty-yard line have triggered an epileptic fit! He's swallowing his tongue! Shit in his mouth!"

Nobody does dick.

"You don't understand! He's suffocating! But a little feces in the ol' pie hole will snap an epileptic right out of their convulsion. They love it. Try it at home."

No response.

"The Skabbs's chrome-plated colostomy bag is full of shit! Just like the Skabbs. Brother, can you spare a dump?" Ha!

The pun is lost on them. Where's Telly Bawdhaw when you need him?

"You don't understand! He's going to die!"

Then it hits me. They want him to die. For real. I thought this was just a movie. Or a really shitty book.

I try to run to him but one of the movie extras holds me while the other loops a rope around my muzzle. I wriggle and scratch and almost get loose until one of the bastards slams his fist into my mutilated shoulder. The pain sends me to the ground. I can do nothing but watch as the only friend I've ever had struggles in his last breath, and goes limp.

Traffic Buster is dead.

The stunt double is sitting on top of the body, smiling.

The Skabbs laughs.

The governor pronounces final sentence: "Thomas Jefferson, Jesus Christ, and TB. Now just icons. All dead."

Everything goes red. Fury. Ineffable fury. All my rage at the ugliness, unfairness, greed, stupidity, and evil of the human world is focused into this tiny moment. The poison I harbor for a society so depraved that the best thing to be said of it is that it's bent on its own destruction will be administered in one scalding torrent.

Wrath.

Jerking my muzzle free of the rope I burst from the movie extra's grip and spring at his head. My open mouth finds his neck. I bite down with such rage that my jaws sink clear through. I feel the crunching of windpipe and the hot spray of blood. I tear my head away, savoring the chunks of ruined trachea and carotid artery in my mouth, and swallow them down whole.

The movie extra instinctively gropes at his neck to discover half of it missing. Blood squirts in the air to the rhythm of his beating heart. Which stops soon enough.

The once distant cry of my ancestor the wolf, now endangered like the rest of the natural world, is ringing in my ears. My face is covered in blood. It leaks from my mouth. I am wild and alive and will have more. I look to the remaining movie extra and peel my lips back in full snarl.

He answers by smashing the crowbar down on my crippled shoulder. The blow forces me to the ground but I feel nothing. My three viable legs are good enough to retaliate with a leap at his wrist. Again I enjoy the tearing of skin, the taste of blood.

"Every generation needs a new revolution," whispers Thomas Jefferson. "God forbid we should ever be twenty years without such a rebellion. The tree of liberty must be refreshed from time to time with the blood of patriots and tyrants."

"Then in the name of liberty, more blood will spill!" howls TB, opening his eyes, grabbing the stunt double by the shoulder and hip, and ripping him clean in half.

TB surges to his feet. Hair grows out of his hands and paws. The dude springs a snout. And please don't forget the afro.

Holy shit! The leper's a motherfucking werewolf! How's that for a lame *deus ex machina!*

My mouth drops open in amazement and I release the chewy wrist of the movie extra who takes off running. The wolfman picks up the stunt double's upper torso and throws it downfield into the end zone. It's a perfect spiral. The upper torso hits the movie extra in the back with such velocity that it turns him into a liquid, but not a gas. Touchdown!

The furry leper then grabs the stunt double's pantsless lower torso and throws the legs, hangnail, and subatomic quarks straight into the disco ball which explodes above us raining thousands of glittering shards all over the field making the Skabbs jealous and weepy.

Gov: "One hell of a halftime show. The dullards at home will love it."

Our team has all the momentum. The ATV Pit Bull looks unsure of what to do and starts to backpedal. I throw down the gauntlet, crouching low to the turf, baring my teeth. "Let's go, you tin-can bête noire. Bring it!"

All gasoline and testosterone, the Pit Bull takes the bait, barking out foam and saliva as it accelerates forward.

Twenty yards away. Not a twitch out of me.

Fifteen yards to impact. I don't move.

Ten yards and speeding right at me. I stay in my crouch.

Five, four, three, two, one! I jump neither left nor right, but stay exactly where I am. Befuddled, the ATV races directly over me. If it had been anything else not so overcompensatingly jacked up, I would've been killed. But as it is, a foot long of manly ground clearance is enough for me to squeeze under untouched. That is until the Pit Bull's pink little pouch dangling between its rear tires speeds into my waiting mouth. Which closes on Max's balls like a steel trap.

The Pit Bull must be motoring 60 miles an hour when its testicles are ripped off. It squeals, shudders, and flips. I turn my

head and watch as the off-road vehicle rolls over and over and over and over and over and onto the Skabbs.

"Guess that's *quad* on *quad*."

"Maybe it's a ménage à *quad*. Ha!"

The impact is horrific. There's mangled chrome everywhere.

I hobble up to the overturned Pit Bull. It can't breathe. Tightly wrapped around under its head is a string of Harley Christmas lights. A chrome cannonball later identified as one of the Skabbs's testicles hangs from the still-blinking string like an electric bolo tie of doom and male inadequacy.

The ATV Pit Bull expires as I drop its wayward scrotum next to it. "All balls and no brain. Purebred."

"That's what the purebred gets for *traveling* without his *wilburys!*" deliciously delivers the werewolf.

A round hole in the roof reveals where the Skabbs's other jeweled family jewel was launched from the tent, from the atmosphere, and into the moon. "Guess they've replaced the *man* in the moon with the *man-ball* in the moon! Ha!" The werewolf is rolling.

Underneath the pile lies the downed Harley. The collision has broken off many of the bloated chrome porcupine's spines allowing my friend, who I grant you is a vicious monster, to poke his paw at the drooling Skabbs and pull from his chest a trembling heart. If it can be called a heart. Small, shriveled, and black, it's more akin to a plus-sized raisin.

The Skabbs's chrome-plated colostomy bag explodes, sending shrapnel of digested baby food and steroids everywhere. American heroes are always messy when they go.

I do the wet-dog shake. Feces fly from my fur. The leper does the same then takes off on all fours into the end zone. He springs ten feet in the air and lands on top of the governor's platform. The gov is startled but buys time by pushing his fluffer in front of him. The werewolf says "Give me head

till you're dead! Ha!" and swings his paw and knocks off the fluffer's head. The film crew continues to roll the camera as the gov buys more time by pushing the gaffer in front of him. By the time the werewolf has finished beating the gaffer with his own leg the gov has armed himself with a hydraulic press and re-oiled himself. The werewolf swings the gaffer's leg, accurately guiding the gafferian foot into the gov's thong, driving the gov into the air and into the hydraulic press. The werewolf presses the press's start button and ad-libs "You're terminated, fucker!" as the gov is smooshed flat. "Guess that's what you politicians mean by *pressing the flesh!* Ha!" The camera zooms in on the gov's crushed thong as its neon light fades out.

TB exits through the tent back door, sees the parked Oldsmobile, tips the valet, crashes the Olds through the tent wall, picks me up at the fifty-yard line, sets fire to the tent, and crashes the Olds out of the tent.

"Oh, you are the great love of my life," I blubber to the new 102-inch plasma television miraculously installed in an Oldsmobile with only 37 inches of headroom by our Lord Jesus the technician from Al & Ed's Autosound.

I cry tears of joy. My life has been fulfilled. The picture quality is sublime.

The plasma television lets out a moan and ejaculates all over me.

"It's one of those multi-orgasmic plasma televisions!"

"I guess that means there's more to *come!*" Ha!

The werewolf chokes back his tears from noxious diesel generator fumes. "If we had held out a little longer on the football field they would have had enough time to upgrade the backseat diesel generator with some newborn babies, midgets, electronic gadgets, and big ol' titties. The things you need to create *buzz*." The werewolf pours himself a mug of sludge from the newly installed drum of Starbucks. The chrome on the barrel matches the chrome trim glued everywhere which matches the glittering

Arby's wrappers glued to human heads on our wheels which match the Arby's corporate sponsor logo on the car hood which matches the hundreds of other corporate sponsor logos slapped all over the Olds. "Wow. The audiences will be standing and cheering when they get a load of all these upgrades in the movie's triumphant final scene."

"Are you sure all the glimmering chrome and flashing Christmas lights won't cause you to have an epileptic fit? Oh, wait! I forgot! All this time it was *the full moon* that sent you twitching like Margot Kidder, you dirty motherfucker!" I say in a hurt tone as the full moon glimmers off our upgraded hundred-foot chrome smokestack tailpipe from Dow.

"I never meant to hurt you. I tried to tell you the truth, to show you the real me, but you kept shitting in my mouth."

"A relationship can't survive secrets. That's straight from Dr. Phil. Since you're a werewolf do you want to devour his succulent canned-ham head too?"

"Look. Here's the truth. Epilepsy does not really exist. It's a completely fabricated disease faked by lycanthropes ashamed of their lycanthropy. When you see an 'epileptic' on the street convulsing you must immediately stop them by shitting in their mouth and/or shooting them through the heart with a silver bullet."

"OK. But please at least tell me the leprosy is for real."

"Sure, baby. Now is it time for the make-up sex?"

"Ooh, what hairy paws you have! That's what happens to children who masturbate to ova."

So I forgive the big lug. You can't really stay mad at a creature with more fur on its back than a Greek woman. Some also have small penises. (Source: *Rick Steves' Greek Escapes*.)

The rough dirt road eventually spills out onto one that's paved which eventually spills out onto a highway. It's I-40. To the west is Los Angeles. To the east is Arizona. We must choose.

"Look," I say, "I think we could really use a change. Not that

Southern California's thousands of cemented miles of spirit-wilting blight aren't great, but consider Arizona—you know, for some different scenery. We could lie low there for a while, enjoy radiant desert vistas, eat some peyote. Oh, I'm not saying we retire from the whole traffic-busting mass-murder racket. I just think we need a few weeks off; let things cool down. Then, refreshed and invigorated, we get ourselves a new tarp and go for a drive. Plenty of Escalades and sprawl around Phoenix to keep us entertained."

I almost have him convinced. Then a single pair of head-lights appears on the highway. The serenity of the desert at the midnight hour is ruined by one speeding Cadillac, headed to Los Angeles. The werewolf scowls and jams the accelerator in pursuit.

The Cadillac commercial features a female model perfectly modern in her perfect beauty and soullessness, driving her new Cadillac. While at the wheel the model looks into the camera with perfect empty-headed smugness and reads these lines: "Hmmm. Gossip magazines...hand-dipped truffles...Italian leather furniture...definitely a pan-seared top sirloin...and pulling up to the boys' club in one of these. Oh, these are just a few of my favorite things."

"Ah, you see. With the purchase of a Cadillac, the ladies can show the world that they are every bit as fatuously superficial as a male," admires the werewolf.

With all the misplaced arrogance one expects from a perfect bourgeois know-nothing, the model asks: "When you turn on your car, can it return the favor?"

"No. His Oldsmobile does not turn him on. But your unfertilized gametes do," I apologize to her.

"At least her eggs are real life. If she hasn't had them laminated for easier showing."

"Wrong, leper. Life is about the insensate beauty of material objects."

"That would perfectly describe their perfect female in this commercial."

"Stay away from the white woman, you black endocrinally challenged savage!"

The werewolf guns the engine. "Get out of my dreams, and into my car. Or at least *onto* my car," the loudspeaker broadcasts as he rams the lovely from behind, thrusting his snowplow into her never-before-plowed rear. She squeals as the hirsute gentleman splits open her trunk. "Not much junk in this trunk," he compliments or criticizes depending on your socioeconomic standing. But he's in a playful mood, and slows, savoring the feel of her car boot (or is it booty? Ha!) all over his Cutlass. Suddenly he pulls out (the tease!) only to wickedly pound his wedge ever deeper into her quivering, red-hot (actually on fire) cleft. Yes. Daddy is indeed home.

The werewolf lights a cigarette. He basks in the afterglow of that manliest of pleasures: to rip a lady's Cadillac completely in two.

His lady, ripped in two, explodes beneath him like a Palestinian under a Caterpillar. "Tsk tsk. Messy lady," he lovingly chides.

"Ah, the rapture."

"Ah, the *rupture.*"

"Ha!"

"Ha!"

"Now that you've turned modernity's representation of the aesthetically and spiritually perfect woman into a grease spot we can double back and head to Arizona."

"Afraid not. The disease in the Cadillac was a symbol. A symbol of Los Angeles. And a sign. A sign that we need to finish this job. Which is to finish Los Angeles."

"There's plenty to finish in Phoenix. There's plenty to finish everywhere else in the United States!"

"Yeah, there is plenty to finish everywhere else in this ever

more homogenized, Americanized world. But Los Angeles is getting to where the world is going first. It starts there. With its 'entertainment' industry built to sell and stupefy. With its tens of millions of clones worshipping their gossip magazines, Italian leather whatever, Cadillacs; droves of humanoids, more plastic than flesh. Los Angeles is the epicenter from where the shock waves of abstract materialism radiate out to the rest of the globe."

Bill Hicks: "If you're looking for some ideas, you're free to consult my *Arizona Bay* stand-up routine where I suggest that Los Angeles dropping into the ocean due to a huge earthquake would be the ultimate feng shui upgrade."

TB: "And I can't think of anything more fashionable than a huge earthquake caused by a 1994 Oldsmobile Cutlass Supreme detonating its hybrid 3.1-liter V-6/cold-fusion nuclear engine inside the San Andreas Fault."

Bill Hicks: "Causing L.A. to be flushed away."

TB: "You don't have to be gay to appreciate those redecorating possibilities."

Telly Bawdhaw: "The whole of Los Angeles, the shallowest of the shallow, in not so shallow water. *Heehaw!*"

"Leaving a cool ocean breeze blowing into *Arizona Bay*," whispers Bill Hicks.

"*Arizona Bay*," repeats TB.

Guano: "Hey, I've got no problem with utterly annihilating the planetary pinnacle of avarice. And if you want to start trimming back the suffocating human population you might as well start with a couple dozen million of the basest of the base. But using a nuclear detonation to do it? Isn't that counter to the wise long-term thinking we pay our publicists top dollar to say we stand for?"

TB: "Nuclear weapons are the height of man's hubris. As if any single species has the right to destroy the entirety of its kind, and take all other complex life on Earth with it. Sheer

hubris; and insanity. No one yielded man this right. Except for maybe Jesus. See the fundamentalists next door for Bible-passage proof. Or the billions of nationalistic flag-suckers next door to them."

Guano: "Well, yeah. That's my point. To conceive of, build, and stockpile weapons that exterminate worldwide life is arrogant lunacy. And for you to use such a weapon on the arrogant lunatics would make you an arrogant lunatic."

TB: "Ah, yes. You say I'm a hypocrite. And that may be true, because, after all, I am a man."

Guano: "You can hardly tell with all the yak hair glued to your face by the makeup crew."

TB: "Yeah. You'd think they would have spent more on special effects for this piece-of-shit movie."

Guano: "They'll superimpose in a more realistic-looking werewolf during the editing process."

TB: "In this modern society, we all live in hypocrisy. Just as in life itself, you can only gauge such things by a matter of degrees."

Guano: "Using a nuclear weapon to stop a culture that justifies nuclear weapons seems on the far end of the hypocrisy spectrum."

TB: "I prefer to categorize it as less hypocritical and more ironic. All societies, even the healthiest ones, eventually fail. Nothing lasts forever. *All things die*—and we are still bound to this one universal of the natural world, whether we acknowledge it or not. So if all societies are doomed to die, the logical question is: When, inevitably, a society armed with technological horrors that can instantly kill the whole planet begins to decline, what happens to these weapons? Of course, there is no pat answer, but it's not irrational to postulate that in its decline, someone in this society will decide to use the planet-killers. Maybe it's some religious maniac in a position of power who sees humanity ravaged by a plague or some other 'act of God' and decides

to lend God a hand. Maybe the maniac simply sees the world in moral decline and hears Jesus tell him to cleanse it with radioactive fire. Maybe it's your standard chieftain who believes a little too much in the national myths and out of fear decides to incinerate the up-and-coming tribe across the ocean. Maybe (quite likely, actually) it all plays out after human overpopulation and an unsustainable economic system trigger an ecological collapse leading to wars over scarce environmental resources, provoking the losing side's madman, facing defeat and death, to use his nukes. Maybe there's no madman directly involved but one missile still gets uppity and launches by technological error or human accident which starts a wider nuclear conflagration. The point being, given enough time and unknowable events, it's unreasonable to assume a society's nuclear weapons *won't* be exploded.

"Human history is the history of societies being born and built, only to decline and die so that other societies may be born to take their place. (After all, there aren't any Sumerians running around anymore because if there were, America would have killed them for their oil and ziggurats. I mean, to free them.) But a nuclear-armed society does not allow for this natural societal life cycle of death and rebirth to continue. A nuclear-armed society in its death throes will make sure that *nothing* lives past it. That is arrogant, insane, and by any meaningful definition, evil."

Guano: "Yup. But back to my original point. You're being a massive hypocrite in using a nuclear weapon to stop them from using their nuclear weapons."

TB: "Back to my ultimate point. It's less hypocrisy and more irony that given what this society's future is, the city leading this society to its future is destroyed first as the result of a nuclear explosion."

Guano: "Fine. But I don't think I can outrun a nuclear detonation on only three good legs."

The werewolf pulls the Olds over to the side of the highway. Then he sits there and stares at the steering wheel. "What are you doing?" I sigh. "Los Angeles ain't gonna come to us."

"I suppose not," he says.

"Oh, what is this? Look, I was just kidding about not being able to outrun a nuclear blast with only three good legs. Besides, I don't really have to outrun a nuclear explosion—just a magnitude 11 earthquake caused by a nuclear explosion, right?"

He turns his head and looks at me. "I love you, boy. I always have, and I always will." He gets out of the Olds, walks around it, opens my door, lifts me out of the car taking care not to touch my gored shoulder, and sets me down on the side of the road. I don't know what to say, so I say nothing and try to get back in the car. He gently stops me with his hand while shutting the passenger door.

"What are you doing?" I ask.

He kneels down and strokes my head. "This is something I need to finish…alone."

"I can help. I want to help." I stare at the pavement, searching for something eloquent to say but only find the pitiable: "We've always been there for each other. *Please.*"

"Head to Arizona. I'll come for you there."

"Bullshit. You won't. They'll kill you."

"They can't kill me. Only silver can kill a werewolf."

"I'm pretty sure a 100 megaton nuclear detonation also counts."

"I'll jump out of the Olds just before she drops into the fault."

"An earthquake powerful enough to sink Los Angeles into the ocean may have some adverse effects on someone standing at the fault line. Also, I don't think ducking the abovementioned 100 megaton explosion will be a simple matter. Even if you are Lon Chaney on performance enhancers."

He looks west, wincing at the light pollution overpowering the night horizon, then back at me. "I couldn't have asked for a better partner. Or a truer friend."

"And friends are there for one another!"

"Friends *protect* each other. Even if it means letting go."

"You'd rather sacrifice yourself up to martyrdom than risk taking responsibility for a loved one. Well, we're a little late in the game for that. You're a coward. You're running."

"This is a hard thing I do. But I don't do it because I'm afraid." He's weeping, choking on the words.

"If this life has any meaning, it's to hold tight to the ones worthy of love. Crenshaw, all we have is each other. It's all we've ever had. But don't you get it? That's good enough."

He says nothing, turning away from me.

"But you're so torn up by hatred that you're willing to abandon the one decent thing in your life to get one last shot at them."

He walks to the driver's door.

"They've always considered us the losers. And for the first time, they're right."

He gets in the car.

I'm being left again. Rejection. Abandonment. *I've never been good enough.*

"You've always been good enough, Guano. They're the ones not good enough for you."

"Don't. Please. They're not worth it, Crenshaw. But *we* are."

He pauses. I catch a glimpse of his tear-stained eye. Then he's gone.

END OF THE NIGHTMARE

(I'M SPEAKING OF THIS BOOK)

EPILOGUE

So Lady Fortuna decides to stop pissing on me for a sec. I've hobbled east on I-40 for a couple miles when a midnight blue Karmann Ghia pulls over. It's a thirty-something couple making a midnight run to Arizona. As luck would have it, she's a veterinary surgeon taking a new job there. He's an idiot.

After surgery I spend my days bored at home with her man who spends his days playing with himself. Good work if you can get it. Then I notice it's raining piss again. Arizona is hot as balls. And I still have no balls despite my request to tack on a duo of thirty-pound medicine balls. I mean, if I'm already on the table getting shoulder work done is it really so inconvenient to slap a couple chumlies on? But no. My insurance company turned down the request because man-ball chrome plating and cancer treatment are considered elective procedures. As if I were actually insured. I mean, this ain't fucking Canada or pretty much anywhere else in the First World.

Arizona is hot as balls because there is no Arizona Bay. Something went wrong with TB's plan.

Here's what went wrong with TB's plan (as I would later learn watching the reruns in syndication): Oh, sure. There's a 100 megaton nuclear explosion. But Southern California does not fall into the ocean because the San Andreas Fault has no crevice whatsoever at its fault line making the whole nuclear-

explosion-inside-the-San-Andreas-crevice-causing-a-massive-earthquake idea completely implausible. A first for this book. And completely unoriginal. Lex Luthor tried the same lame thing in the original *Superman* movie. Turns out TB should have just driven the Olds to the middle of Bel Air which makes a fine ground zero (try this at home) and incinerated everything within twenty miles in all directions.

But instead he just had to listen to Bill Hicks.

So I'm sitting at home watching the reruns when they interrupt this broadcast for some breaking news from California. *"TB is alive!"* screams a lump of makeup and silicone implants. I leap to all fours, ignoring the pain in my reconstructed shoulder. Could it really be? They go live to Los Angeles. And buy God, there's a Cadillac Escalade splitting traffic!

A *real* Cadillac Escalade! No tarp with shiny Christmas tree tinsel over a shitty Oldsmobile need apply!

The overhead helicopter camera zooms in on the Escalade, paying special attention to the hundreds of corporate sponsor logos glued all over it. A special in-Escalade camera shows the car interior adorned with newborn babies, midgets, electronic gadgets, and big ol' titties that are generating quite the buzz. Access to the in-Escalade camera is available on pay-per-view for just $49.95. Operators are standing by.

The Escalade finishes knifing through I-405 gridlock and pulls into the winner's circle, which is Bel Air. There to greet it is the governor in his 18-wheeler covered in corporate sponsor logos. The TV news is informing the populace how the semi's trailer is a mobile Starbucks that serves underprivileged children who normally couldn't afford much-needed caffeine and sugar. This latest reform to address the crime of capitalism was initiated by Governor Adrenal Wartzenfegger and is being continued by the actor now playing the role of Governor Adrenal Wartzenfegger in this, the sequel. The new same-old governor portraying the old same-old governor were from rival political

parties and prove the superiority of our two-party dictatorship, glows *The New York Times.*

The director of the film crew nailed to the top of the tractor-trailer barks instructions as the camera zooms in on the Escalade's Give Whitey Five flag which I didn't remember having all the star-spangled red, white, and blue.

"There's TB!" applauds the lump of makeup and silicone implants. The in-studio audience claps and bleats as per the instudio "clap and bleat" blinking sign.

"Huh. Dissent really sells," observes the guy sitting next to me playing with himself.

TB sports a bald head that resembles a finely aged goiter which he slaps a rubber chicken over that squawks *"Got Man!santo?"* (Cue clapping and bleating.) TB's jive-talking dog sidekick has glued-on white fur and is in blackface. *"Fo' shizzle! Fo' shizzle!"* he barks while down on all four hands and knees; as usual.

"Who says you can't teach an old dog new tricks! *Heehaw!"* delivers TB.

America is standing and cheering. It does huge box office.

Holy shit, does this movie suck. Almost as bad as *Crash.*

www.givewhiteyfive.com

CPSIA information can be obtained at www.ICGtesting.com
Printed in the USA
BVOW07s0932250614

357336BV00001B/31/P